O9-BUB-414

THE HEIR

ALSO BY KIERA CASS

The Selection

The Elite

The One

The Selection Stories: The Prince & The Guard

The Queen (available as an ebook only)

KIERA CASS

An Imprint of HarperCollins*Publishers*

HarperTeen is an imprint of HarperCollins Publishers.

The Heir

www.epicreads.com

Library of Congress Control Number: 2015933400
ISBN 978-0-06-234985-9 (trade)
ISBN 978-0-06-240550-0 (special edition)
ISBN 978-0-06-239746-1 (special edition)
ISBN 978-0-06-239130-8 (international edition)
ISBN 978-0-06-240918-8 (special international edition)
ISBN 978-0-06-239745-4 (special edition)

Typography by Sarah Hoy
16 17 18 19 CG/RRDH 20 19 18 17 16 15
❖
First Edition

To Jim and Jennie Cass.

For lots of reasons, but mostly for making Callaway.

THE HEIR

CHAPTER 1

I COULD NOT HOLD MY breath for seven minutes. I couldn't even make it to one. I once tried to run a mile in seven minutes after hearing some athletes could do it in four but failed spectacularly when a side stitch crippled me about halfway in.

However, there was one thing I managed to do in seven minutes that most would say is quite impressive: I became queen.

By seven tiny minutes I beat my brother Ahren into the world, so the throne that ought to have been his was mine. Had I been born a generation earlier, it wouldn't have mattered. Ahren was the male, so Ahren would have been the heir.

Alas, Mom and Dad couldn't stand to watch their firstborn be stripped of a title by an unfortunate but rather lovely set of breasts. So they changed the law, and the people rejoiced, and I was trained day by day to become the next ruler of Illéa.

What they didn't understand was that their attempts to make my life fair seemed rather *unfair* to me.

I tried not to complain. After all, I knew how fortunate I was. But there were days, or sometimes months, when it felt like far too much was piled on me, too much for any one person, really.

I flipped through the newspaper and saw that there had been yet another riot, this time in Zuni. Twenty years ago, Dad's first act as king was to dissolve the castes, and the old system had been phased out slowly over my lifetime. I still thought it was completely bizarre that once upon a time people lived with these limiting but arbitrary labels on their backs. Mom was a Five; Dad was a One. It made no sense, especially since there was no outward sign of the divisions. How was I supposed to know if I was walking next to a Six or a Three? And why did that even matter?

When Dad had first decreed that the castes were no more, people all over the country had been delighted. Dad had expected the changes he was making in Illéa to be comfortably in place over the course of a generation, meaning any day now everything should click.

That wasn't happening—and this new riot was just the most recent in a string of unrest.

"Coffee, Your Highness," Neena said, setting the drink on my table.

"Thank you. You can take the plates."

I scanned the article. This time a restaurant was burned to the ground because its owner refused to promote a waiter to a position as a chef. The waiter claimed that a promotion had been promised but was never delivered, and he was sure it was because of his family's past.

Looking at the charred remains of the building, I honestly didn't know whose side I was on. The owner had the right to promote or fire anyone he wanted, and the waiter had the right not to be seen as something that, technically, didn't exist anymore.

I pushed the paper away and picked up my drink. Dad was going to be upset. I was sure he was already running the scenario over and over in his head, trying to figure out how to set it right. The problem was, even if we could fix one issue, we couldn't stop every instance of post-caste discrimination. It was too hard to monitor and happening far too often.

I set down my coffee and headed to my closet. It was time to start the day.

"Neena," I called. "Do you know where that plum-colored dress is? The one with the sash?"

She squinted in concentration as she came over to help.

In the grand scheme of things, Neena was new to the palace. She'd only been working with me for six months, after my last maid fell ill for two weeks. Neena was acutely attuned to my needs and much more agreeable to be around, so I kept her on. I also admired her eye for fashion.

Neena stared into the massive space. "Maybe we should reorganize."

"You can if you have the time. That's not a project I'm interested in."

"Not when I can hunt down your clothes for you," she teased.

"Exactly!"

She took my humor in stride, laughing as she quickly sorted through gowns and pants.

"I like your hair today," I commented.

"Thank you." All the maids wore caps, but Neena was still creative with her hairdos. Sometimes a few thick, black curls would frame her face, and other times she twisted back strands until they were all tucked away. At the moment there were wide braids encircling her head, with the rest of her hair under her cap. I really enjoyed that she found ways to work with her uniform, to make it her own each day.

"Ah! It's back here." Neena pulled down the knee-length dress, fanning it out across the dark skin of her arm.

"Perfect! And do you know where my gray blazer is? The one with the three-quarter sleeves?"

She stared at me, her face deadpan. "I'm definitely rearranging."

I giggled. "You search; I'll dress."

I pulled on my outfit and brushed out my hair, preparing for another day as the future face of the monarchy. The outfit was feminine enough to soften me but strong enough that I'd be taken seriously. It was a fine line to walk, but I did it every day.

Staring into the mirror, I talked to my reflection.

"You are Eadlyn Schreave. You are the next person in line

to run this country, and you will be the first girl to do it on your own. No one," I said, "is as powerful as you."

Dad was already in his office, brow furrowed as he took in the news. Other than my eyes, I didn't look much like him. Or Mom, for that matter.

With my dark hair, oval-shaped face, and a hint of a tan that lingered year round, I looked more like my grandmother than anyone else. A painting of her on her coronation day hung in the fourth-floor hallway, and I used to study it when I was younger, trying to guess at how I would look as I grew. Her age in the portrait was near to mine now, and though we weren't identical, I sometimes felt like her echo.

I walked across the room and kissed Dad's cheek. "Morning."

"Morning. Did you see the papers?" he asked.

"Yes. At least no one died this time."

"Thank goodness for that." Those were the worst, the ones where people were left dead in the street or went missing. It was terrible, reading the names of young men who'd been beaten simply for moving their families into a nicer neighborhood or women who were attacked for trying to get a job that in the past would not have been open to them.

Sometimes it took no time at all to find the motive and the person behind these crimes, but more often than not we were faced with a lot of finger-pointing and no real answers. It was exhausting for me to watch, and I knew it was worse for Dad.

"I don't understand it." He took off his reading glasses and rubbed his eyes. "They didn't want the castes anymore. We took our time, eliminated them slowly so everyone could adjust. Now they're burning down buildings."

"Is there a way to regulate this? Could we create a board to oversee grievances?" I looked at the photo again. In the corner, the young son of the restaurant owner wept over losing everything. In my heart I knew complaints would come in faster than anyone could address them, but I also knew Dad couldn't bear doing nothing.

Dad looked at me. "Is that what you would do?"

I smiled. "No, I'd ask my father what he would do."

He sighed. "That won't always be an option for you, Eadlyn. You need to be strong, decisive. How would you fix this one particular incident?"

I considered. "I don't think we can. There's no way to prove the old castes were why the waiter was denied the promotion. The only thing we can do is launch an investigation into who set the fire. That family lost their livelihood today, and someone needs to be held responsible. Arson is not how you exact justice."

He shook his head at the paper. "I think you're right. I'd like to be able to help them. But, more than that, we need to figure out how to prevent this from happening again. It's become rampant, Eadlyn, and it's frightening."

Dad tossed the paper into the trash, then stood and walked to the window. I could read the stress in his posture. Sometimes his role brought him so much joy, like visiting the schools he'd worked tirelessly to improve or seeing communities flourish in the war-free era he'd ushered in. But those instances were becoming few and far between. Most days he was anxious about the state of the country, and he had to fake his smiles when reporters came by, hoping that his sense of calm would somehow spread to everyone else. Mom helped shoulder the burden, but at the end of the day the fate of the country was placed squarely on his back. One day it would be on mine.

Vain as it was, I worried I would go gray prematurely.

"Make a note for me, Eadlyn. Remind me to write Governor Harpen in Zuni. Oh, and put to write it to Joshua Harpen, not his father. I keep forgetting he was the one who ran in the last election."

I wrote his instructions in my elegant cursive, thinking how pleased Dad would be when he looked at it later. He used to give me the worst time over my penmanship.

I was grinning to myself when I looked back at him, but my face fell almost immediately when I saw him rubbing his forehead, trying so desperately to think of a solution to these problems.

"Dad?"

He turned and instinctively squared his shoulders, like he needed to act strong even in front of me.

"Why do you think this is happening? It wasn't always like this."

He raised his eyebrows. "It certainly wasn't," he said, almost to himself. "At first everyone seemed pleased. Every time we removed a new caste, people held parties. It's only been in the last few years, since all the labels have officially been erased, that it's gone downhill."

He stared back out the window. "The only thing I can think is that those who grew up with the castes are aware of how much better this is. Comparatively, it's easier to marry or work. A family's finances aren't capped by a single profession. There are more choices when it comes to education. But those who are growing up without the castes and are still running into opposition . . . I guess they don't know what else to do."

He looked at me and shrugged. "I need time," he muttered. "I need a way to put things on pause, set them right, and press play again."

I noted the deep furrow in his brow. "Dad, I don't think that's possible."

He chuckled. "We've done it before. I can remember. . . ."

The focus in his eyes changed. He watched me for a moment, seeming to ask me a question without words.

"Dad?"

"Yes."

"Are you all right?"

He blinked a few times. "Yes, dear, quite all right. Why don't you get to work on those budget cuts. We can go over your ideas this afternoon. I need to speak with your mother."

"Sure." Math wasn't a skill that came to me naturally, so I had to work twice as long on any proposals for budget cuts or financial plans. But I absolutely refused to have one of Dad's advisers come behind me with a calculator to clean up my mess. Even if I had to stay up all night, I always made sure my work was accurate.

Of course, Ahren was naturally good at math, but he was never forced to sit through meetings about budgets or rezoning or health care. He got off scot-free by seven stupid minutes.

Dad patted me on the shoulder before dashing out of the room. It took me longer than usual to focus on the numbers. I couldn't help but be distracted by the look on his face and the unmistakable certainty that it was tied to me.

CHAPTER 2

AFTER WORKING ON THE BUDGET report for a few hours, I decided I needed a break and retreated to my room to get a hand massage from Neena. I loved those little bits of luxury in my day. Dresses made to my exact measurements, exotic desserts flown in simply because it was Thursday, and an endless supply of beautiful things were all perks; and they were easily my favorite parts of the job.

My room overlooked the gardens. As the day shifted, the light changed to a warm, honey color, brightening the high walls. I focused on the heat and Neena's deliberate fingers.

"Anyway, his face got all funny. It was kind of like he disappeared for a minute."

I was trying to explain Dad's out-of-character departure this morning, but it was hard to get it across. I didn't even know if he found Mom or not, as he never came back to the office.

"Do you think he's sick? He does seem tired these days." Neena's hands worked her magic as she spoke.

"Does he?" I asked, thinking that Dad didn't seem tired exactly. "He's probably just stressed. How could he not be with all the decisions he has to make?"

"And someday that will be you," she commented, her tone a mix of genuine worry and playful amusement.

"Which means you will be giving me twice as many massages."

"I don't know," she said. "I think in a few years I might like to try something new."

I scrunched my face. "What else would you do? There aren't many positions better than working in the palace."

There was a knock on the door, and she didn't have a chance to answer the question.

I stood, throwing my blazer back on to look presentable, and gave a nod to Neena to let my guests in.

Mom came around the door, smiling, with Dad contentedly trailing her steps. I couldn't help but notice it was always this way. At state events or important dinners, Mom was beside Dad or situated right behind him. But when they were just husband and wife—not king and queen—he followed her everywhere.

"Hi, Mom." I walked over to hug her.

Mom tucked my hair behind my ear, smiling at me. "I like this look."

I stood back proudly and smoothed out my dress with my hands. "The bracelets really set it off, don't you think?"

She giggled. "Excellent attention to detail." Every once in

a while Mom let me pick out jewelry or shoes for her, but it was rare. Mom didn't find it as much fun as I did, and she didn't rely on the extras for beauty. In her case, she really didn't need it. I liked that she was classic.

Mom turned and touched Neena's shoulder. "You're excused," she said quietly.

Neena instantly curtsied and left us alone.

"Is something wrong?" I asked.

"No, sweetheart. We simply want to speak in private." Dad held out a hand and ushered us all to the table. "We have an opportunity to talk to you about."

"Opportunity? Are we traveling?" I adored traveling. "Please tell me we're finally going on a beach trip. Could it just be the six of us?"

"Not exactly. We wouldn't be going somewhere so much as having visitors," Mom explained.

"Oh! Company! Who's coming?"

They exchanged glances, then Mom continued talking. "You know that things are precarious right now. The people are restless and unhappy, and we cannot figure out how to ease the tension."

I sighed. "I know."

"We're seeking a way to boost morale," Dad added.

I perked up. Morale boosting typically involved a celebration. And I was always up for a party.

"What did you have in mind?" I started designing a new dress in my head and dismissed it almost as quickly. That wasn't what needed my attention at the moment.

"Well," Dad started, "the public responds best to something positive with our family. When your mother and I were married, it was one of the best seasons in our country. And do you remember how people threw parties in the street when they found out Osten was coming?"

I smiled. I was eight when Osten was born, and I'd never forget how excited everyone got just over the announcement. I heard music playing from my bedroom practically until dawn.

"That was marvelous."

"It was. And now the people look to you. It won't be long before you're queen." Dad paused. "We thought that perhaps you'd be willing to do something publicly, something that would be exciting for the people but also might be very beneficial to you."

I narrowed my eyes, not sure where this was going. "I'm listening."

Mom cleared her throat. "You know that in the past, princesses were married off to princes from other countries to solidify our international relations."

"I did hear you use the past tense there, correct?"

She laughed, but I wasn't amused. "Yes."

"Good. Because Prince Nathaniel looks like a zombie, Prince Hector dances like a zombie, and if the prince from the German Federation doesn't learn to embrace personal hygiene by the Christmas party, he shouldn't be invited."

Mom rubbed the side of her head in frustration. "Eadlyn, you've always been so picky."

Dad shrugged. "Maybe that's not a bad thing," he said, earning a glare from Mom.

I frowned. "What in the world are you talking about?"

"You know how your mother and I met," Dad began.

I rolled my eyes. "Everyone does. You two are practically a fairy tale."

At those words their eyes went soft, and smiles washed over their faces. Their bodies seemed to tilt slightly toward each other, and Dad bit his lip looking at Mom.

"Excuse me. Firstborn in the room, do you mind?"

Mom blushed as Dad cleared his throat and continued. "The Selection process was very successful for us. And though my parents had their problems, it worked well for them, too. So . . . we were hoping. . . ." He hesitated and met my eyes.

I was slow to pick up on their hints. I knew what the Selection was, but never, not even once, had it been suggested as an option for any of us, let alone me.

"No."

Mom put up her hands, cautioning me. "Just listen—"

"A Selection?" I burst out. "That's insane!"

"Eadlyn, you're being irrational."

I glared at her. "You promised—*you promised*—you'd never force me into marrying someone for an alliance. How is this any better?"

"Hear us out," she urged.

"No!" I shouted. "I won't do it."

"Calm down, love."

"Don't talk to me like that. I'm not a child!"

Mom sighed. "You're certainly acting like one."

"You're ruining my life!" I ran my fingers through my hair and took several deep breaths, hoping it would help me think. This couldn't happen. Not to me.

"It's a huge opportunity," Dad insisted.

"You're trying to shackle me to a stranger!"

"I told you she'd be stubborn," Mom muttered to Dad.

"Wonder where she gets that from," he shot back with a smile.

"Don't talk about me like I'm not in the room!"

"I'm sorry," Dad said. "We just need you to consider this."

"What about Ahren? Can't he do it?"

"Ahren isn't going to be the future king. Besides, he has Camille."

Princess Camille was the heir to the French throne, and a few years ago she'd managed to bat her lashes all the way into Ahren's heart.

"Then make them get married!" I pleaded.

"Camille will be queen when her time comes, and she, like you, will have to ask her partner to marry her. If it was Ahren's choice, we'd consider it; but it's not."

"What about Kaden? Can't you have him do it?"

Mom laughed humorlessly. "He's fourteen! We don't have that kind of time. The people need something to be excited about now." She narrowed her eyes at me. "And, honestly, isn't it time you look for someone to rule beside you?"

Dad nodded. "It's true. It's not a role that should be shouldered alone."

"But I don't want to get married," I pleaded. "Please don't

make me do this. I'm only eighteen."

"Which is how old I was when I married your father," Mom stated.

"I'm not ready," I urged. "I don't want a husband. Please don't do this to me."

Mom reached across the table and put her hand on mine. "No one would be doing anything to you. You would be doing something for your people. You'd be giving them a gift."

"You mean faking a smile when I'd rather cry?"

She gave me a fleeting frown. "That has always been part of our job."

I stared at her, silently demanding a better answer.

"Eadlyn, why don't you take some time to think this over?" Dad said calmly. "I know this is a big thing we're asking of you."

"Does that mean I have a choice?"

Dad inhaled deeply, considering. "Well, love, you'll really have thirty-five choices."

I leaped up from my chair, pointing toward the door.

"Get out!" I demanded. "Get! Out!"

Without another word they left my room.

Didn't they know who I was, what they'd trained me for? I was Eadlyn Schreave. No one was more powerful than me.

So if they thought I was going down without a fight, they were sadly mistaken.

CHAPTER 3

I DECIDED TO TAKE DINNER in my room. I didn't feel like seeing my family at the moment. I was irate with all of them. At my parents for being happy, at Ahren for not picking up the pace eighteen years ago, at Kaden and Osten for being so young.

Neena circled me, filling my cup as she spoke. "Do you think you'll go through with it, miss?" she asked.

"I'm still trying to figure a way out."

"What if you said you were already in love with somebody?"

I shook my head as I poked at my food. "I insulted my three most likely candidates right in front of them."

She set a small plate of chocolates in the middle of the table, guessing correctly that I'd probably want those more than the caviar-garnished salmon.

"Perhaps a guard then? Happens to the maids often enough," she suggested with a giggle.

I scoffed. "That's fine for them, but I'm not that desperate."

Her laughter faded.

I saw immediately that I had offended her, but that was the truth. I couldn't settle for any old person, let alone a guard. Even considering it was a waste of time. I needed a way out of this whole situation.

"I don't mean it like that, Neena. It's just that people expect certain things from me."

"Of course."

"I'm done. You can go for the night; I'll leave the cart in the hallway."

She nodded and left without another word.

I grazed on the chocolates before completely giving up on the food and slipped into my nightgown. I couldn't reason with Mom and Dad right now, and Neena didn't understand. I needed to talk to the only person who might see my side, the person who sometimes felt like he was half of me. I needed Ahren.

"Are you busy?" I asked, cracking open his door.

Ahren was sitting at his desk, writing. His blond hair was end-of-the-day messy, but his eyes were far from tired, and he looked so much like the pictures of Dad when he was younger it was eerie. He was still dressed from dinner but had taken off his coat and tie, settling in for the evening.

"Knock, for goodness' sake."

"I know, I know; but it's an emergency."

"Then get a guard," he snapped back, returning to his papers.

"That's already been suggested," I muttered to myself. "I'm serious, Ahren; I need your help."

Ahren peeked over his shoulder at me, and I could see he was already planning to give in. He used his foot to push out the seat next to him casually. "Step into my office."

Sitting, I sighed. "What are you writing?"

He quickly piled papers on top of the one he'd been working on. "A letter to Camille."

"You know you could simply phone her."

He grinned. "Oh, I will. But then I'll send her this, too."

"That makes no sense. What could you possibly have to talk about that would fill an entire phone call and a letter?"

He tilted his head. "For your information, they serve different purposes. The calls are for updates and to see how her day went. The letters are for the things I can't always say out loud."

"Oh, really?" I leaned over, reaching for the paper.

Before I could even get close, Ahren's hand gripped my wrist. "I will murder you," he vowed.

"Good," I shot. "Then you can be the heir, and you can go through a Selection and kiss your precious Camille goodbye."

He scrunched his forehead. "What?"

I slumped back into my chair. "Mom and Dad need to

boost morale. They've decided that, for the sake of Illéa," I said in mock patriotism, "I need to go through a Selection."

I was expecting abject horror. Perhaps a sympathetic hand on my shoulder. But Ahren threw back his head and laughed.

"Ahren!"

He continued to howl, pitching himself forward and hitting his knee.

"You're going to wrinkle your suit," I warned, which only made him laugh harder. "For goodness' sake, stop it! What am I supposed to do?"

"As if I know! I can't believe they think this would even work," he added, his smile still not fading.

"What's that supposed to mean?"

He shrugged. "I don't know. I guess I thought, if you ever did get married, it'd be down the line. I think everyone assumed that."

"And what is *that* supposed to mean?"

The warm touch I'd been hoping for finally came as he reached for my hand. "Come on, Eady. You've always been independent. It's the queen in you. You like to be in charge, do things on your own. I didn't think you'd partner up with anyone until you at least got to reign for a while."

"Not like I really had a choice in the first place," I mumbled, tilting my head to the floor but still looking to my brother.

He gave me a little pout. "Poor little princess. Don't want to rule the world?"

I swatted his hand away. "Seven minutes. It should have

been you. I'd much rather sit alone and scribble away instead of do all that stupid paperwork. And this ridiculous Selection nonsense! Can't you see how dreadful this is?"

"How did you get roped into this anyway? I thought they'd done away with it."

I rolled my eyes again. "It has absolutely nothing to do with me. That's the worst part. Dad's facing public opposition, so he's trying to distract them." I shook my head. "It's getting really bad, Ahren. People are destroying homes and businesses. Some have died. Dad isn't completely sure where it's coming from, but he thinks it's people our age, the generation that grew up without castes, causing most of it."

He made a face. "That doesn't make sense. How could growing up without those restrictions make you upset?"

I paused, thinking. How could I explain what we could only really guess at? "Well, I grew up being told I was going to be queen one day. That was it. No choice. You grew up knowing you had options. You could go into the military, you could become an ambassador, you could do plenty of things. But what if that wasn't really happening? What if you didn't have all the opportunities you thought you would?"

"Huh," he said, following. "So they're being denied jobs?"

"Jobs, education, money. I've heard of people refusing to let their kids get married because of old castes. Nothing is happening the way Dad thought it would, and it's nearly impossible to control. Can we force people to be fair?"

"And that's what Dad's trying to figure out now?" he asked, skeptical.

"Yes, and I'm the smoke-and-mirror act diverting their attention while he comes up with a plan."

He chuckled. "That makes much more sense than you suddenly being romantically inclined."

I cocked my head. "Let it go, Ahren. So I'm not interested in marriage. Why does that matter? Other women can stay single."

"But other women aren't expected to produce an heir."

I hit him again. "Help me! What do I do?"

His eyes searched mine, and I knew, as easily as I could read any emotion in him, that he saw I was terrified. Not irritated or angry. Not outraged or repulsed.

I was scared.

It was one thing to be expected to rule, to hold the weight of millions of people in my hands. That was a job, a task. I could check things off lists, delegate. But this was much more personal, one more piece of my life that ought to be mine but wasn't.

His playful smile disappeared, and he pulled his chair closer to mine. "If they're looking to distract people, maybe you could suggest other . . . opportunities. A possible marriage isn't the only choice. That said, if Mom and Dad came to this conclusion, they might have already exhausted every other option."

I buried my head in my hands. I didn't want to tell him I tried to offer up him as an alternative or that I thought Kaden might even be acceptable. I sensed he was right, that the Selection was their last hope.

"Here's the thing, Eady. You'll be the first girl to hold the throne fully in her own right. And people expect a lot from you."

"Like I don't already know that."

"But," he continued, "that also gives you a lot of bargaining power."

I raised my head marginally. "What do you mean?"

"If they really need you to do this, then negotiate."

I sat up straight, my mind running around in circles, trying to think of what I could ask for. There might be a way to get through this quickly, without it even ending in a proposal.

Without a proposal!

If I spoke fast enough, I could probably get Dad to agree to practically anything so long as he got his Selection out of it.

"Negotiate!" I whispered.

"Exactly."

I stood up, grabbed Ahren by his ears, and planted a kiss on his forehead. "You are my absolute hero!"

He smiled. "Anything for you, my queen."

I giggled, shoving him. "Thanks, Ahren."

"Get to work." He waved me toward the door, and I suspected he was actually more eager to get back to his letter than he was for me to come up with a plan.

I dashed from the room, heading to my own to fetch some paper. I needed to think.

As I rounded the corner, I ran smack into someone, falling backward onto the carpet.

"Ow!" I complained, looking up to see Kile Woodwork, Miss Marlee's son.

Kile and the rest of the Woodworks had rooms on the same floor as our family, a singularly huge honor. Or irritation, depending on how one felt about the Woodworks.

"Do you mind?" I snapped.

"I wasn't the one running," he answered, picking up the books he'd dropped. "You ought to be looking where you're going."

"A gentleman would offer his hand right now," I reminded him.

Kile's hair flopped across his eyes as he looked over at me. He was in desperate need of a cut and a shave, and his shirt was too big for him. I didn't know who I was more embarrassed for: him for looking so sloppy or my family for having to be seen with such a disaster.

What was especially irritating was that he wasn't always so scruffy, and he didn't have to be now. How hard would it be to run a brush through his hair?

"Eadlyn, you've never thought I was a gentleman."

"True." I pulled myself up without help and brushed off my robe.

For the last six months I had been spared Kile's less-than-thrilling company. He'd gone to Fennley to enroll in some accelerated course, and his mother had been lamenting his absence ever since the day he left. I didn't know what he was studying, and I didn't particularly care. But he was back now, and his presence was another stressor on an ever-growing list.

"And what would make such a lady run like that in the first place?"

"Matters you are far too dim to comprehend."

He laughed. "Right, because I'm such a simpleton. It's a miracle I manage to bathe myself."

I was about to ask if he did bathe, because he looked like he'd been running away from anything that resembled a bar of soap.

"I hope one of those books is a primer on etiquette. You seriously need a refresher."

"You're not queen yet, Eadlyn. Take it down a notch." He walked away, and I was furious with myself for not getting the last word.

I pressed on. There were bigger problems in my life right now than the state of Kile's manners. I couldn't waste my time quibbling with people or being distracted by anything that couldn't put the Selection to death.

CHAPTER 4

"I WANT TO BE CLEAR," I said, sitting down in Dad's office. "I have no desire to get married."

He nodded. "I understand that you don't want to get married today, but it was always something you'd have to do, Eadlyn. You're obligated to continue the royal line."

I hated it when he talked about my future like that, like sex and love and babies weren't happy things but duties performed to keep the country running. It took every speck of joy out of the prospect.

Of all the things in my life, shouldn't those be the real pleasures, the best parts?

I shook the worry away and focused on the task at hand.

"I understand. And I agree that it's important," I replied diplomatically. "But weren't you ever worried when you went through your Selection that no one in the pool was right for you? Or that maybe they were there for the wrong reason?"

His lips hitched up in a smile. "Every waking moment, and half the time I slept."

He'd told me a handful of vague stories about one girl who'd been so pliable he could hardly stand her and another who had tried to manipulate the process at every turn. I didn't know many names or details, and that was fine with me. I had never liked to imagine Dad possibly falling in love with anyone but Mom.

"And don't you think that as the first woman to fully control the crown, there should be . . . some standards set for who might rule beside me?"

He tilted his head. "Go on."

"I'm sure there's some sort of vetting process in place to make sure an actual psychopath doesn't make his way into the palace, yes?"

"Of course." He grinned as if this wasn't a valid concern.

"But I don't trust just anyone to do this job with me. So"—I sighed deeply—"I will agree to go through with this ridiculous stunt if you make me a few tiny promises."

"It's not a stunt. It's had an excellent track record. But please, dear girl, tell me what you want."

"First, I want the contestants to have the freedom to leave of their own free will. I won't have someone feeling obligated to stay if they don't care for me or the life they'd have to lead in the palace."

"I fully agree to that," he said forcefully. Seemed like I had touched a nerve.

"Excellent. And I know you might be opposed to the idea, but if by the end of this I can't find anyone suitable, then we call the whole thing off. No prince, no wedding."

"Ah!" he said, leaning forward in his chair and pointing a calculating finger at me. "If I allow that, you'll turn them all away the first day. You won't even try!"

I paused, thinking. "What if I guaranteed you a timeline? I would keep the Selection running for, say, three months and weigh my options for at least that amount of time. After then, if I haven't found a suitable match, all the contestants are released."

He ran his hand across his mouth and shifted in his chair a little before pressing his eyes into mine. "Eadlyn, you know how important this is, don't you?"

"Of course," I replied instantly, very aware of how serious this was. I sensed one wrong move would set my life on a course I could never correct.

"You need to do this and do it well. For everyone's sake. Our lives, all of them, are given over in service to our people."

I looked away. If anything, it felt like Mom, Dad, and I were the trinity of sacrifice here, with the others doing as they pleased.

"I won't let you down," I promised. "You do what you must. Make your plans, find a way to appease our public, and I will give you an acceptable window of time to pull it all together."

His eyes darted toward the ceiling in thought. "Three months? And you swear you'll try?"

I held up my hand. "I give you my word. I'll even sign something if you like, but I can't promise you I'll fall in love."

"Wouldn't be so sure if I was you," he said knowingly. But I wasn't him, and I wasn't Mom. No matter how romantic he thought this was, all I could think of were the thirty-five loud, obnoxious, weird-smelling boys who were about to invade my home. Nothing about that sounded magical.

"It's a deal."

I stood, practically ready to dance. "Really?"

"Really."

I took his hand and sealed my future with a single shake. "Thank you, Dad."

I left the room before he could see how big my smile was. I had already been running through how I could get most of the boys to leave of their own volition. I could be intimidating when I needed to be or find ways to make the palace a very unwelcoming environment. I also had a secret weapon in Osten, who was the most mischievous of us all and would help me if I asked him to, probably with minimal persuasion.

I admired the thought of a common boy feeling brave enough to face the challenge of becoming a prince. But no one was going to tie me down before I was ready, and I was going to make sure those poor suckers knew what they were signing up for.

They kept the studio cold, but once the lights came on, we might as well have been in an oven for all the good it did. I'd learned years ago to keep my clothing choices for the *Report* airy, which was why my dress tonight fell off my shoulders. My look was classy, as always, but not something that would subject me to a heatstroke.

"That's the perfect dress," Mom commented, pulling at the little ruffles on the sleeves. "You look lovely."

"Thank you. So do you."

She smiled as she continued to straighten my dress. "Thank you, sweetheart. I know you're feeling a little overwhelmed, but I think a Selection will be good for everyone. You're alone a lot, and it's something we would have to think about eventually, and—"

"And it will make the people happy. I know."

I tried to hide the misery in my voice. We had technically moved past selling off the royal daughters, but . . . this didn't feel that different. Didn't she get that?

Her eyes moved from the gown to my face. Something in them told me she was sorry.

"I know you feel like this is a sacrifice; and it's true that when you live a life of service, there are many things you do, not because you want to, but because you must." She swallowed. "But through this I found your father, and I found my closest friends, and I learned that I was stronger than I ever thought I could be. I know about the agreement you made with your dad, and if this ends without you finding the right person, so be it. But please, let yourself experience something here. Sharpen yourself, learn something. And try not to hate us for asking you to do it."

"I don't hate you."

"You at least considered it when we proposed this," she said with a grin. "Didn't you?"

"I'm eighteen. I'm genetically encoded to fight with my parents."

"I don't mind a good fight so long as you still know how much I love you in the end."

I reached to hug her. "And I love you. Promise."

She held me for a moment, then pulled away, smoothing my dress to make sure I was still immaculate before she went to find Dad. I walked to take my seat next to Ahren, who wiggled his eyebrows at me teasingly. "Looking good, sis. Practically bridal."

I swung my skirt and sat down gracefully. "One more word and I will shave your head in your sleep."

"I love you, too."

I tried not to smile but failed. He just always knew.

The room filled with the palace household. Miss Lucy sat alone, as General Leger was on rounds, and Mr. and Mrs. Woodwork sat behind the cameras with Kile and Josie. They were the Woodworks' only children, and I knew Miss Marlee meant the world to Mom, so I kept it to myself that I thought her kids were the absolute worst. Kile wasn't as obnoxious as Josie, but, in all the years I'd known him, he'd never made anything remotely close to an interesting conversation. So help me, if I ever got a bad case of insomnia, I'd hire him to sit in my room and talk. Problem solved. And Josie . . . I didn't have words for how wretched that girl was.

Dad's advisers filed in, bowing as they came. There was only one woman in Dad's cabinet, Lady Brice Mannor. She was lovely and petite, and I was never sure how someone so demure managed to stay afloat in the political arena. I'd never heard her raise her voice or get angry, but people listened to her. The men didn't listen to me unless I was stern.

Her presence made me curious though. What would happen if I, as queen, made my entire board of counselors women?

That might be an interesting experiment.

The chairmen and advisers delivered their announcements and updates, and finally, Gavril turned to me.

Gavril Fadaye had slicked-back silver hair but a very handsome face. He'd been talking recently about retirement, but after an announcement this big, he'd have to stick around a bit longer.

"Tonight, Illéa, to conclude our program, we have some very exciting news. And there is no one better to deliver it than our future queen, the beautiful Eadlyn Schreave."

He swept his hand grandly in my direction, and I smiled widely as I walked across the carpeted stage to polite applause.

Gavril gave me a quick embrace and a kiss on each cheek. "Princess Eadlyn, welcome."

"Thanks, Gavril."

"Now, I have to be honest. It feels like only yesterday I was announcing the birth of you and your brother Ahren. I can't believe it's been more than eighteen years!"

"It's true. We're all grown up." I looked toward my family, sharing a warm gaze.

"You're on the edge of making history. I think all of Illéa is eager to see what you'll do a few years down the road when you become queen."

"That'll certainly be an exciting time, but I'm not sure I want to wait that long to make history." I gave him a playful nudge with my elbow, and he mocked surprise.

"Why don't you tell us what you have in mind, Your Highness?"

I squared my shoulders in front of camera C and smiled. "Our great country has gone through many changes over the years. In my parents' lifetimes alone we've seen the rebel forces within our country practically run into extinction, and though we still face challenges, the caste system no longer divides our people along imaginary lines. We live in an era of extraordinary freedom, and we wait with anticipation to see our nation become everything it possibly can."

I remembered to smile and speak articulately. Years of lessons on how to address an audience had drilled the proper technique into me, and I knew I was hitting every last point I was meant to as I delivered my announcement.

"And that's great . . . but I'm still an eighteen-year-old girl." The small audience of guests and advisers giggled. "It gets a little boring when you spend the majority of the day in an office with your dad. No offense, Your Majesty," I added, turning to Dad.

"None taken," he called back.

"And so I've decided it's time for a change of pace. It's time to search, not just for someone to be a coworker with me in this very demanding job, but for a partner to walk with me through life. To do that, I'm hoping Illéa will indulge my deepest wish: to have a Selection."

The advisers gasped and muttered. I saw the shocked faces of the staff. It became clear that the only person who was already in on this was Gavril, which surprised me.

"Tomorrow, letters will be sent to all the eligible young men in Illéa. You'll have two weeks to decide whether you would like to compete for my hand. I realize, of course, that this is uncharted territory. We've never had a female-run Selection before. Still, even though I have three brothers, I'm very excited to meet another prince of Illéa. And I'm hoping that all of Illéa will celebrate with me."

I gave a small curtsy and retreated to my seat. Mom and Dad were beaming proudly at me, and I tried to tell myself that their reaction was enough, though I felt like my blood was trembling in my veins. I couldn't help but think I'd missed something, that there was a gaping hole in the net I'd set up to catch myself.

But there was nothing I could do. I'd just thrown myself off the ledge.

CHAPTER 5

I KNEW WE HAD AN arsenal of staff working at the palace, but I was convinced the majority of them had been in hiding until today. As the announcement of this unexpected Selection spread, it wasn't simply the maids and butlers running around in preparation, but people I'd never even seen before.

My daily workload of reading reports and sitting in on meetings shifted as I became the focal point of the Selection preparations.

"This is slightly less expensive, Your Highness, but it is still incredibly comfortable and would work well with the existing decor." A man held out a very large swatch of fabric, which he draped over the previous two options.

I touched it, enchanted by the texture of cloth as I usually was, though this was clearly not intended to be worn.

"I'm not sure I understand why we're doing this," I confessed.

The man, one of the palace decorators, pressed his lips together. "It has been suggested that some of the guest rooms are a bit feminine and that your suitors might be more comfortable in something like this," he said, pulling out yet another option. "We can make a room look entirely different with a simple bedspread," he assured me.

"Fine," I said, thinking it was a little unnecessary to get this worked up over some sheets. "But do I need to make this decision?"

He smiled kindly. "Your fingerprints will be all over this Selection, miss. Even if you don't choose, people will assume you did. We might as well get your authority on all things."

I stared at the fabric, more than a little exhausted thinking about how all these silly details would point back to me. "This one." I chose the least-expensive option. It was a deep green and would be perfectly acceptable for a three-month stay.

"Very wise, Your Highness," the decorator complimented. "Now, should we consider adding new art as well?" He clapped his hands, and a stream of maids walked in carrying paintings. I sighed, knowing my afternoon was lost.

The following morning I was summoned to the dining hall. Mom came with me, but Dad couldn't be pulled away from his work.

A man I assumed was our head chef bowed to us, not able to go very low because of his wide stomach. His face was closer to red than white, but he didn't sweat, which made me think that all the years in the kitchen had simply steamed him.

"Thank you for joining us, Your Majesty, Your Highness. The kitchen staff has been working day and night to find appropriate options for the first dinner once your suitors arrive. We want to serve seven courses, obviously."

"Of course!" Mom replied.

The chef smiled at her. "Naturally, we would like your approval for the final menu."

I groaned internally. A true seven-course meal could take six hours from the first sip of a cocktail to the final bite of chocolate. How long would it take to sample several different options for each course?

About eight hours, it turned out, and I had a dreadful stomachache for the rest of the day, which made me less than enthusiastic when someone came asking about music selections for the evening of the first dinner.

The hallways were like crowded streets, and every corner of the palace was noisy with speedy preparations. I endured it as best I could until Dad stopped me in passing one day.

"We were thinking about making a special room for the Selected. What do you think about—"

"Enough!" I sighed, exasperated. "I don't care. I have no idea what a boy would like in a recreational space, so I suggest you ask someone with some testosterone. And as for me, I'll be in the garden."

Dad could tell I was near a breaking point, and he let

me pass without a fight. I was thankful for the momentary respite.

I lay on my stomach in my bikini on a blanket in the open stretch of grass that spread out just before the forest. I wished, as I had so many times before, that we had a pool. I was pretty good at getting my way, but Dad never budged on the pool issue. When the palace was mine, that was the first thing on the agenda.

I sketched dresses in my book, trying to relax. As the sun warmed me, the quick scratch of my pencil blended with the sound of rustling leaves, making a lovely, tranquil song. I mourned the loss of peace in my life. *Three months,* I recited. *Three months, and then everything goes back to normal.*

A piercing laugh polluted the stillness of the garden. "Josie," I muttered to myself. Shading my eyes, I turned and saw her walking toward me. She was with one of her friends, an upper-class girl she'd chosen to associate with specifically because the company in the palace wasn't enough for her.

I closed my book, hiding my designs, and turned onto my back simply to take in the sun.

"It will be a good experience for everyone," I heard Josie remark to her friend. "I don't get to interact with boys very often, so it'll be nice to have an opportunity to talk to some. One day, when my wedding is arranged, I'd like to be able to carry on a conversation."

I rolled my eyes. If I thought I'd have the slightest attachment to these boys, it would have bothered me that she thought they were here for her. Then again, Josie thought everything existed for her. And the idea that she was so important that her marriage would need to be arranged on her behalf was comical. She could marry anyone off the street and no one would care one way or the other.

"I hope I'll be able to visit during the Selection," her friend replied. "It'll be so fun!"

"Of course, Shannon! I'll make sure all my friends get to come often. It'll be valuable for you as well."

How kind of her to offer up my home and events as learning opportunities for her little buddies. I took a deep breath. I needed to focus on relaxing.

"Eadlyn!" Josie cried, spotting me.

I groaned, then raised a hand to acknowledge her, hoping the silence would convey my wish for privacy.

"How excited are you for the Selection?" she yelled, continuing over.

I wasn't going to holler like a farmhand, so I said nothing. Eventually, Josie and her friend were standing above me, blocking the sun.

"Didn't you hear me, Eadlyn? Aren't you excited for the Selection?"

Josie never addressed me properly.

"Of course."

"Me, too! I think it'll be exciting to have all the company."

"You won't have any company," I reminded her. "These boys are *my* guests."

She tipped her head like I was stating the obvious. "I

know! But it'll still be nice to have more people around."

"Josie, how old are you?"

"Fifteen," she answered proudly.

"I thought so. If you really want to, I'm sure you could get out and meet people of your own accord now. You're certainly old enough."

She smiled. "I don't think so. That's not exactly appropriate."

I didn't want to get into this argument again. *I* was the one who couldn't pick up and leave the palace without warning. Security sweeps, proper announcements, and protocol reviews were all necessary before I could even consider it.

Also, I constantly had to be aware of the company I kept. I couldn't be seen with just anyone. An unflattering picture wasn't simply taken; it was documented, stored, and resurrected whenever the newspapers needed to criticize me. I had to be relentlessly on my toes to avoid anything that could possibly tarnish my image, my family's image, or the country at large.

Josie was a commoner. She didn't have any such restrictions.

Not that it stopped her from acting like she did.

"Well, at least you have some company for today, then. If you two don't mind, I'm trying to rest."

"Certainly, Your Highness." Her friend bowed her head. Okay, she wasn't too bad.

"I'll see you at dinner!" Josie was a little too enthusiastic about it.

I tried to lull myself back into relaxation, but Josie's piercing voice kept finding its way over to me, and I eventually scooped up my blanket and sketches, and headed inside. If I couldn't enjoy myself here, I might as well figure out something else to do.

After being so exposed to the bright Angeles sun, the palace halls looked like twilight as I waited for my eyes to adjust. I blinked hard, trying to make out the face of the person coming toward me. It was Osten, carrying two notebooks as he rushed down the hall.

He shoved the books into my arms. "Hide these in your room, okay? And if anyone asks, you haven't seen me."

As quickly as he appeared, he vanished. I sighed, knowing that even attempting to comprehend would be pointless. I sometimes couldn't stand the pressure placed on me from being born first, but thank goodness it was me and not Osten. Every time I tried to imagine him at the helm, it gave me a headache.

I flipped through the notebooks, curious as to what he was plotting. Turned out they weren't his at all. They were Josie's. I recognized her babyish handwriting, and, if that hadn't given it away, the sheets of her and Ahren's names in hearts made it all too obvious. It wasn't just Ahren's name though. A few pages later she was in love with all four members of Choosing Yesterday, a popular band, and just after that it was some actor. Anyone with any sort of clout would do, it seemed.

I decided to set the books on the floor by the doors to the

garden. Whatever Osten had planned, there was no way it would be as distressing as her stumbling across them when she came inside, with no clue as to how they'd gotten there or who had seen them.

For someone who prided herself on being so close to the royal family, she really should have learned a lesson or two in discretion by now.

When I got to my room, Neena was at the ready, grabbing my blanket to place in the wash. I threw something on, not really in the mood to think about my outfit too much today. As I was about to fix my hair, I noticed some files on the table.

"Lady Brice dropped those off for you," Neena said.

I stared at the folders. Though it was my first piece of actual work in a week, I couldn't be bothered. "I'll get to them later," I promised, knowing that I probably wouldn't. I'd maybe look at them tomorrow. Today was mine.

I pinned back my hair, double-checked my makeup, and went to look for Mom. I could use the company, and I felt pretty confident that she wouldn't ask me to pick out furniture or food.

I found her alone in the Women's Room. A plaque beside the door declared that the space was actually titled the Newsome Library, but I'd never heard anyone call it by that name except for Mom on occasion. It was the space where the women congregated, so the original label seemed more practical, I supposed.

I could tell Mom was in there before I even opened the

door because I heard her playing the piano, and her sound was unmistakable. She loved to tell the story of how Dad made her pick out four brand-new pianos, each with various attributes, after they were married. They were placed all over the palace. One was in her suite, a second in Dad's, one here, and another in a largely unused parlor on the fourth floor.

I was still jealous of how easy she made it look. I remembered her warning me that one day time would take the dexterity out of her hands, and she'd only be able to plunk away at one or two keys at a time. So far time had failed.

I tried to be quiet, but she heard me all the same.

"Hello, darling," she called, pulling her fingers away from the keys. "Come sit with me."

"I didn't mean to interrupt." I walked across the room, settling next to her on the bench.

"You didn't. I was clearing my head, and I feel much better now."

"Is something wrong?"

She smiled distractedly and rubbed her hand over my back. "No. Just the everyday wear and tear of the job."

"I know what you mean," I said, running my fingers along the keys, not actually making any sound.

"I keep thinking that I've gotten to a point where I've seen it all, where I've mastered everything about being queen. No sooner do I think it than everything changes. There are . . . Well, you have enough to worry about today. Let's not bother with it."

With some work she pasted a smile back onto her face, and while I wanted to know what was troubling her—because, in the end, all those troubles also fell on me—she was right. I simply couldn't deal with it today.

It seemed she hardly could either.

"Do you ever regret it?" I asked, seeing the sadness in her eyes despite her efforts. "Entering the Selection and ending up queen?"

I was grateful she didn't just immediately say yes or no but actually considered the question.

"I don't regret marrying your father. I sometimes wonder about the life I would have had without the Selection, or if I had still come to the palace but lost. I think I would have been fine. Not unhappy exactly, but not aware of what else there could have been for me. But the path to him was a difficult one, mostly because I didn't want to walk it."

"At all?"

She shook her head. "It wasn't my idea to enter the Selection."

My mouth fell open. She'd never told me that. "Whose was it?"

"That's not important," she answered quickly. "But I can tell you that I understand your reservations. I think the process will teach you a lot about yourself. I hope you'll trust me on this."

"It'd be a lot easier to trust you if I knew you were doing this for me and not to buy yourself some peace." The words came out sharper than I meant them to.

She took a deep breath. "I know you think this is selfish, but you'll see. One day the welfare of the country will be on your shoulders, and you'll be surprised at what you'd try in order to keep it all from crumbling. I never thought we'd have another Selection, but plans change when that much is demanded of you."

"Plenty is demanded of me now," I shot back.

"One, watch your tone," she warned. "And two, you only see a fraction of the work. You have no idea how much pressure is placed on your father."

I sat there, silent. I wanted to leave. If she didn't like my tone, then why did she push me?

"Eadlyn," she began quietly. "The timing of this happened to fall when it did. But, honestly, sooner or later I would have done something."

"What do you mean?"

"You seem shut off in a way, disconnected from your people. I know you're constantly worried about the demands you will face as queen, but it's time you see the needs of others."

"You don't think I do that now?" Did she see what I did all day?

She pressed her lips together. "No, honey. Not if it comes before your comfort."

I wanted to scream at her, and at Dad, too. Sure, I took shelter in long baths or a drink with dinner. I didn't think that was too much to ask for considering what I sacrificed.

"I didn't realize you thought I was so flawed." I stood, turning away.

"Eadlyn, that's not what I'm saying."

"It is. That's fine." I made my way to the door. The accusation filled me with so much rage I could barely stand it.

"Eadlyn, darling, we want you to be the best queen you can be, that's all," she pleaded.

"I will," I answered, one foot in the hallway. "And I certainly don't need a boy to show me how to do that."

I tried to calm myself before walking away. It felt like the universe was plotting against me, its arms taking turns swatting me down. I repeated in my head that it was only three months, only three months . . . until I heard someone crying.

"Are you sure?" It sounded like General Leger.

"I talked with her this morning. She decided to keep it." Miss Lucy pulled in a jagged breath.

"Did you tell her that we could give that baby everything? That we had more money than we could ever spend? That we'd love it, no matter its faults?" General Leger's words fell out in a whispered rush.

"All that and more," Miss Lucy insisted. "I knew there was a huge chance of the baby being born with mental issues. I told her we'd be able to tend to any need he had, that the queen herself would see to it. She said she talked with her family, and they agreed to help her, and that she never really wanted to let the baby go in the first place. She only looked into adoption because she thought she'd be alone. She apologized, like that could fix it."

Miss Lucy sniffed as if she was trying to quiet her sobs. I

drew close to the corner of the passage, listening

"I'm so sorry, Lucy."

"There's nothing to be sorry for. It's not your fault." She said those words kindly, bravely. "I think we need to accept that it's over. Years of treatments, so many miscarriages, *three* failed adoptions . . . we just need to let it go."

There was a long silence before General Leger answered. "If that's what you think is best."

"I do," she said, her voice sounding assertive, before she sank into tears again. "I still can't believe I'll never be a mother."

A second later her cries were muffled, and I knew her husband had pulled her to his chest, trying to comfort her as best he could.

All these years I had thought the Legers had chosen to be a childless couple. Miss Lucy's struggles had never made it into conversation when I was in the room, and she seemed content enough to play with us as children and send us on our way. I'd never considered that it might have been an unfortunate circumstance thrust on them.

Was my mother right? Was I not as observant or caring as I thought? Miss Lucy was one of my favorite people in the world. Shouldn't I have been able to see how sad she was?

CHAPTER 6

THIRTY-FIVE MASSIVE BASKETS SAT IN the office, filled with what must have been tens of thousands of entries, all left in their envelopes to protect the gentlemen's anonymity. I tried to give off an air of eager anticipation for the sake of the camera, but I felt like I might vomit into one of those baskets at any given moment.

That would be one way to narrow the pool.

Dad placed a hand on my back. "All right, Eady. Just walk to each basket and select an envelope. I'll hold them for you so your hands don't get full. Then we'll open them live tonight on the *Report*. It's that easy."

For something so simple, it seemed incredibly daunting. Then again, I'd felt overwhelmed since we announced the Selection, so this shouldn't have been a surprise.

I adjusted my favorite tiara and smoothed out my iridescent

gray dress. I wanted to make sure I looked positively radiant today, and when I'd checked my reflection before heading downstairs, even I was a little intimidated by the girl in the mirror.

"So I literally select each one myself?" I whispered, hoping the cameras weren't watching too closely.

He gave me a tiny smile and spoke softly. "It's a privilege I never had. Go ahead, love."

"What do you mean?"

"Later. Go on now." He gestured toward the piles and piles of entries.

I took a deep breath. I could do this. No matter what people were hoping for, I had a plan. And it was foolproof. I would walk away from this unscathed. Just a few months of my life—nothing, in the grand scheme of things—and then I'd go back to the work of becoming queen. Alone.

So why are you stalling?

Shut up.

I walked to the first basket, with a label declaring the contestants were all from Clermont. I pulled one from the side, cameras flashed, and the handful of people in the room actually applauded. Mom wrapped her arm around Ahren in excitement, and he sneakily made a face at me. Miss Marlee sighed with delight, but Miss Lucy was absent. Osten was missing, too, which was no surprise, but Kaden stood by, observing the whole thing with interest.

I used different techniques for different bins. On one, I plucked the envelope from the very top. On the next, I buried my arm to fish out my choice. The onlookers seemed incredibly amused when I got to Carolina, Mom's home province, picked up two envelopes, and weighed them in my hands for a few seconds before dropping one back in.

I placed the last entry in Dad's hands, and there was more clapping and camera flashes. I gave what I hoped was an enthusiastic smile before the reporters all exited the room, off to give their exclusive stories. Ahren and Kaden left, joking as they went, and Mom gave me a quick kiss on the head before she followed them. We were speaking again but didn't have much to say.

"You did marvelously," Dad said once we were alone, a genuine tone of awe in his voice. "Really, I understand how nerve-racking this can feel, but you were wonderful."

"How do you know though?" I placed my hands on my hips. "If you didn't pick out the entries yourself?"

He swallowed. "You've heard the broad strokes of how your mother and I found each other. But there are tiny details that are best left in the drawer. The only reason I am telling you this is because I think it will help you to see how fortunate you are."

I nodded, not sure where he was going.

He took a breath. "My Selection wasn't a farce, but it wasn't that far off. My father chose all the contestants by hand, picking young women with political alliances, influential families, or enough charm to make the entire country worship the ground they walked on. He knew he had to make it varied enough to seem legit, so there were three

Fives thrown into the mix but nothing below that. The Fives were meant to be little more than throwaways to keep anyone from being suspicious."

I realized my mouth was gaping open and shut it immediately. "Mom?"

"Was meant to be gone almost immediately. Truth be told, she barely made it past my father's attempts to sway my opinion or remove her himself. And look at her now." His whole face changed. "Though it was hard for me to imagine, she is even more beloved as queen than my mother. She has made four beautiful, intelligent, strong children. And she has been the source of every happiness in my life."

He flipped idly through the envelopes in his hands. "I'm not sure if fate or destiny is real. But I can tell you that sometimes the very thing you've been hoping for will walk through the door, determined to fend you off. And still, somehow, you will find that you are enough."

Until then I'd never had a reason to doubt that I'd seen the whole picture of my parents' love story. But between Dad's confession that Mom wasn't even supposed to be a choice and Mom's revelation that she didn't want to be a part of the choosing in the first place, I wondered how they had managed to find each other at all.

It was clear from Dad's expression, he could barely believe it himself.

"You're going to do great, you know?" he said, beaming proudly.

"What makes you think so?"

"You're like your mother, and my mother, too. You're determined. And, perhaps most important, you don't like to fail. I know this will all work out, if only because you'll refuse to allow it to go any other way."

I nearly told him, nearly confessed I had come up with pages of ideas to drive these boys away. Because he was right: I didn't want to fail. But for me, failure meant having my life led by someone else.

"I'm sure everything will turn out just as it should," I said, a whisper of regret hanging in my voice.

He lifted a hand and placed it on my cheek. "It usually does."

CHAPTER 7

In the studio, the set was slightly rearranged. Typically, Ahren and I were the only ones who sat on camera with my parents, but tonight Kaden and Osten were given seats onstage as well.

Dad's officials were in a cluster of seats on the opposite side, and in the middle a bowl waited with all the envelopes I'd picked earlier. Beside it was an empty bowl for me to place them in as they were opened. I had reservations about reading out the names myself, but at least it gave the appearance of control. I liked that.

Behind the cameras, seats were filled with other members of our household. General Leger was there, kissing Miss Lucy on her forehead and whispering something to her. It had been a few days since I'd overheard their conversation, and I still felt awful for her. Of all the people in the world who ought to be parents, it was the Legers. And of all the people in the world who ought to have the ability to fix things, it was the Schreaves.

Still, I was lost as to how to help.

Miss Marlee was shushing Josie, probably for laughing at a joke Josie made herself that lacked any level of humor. I'd never understand how someone so wonderful had birthed such awful people. My favorite tiara? The one I was wearing? It was only my favorite because Josie bent my first favorite and lost two stones out of the second. She wasn't even supposed to touch them. Ever.

Beside her, Kile was reading a book. Because, clearly, everything going on in our country and home was too boring for him. What an ingrate.

He peeked up from his book, saw me watching, made a face, and went back to reading. Why was he even here?

"How are you feeling?" Mom was suddenly beside me, her arm around my shoulder.

"Fine."

She smiled. "There's no way you're fine. This is terrifying."

"Why, yes, yes it is. How kind of you to subject me to such a delightful thing."

Her giggle was tentative, testing to see if we were on good terms again.

"I don't think you're flawed," she said quietly. "I think you're a thousand wonderful things. One day you'll know what it's like to worry for your children. And I worry for you more than the others. You're not just any girl, Eadlyn. You're *the* girl. And I want everything for you."

I wasn't sure what to say. I didn't want for us to fight right now, not with something this big coming. Her arm was still on my shoulder, so I wrapped mine around her back, and she kissed my hair, just under my tiara.

"I feel very uncomfortable," I confessed.

"Just remember how the boys are feeling. This is huge for them as well. And the country will be so pleased."

I concentrated on my breathing. Three months. Freedom. A piece of cake.

"I'm proud of you," she said, giving me a final squeeze. "Good luck."

She walked away to greet Dad, and Ahren strode toward me, smoothing out his suit. "I cannot believe this is actually happening," he said, genuine excitement coloring his tone. "I'm really looking forward to the company."

"What, is Kile not enough for you?" I darted my eyes at him again, and he still had his nose buried.

"I don't know what you have against Kile. He's really smart."

"Is that code for boring?"

"No! But I'm excited to meet different people."

"I'm not." I crossed my arms, partly frustrated, partly protecting myself.

"Aww, come on, sis. This is going to be fun." He surveyed the room and dropped his voice to a whisper. "I can only imagine what you have in store for those poor saps."

I tried to suppress my smile, but I was anticipating watching them squirm.

He picked up one of the envelopes and bopped me on the nose with it. "Get ready now. If you have a basic grasp of the English language, you should manage this part just fine."

"Such a pain," I said, punching his arm. "I love you."

"I know you do. Don't worry. This is going to be easy."

We were instructed to take our seats, and Ahren threw the envelope back down, taking my hand to walk me to my place. The cameras started rolling, and Dad began the *Report* with an update about an approaching trade agreement with New Asia. We worked so closely with them now, it was hard to imagine a time we were actually at war. He touched on the growing immigration laws, and all his advisers spoke, including Lady Brice. It simultaneously felt like it dragged on forever and passed in an instant.

When Gavril announced my name, it took me a second to remember exactly what I was supposed to be doing. But I stood and walked across the stage, and assumed my place in front of the microphone.

I flashed a smile and looked straight into the camera, knowing every TV in Illéa was on tonight. "I'm sure you're all as excited as I am, so let's skip ceremony and get right to what everyone is dying to hear. Ladies and gentlemen, here are the thirty-five young men invited to participate in this groundbreaking Selection."

I reached into the bowl and pulled out the first envelope. "From Likely," I read, pausing to open it, "Mr. MacKendrick Shepard."

I held up his photograph, and the room applauded as I set it in the other bowl and moved back for the next entry.

"From Zuni . . . Mr. Winslow Fields."

There was a smattering of applause after every name.

Holden Messenger. Kesley Timber. Hale Garner. Edwin Bishop.

It felt like I had opened at least a hundred envelopes by the time my hands reached for the final one. My cheeks hurt, and I was hoping Mom wouldn't judge me if I skipped dinner and ate alone in my room. I really thought I'd earned it.

"Ah! From Angeles." I ripped at the paper, pulling out the final entry. I knew my smile must have faltered, but really, it couldn't be helped. "Mr. Kile Woodwork."

I heard the reactions around the room. Several gasps, a handful of laughs, but, most obviously, I could hear Kile's reaction. He dropped his book.

I pulled in a breath. "There you have it. Tomorrow, advisers will be sent out to begin prepping these thirty-five candidates for the adventure before them. And, in one short week, they will arrive at the palace. Until then, join me in congratulating them."

I began the applause, the room followed, and I retreated to my seat, trying not to look as sick as I felt.

Kile's name being in there shouldn't have shaken me the way it did. At the end of the day, none of those boys stood a chance. But something about this felt wrong.

The second Gavril finished signing off, everyone erupted. Mom and Dad walked to the Woodworks. I followed right behind them, Josie's laughter acting as a homing beacon.

"I didn't do it!" Kile insisted. As I approached, our eyes met. I could see he was as upset as I was.

"Does that even matter?" Mom said. "Anyone of age is allowed to put his name in."

Dad nodded. "That's true. It's a bit of a strange situation, but there's nothing illegal about it."

"But I don't want to be a part of this." Kile looked at Dad imploringly.

"Who put your name in?" I asked.

Kile shook his head. "I don't know. It has to be a mistake. Why would I enter when I don't want to compete?"

Mom's eyes were on General Leger, and it looked almost like they were smiling. But there wasn't anything funny about this.

"Excuse me!" I protested. "This is unacceptable. Is anyone going to do anything about it?"

"Pick someone else," Kile offered.

General Leger shook his head. "Eadlyn announced your name in front of the country. You're the candidate from Angeles."

"That's right," Dad agreed. "Reading the names publicly makes it official. We can't replace you."

Kile rolled his eyes. He did that a lot. "Then Eadlyn can eliminate me the first day."

"And send you where?" I asked. "You're already home."

Ahren chuckled. "Sorry," he said, noticing our glares. "That's not going to sit well with the others."

"Send me away," Kile offered, sounding thrilled.

"For the hundredth time, Kile, you're not leaving!" Miss

Marlee said in the firmest voice I'd ever heard her use. She put her hand to her temple, and Mr. Carter wrapped an arm around her, speaking into her ear.

"You want to go somewhere else?" I asked, incredulous. "Isn't a palace good enough for you?"

"It's not mine," he said, raising his voice. "And quite frankly, I'm tired of it. I'm over the rules, I'm over being a guest, and I'm so over your bratty attitude."

I gasped as Miss Marlee thwacked her son over the head.

"Apologize!" she commanded.

Kile pressed his lips together, looking at the ground. I crossed my arms. He wasn't leaving until I got an apology. I'd get it one way or another.

Finally, after a forceful shake of his head, he muttered it under his breath.

I looked away, hardly impressed with his efforts.

"We'll move forward as planned," Dad said. "This is a Selection, just like any of the others. It's about choices. Right now, Kile is one option of many, and Eadlyn could certainly do worse."

Thanks, Dad. I quickly checked Kile's expression. He was staring at the floor, seeming embarrassed and angry.

"For now I think we should all get some food and celebrate. This is a very exciting day."

"That's right," General Leger agreed. "Let's eat."

"I'm tired," I said, turning. "I'll be in my room."

I didn't wait for approval. I didn't owe anyone anything after tonight. I was giving them everything they wanted.

CHAPTER 8

I AVOIDED EVERYONE OVER THE weekend, and no one seemed bothered by it, not even Mom. With the names out there, the Selection felt that much more real, and I was saddened by the dwindling days of solitude.

The Monday before the candidates arrived, I finally rejoined humanity and made my way to the Women's Room. Miss Lucy was there, seeming back to her usual, cheerful self. I kept wishing I could do something to help her. I knew a puppy wasn't a person, but so far my only idea was to get her a pet.

Mom was talking to Miss Marlee, and they waved me over the moment I was through the doorway.

Miss Marlee put her hand on mine as I sat. "I wanted to explain about Kile. He doesn't want to leave because of you. He's been talking about going for a long time, and I thought the semester away would put an end to it. I can't bear to let him go."

"You'll have to let him make his own choice sooner or later," Mom urged. Funny, since she was the one trying to marry her daughter to a stranger.

"I don't understand it. Josie never talks about leaving."

I rolled my eyes. Of course she doesn't.

"But what can you do? You can't force him to stay." Mom poured a cup of tea and set it in front of me.

"I'm hiring another tutor. This one has hands-on experience and can give Kile more than a book could, so I think I've bought some more time. I keep hoping—"

Aunt May burst into the room, looking as if she stepped out of a magazine. I bolted over to her and gave her a bone-crushing hug.

"Your Highness," she greeted.

"Shut up."

She laughed and pulled me back, grasping me by both shoulders and looking into my eyes. "I want to hear everything about the Selection. How are you feeling? Some of those pictures were cute. Are you already in love?"

"Not even close," I replied with a laugh.

"Well, give 'em a few days."

That's how it was with Aunt May. A new love every few months or so. She treated the four of us—and our cousins, Astra and Leo—like we were her kids since she never settled down herself. I particularly enjoyed her company, and the palace always felt more exciting when she was here.

"How long are you staying?" Mom asked, and May held my hand as we crossed back to her.

"Leaving again Thursday."

I gasped.

"I know. I'm going to miss all the excitement!" She pouted at me. "But Leo has a game Friday afternoon, and Astra's dance recital is on Saturday, and I promised I'd be there. She's really coming along," Aunt May said, turning to Mom. "You can tell her mother was an artist."

They shared a smile. "I wish I could go," Mom lamented.

"Why don't we?" I suggested, picking up some cookies for my tea.

Aunt May gave me a questioning look. "You do realize you already have plans for this weekend, right? Big plans? Life-changing plans?"

I shrugged. "I'm not too worried about missing them."

"Eadlyn," Mom reprimanded.

"Sorry! It's just overwhelming. I like the way things are now."

"Where are the pictures?" May asked.

"In my room, on my desk. I'm trying to learn the names, but I haven't gotten very far yet."

May waved her arm at a maid. "Dearie, will you go up to the princess's room and grab the stack of Selection candidates' forms off her desk?"

The maid beamed and curtsied, and I suspected she'd be thumbing through the pile on her way down.

Mom leaned in toward her sister. "I just want to remind

you that, one, they're off-limits, and, two, even if they weren't, you're twice their age."

Miss Marlee and I laughed, while Miss Lucy only smiled. She was much easier on Aunt May than the rest of us.

"Don't tease her," Miss Lucy protested. "I'm sure she has the best intentions."

"Thank you, Lucy. This isn't for me; it's for Eadlyn!" she vowed. "We're going to help her get a head start."

"That's not really how it works." Mom leaned back, drinking her tea with an air of superiority.

Miss Marlee laughed loudly. "This from you! Do we need to remind you of *your* head start?"

"What?" I asked, shocked. How many details had my parents omitted from their story? "What does she mean?"

Mom put down her tea and held up a hand defensively. "I accidentally ran into your father the night before the Selection started, and, I will have you know," she said, more to Miss Marlee than to me, "I could easily have been kicked out for that. It wasn't exactly the first impression you hope for."

I sat there gaping. "Mom, exactly how many rules did you break?"

Her eyes darted up as if she was trying to tally them. "Okay, you know what, go through the pictures all you want; you win."

Aunt May laughed with delight, and I tried to memorize the way her head sloped gracefully to one side and her eyes sparkled. Everything about her was so effortlessly glamorous, and I adored her with a love close to what I held for my mother. While I felt a little slighted by Josie being my closest female playmate growing up, Mom's circle of friends more than made up for it. Aunt May's spirit, Miss Lucy's kindness, Miss Marlee's buoyancy, and Mom's strength were invaluable, and more enlightening than any class I ever took.

The maid came back, placing the pile of forms and pictures in front of me. To my surprise, it was Miss Marlee who grabbed the first handful of applications to graze through. Aunt May was close behind, and while Mom didn't pick up any herself, she did lean over Miss Marlee's shoulder to peek. Miss Lucy looked like she was trying not to be curious but in the end had a pile in her own lap as well.

"Oh, he looks promising." Aunt May shoved a picture in front of me. I stared into a set of dark eyes embedded deep in ebony skin. His hair was cropped short, and he wore a bright smile. "Baden Trains, nineteen, from Sumner."

"He's handsome," Mom gushed.

"Well, obviously," May agreed. "And with a last name like Trains, he probably comes from a family of Sevens. It says here he's in his first year studying advertising. That means either he or someone in his family is very determined."

"True," Miss Marlee agreed. "That's no small feat."

I pulled a couple of the forms over, picking through them.

"So how are you feeling?" Aunt May asked. "Is everything ready to go?"

"I think so." I flipped over an application, scanning for something that might seem remotely interesting. I just didn't care. "For a while everyone was in such a tizzy I thought it might never end. It looks like all the rooms are finished, the food calculations have been made, and now that the list is official, travel arrangements should be done by tomorrow."

"You sound positively thrilled," May teased, poking me.

I sighed, then looked pointedly at Mom. "You might as well know, this isn't completely about me."

"What do you mean, honey?" Miss Lucy asked, setting her pile of papers on her lap, looking between Mom and me with concern.

"Of course we're hoping Eadlyn will find someone worthy of settling down with," Mom began shrewdly. "But as it happens, this is coming at a time when we were in need of a plan to calm the unrest over the castes."

"Ames!" May said. "Your daughter is a decoy?"

"No!"

"Yes," I muttered. Aunt May rubbed my back, and it made me feel so much better to have her there.

"Sooner or later, we would have needed to look at suitors, and this isn't binding. Eadlyn has an agreement with Maxon that if she doesn't fall in love, then the whole thing is off. However, yes, Eadlyn is doing her job as a member of the royal family by creating a little . . . diversion while the population cools down and we investigate what more we could do. And, might I add, it's working."

"It is?" I asked.

"Haven't you looked at the papers? You're the center of everything right now. Local papers are interviewing their candidates, and some provinces are holding parties, hoping their suitor will be the winner. Magazines are talking about possible front-runners, and I saw a segment on the news last night about a few girls who were forming fan clubs and wearing shirts with the names of their favorites plastered all over them. The Selection has consumed the entire country."

"It's true," Miss Marlee confirmed. "Kile living in the palace is no longer a secret."

"Have they also discovered he has no interest in participating?" I asked, more irritation in my voice than I intended. Miss Marlee wasn't to blame for this whole debacle.

"No," she answered with a laugh. "Again, though, that has nothing to do with you."

I smiled back. "Miss Marlee, you heard Mom. He doesn't need to worry. I think Kile and I already know we wouldn't be that great of a match, and there's a chance I'll walk away from this without a fiancé anyway." A one hundred percent chance, to be more accurate. "Don't worry about him hurting my feelings, because I'm just seeing how it goes," I replied, as if this was normal, bringing in a slew of boys for me to pick from. "I'm not upset."

"You said it's taken over everything," May began, concerned. "Do you think it will last?"

"I think it'll hold things off long enough for the people to forget some of the unhappiness that's been so prevalent lately and for us to come up with a way to address issues if they pop up again." Mom sounded confident.

"*When* they pop up," I corrected. "My life might be

exciting for a while, but eventually people will start worrying about themselves again." I went back to looking at the pictures, almost pitying these boys. They had no chance of winning and no idea they were part of a public distraction.

"This is strange," I said, picking up one of the applications. "I don't want to be judgmental, but look at this. I caught three different spelling mistakes on this one."

Mom took the form. "It's possible he was nervous."

"Or an idiot," I offered.

May chuckled.

"Don't be so harsh, sweetie. It's scary on their end, too." Mom handed me the form, and I clipped it back to a picture of a boy with a very innocent face and a head full of wild blond curls.

"Wait, are you scared?" Aunt May asked, worry on my behalf coating her voice.

"No, of course not."

Her expression relaxed back into its normal, beautiful, carefree state. "Can't imagine you being scared of anything." She winked at me.

It was comforting that at least one of us thought so.

CHAPTER 9

WHEN THEY STARTED POURING IN, I fled to my room, sketching in the sunlight on my balcony. Too many boisterous laughs and overly enthusiastic greetings. I wondered how long that camaraderie would last. This was a competition, after all. I mentally added finding ways to pit them against one another to my to-do list.

"I think we should put my hair up, Neena. I want to look mature today."

"Excellent choice, my lady." She scrubbed at my nails. "Any thoughts on a dress?"

"I'm thinking evening gown. Black would do nicely."

She chuckled. "Looking to scare them?"

I couldn't hold back my sly smile. "Only a little."

We giggled together, and I was glad to have her with me. I was going to need her soothing words and calming touches over the next few weeks.

After my hair was dry, we braided and knotted it up like a crown, which only made my tiara look better. I found the black dress I'd worn for a New Year's Eve party last year. It was covered in lace and fitted to the knee before it flared out to the floor. An oval of skin was exposed across my back, and the tiny butterfly sleeves set low across my shoulders. I had to admit it looked even more beautiful in the sun than it did under candles.

My clock struck one, and I made my way downstairs. We had converted one of the libraries on the fourth floor into a Men's Parlor so the Selected could gather and relax during their time in the palace. It was about the same size as the Women's Room and had plenty of places to sit, lots of books, and two televisions.

I was heading to that area of the palace now. We had decided that the suitors would be brought out one at a time to greet me and then escorted to the Men's Parlor to get to know one another.

I saw a cluster of people down the hallway, including my parents and General Leger, and made my way toward them, trying not to let my nerves show. Dad looked stunned and Mom covered her mouth as I approached.

"Eadlyn . . . you seem so grown up." She sighed as she touched my cheek and shoulder and hair, not fixing anything, just checking.

"Probably because I am."

She nodded to herself, tears in her eyes. "You look the

part. I never really thought I passed for a queen, but you . . . wholly perfect."

"Stop it, Mom. You're completely adored. You and Dad brought peace to the country. I haven't done anything."

She placed a finger under my chin. "Not yet. But you're too determined to accomplish nothing."

Before I could respond, Dad approached us. "Ready?"

"Yes," I answered, steadying myself. That wasn't the pep talk I'd been envisioning. "I don't intend to eliminate anyone just yet. I figure everyone deserves at least a day."

Dad smiled. "I think that's wise."

I took a breath. "All right, then. Let's begin."

"Do you want us to stay or go?" Mom asked.

I considered. "Go. For now, anyway."

"As you wish," Dad said. "General Leger and a few guards will be nearby. If you need anything, simply ask. We want you to have a wonderful day."

"Thank you, Daddy."

"No," he said, embracing me, "thank you."

He pulled away and offered his arm to Mom. They walked off, and I felt like I could see their happiness glowing simply in the way they moved.

"Your Highness," General Leger said gently. I turned to see his smiling face. "Nervous?"

I shook my head slightly, almost convincing myself. "Bring the first one out."

He nodded before making eye contact with a butler down the hall. A boy walked out of one of the libraries, straightening his cuff links as he approached. He was lean and a little on the short side, but he had a pleasant enough face.

He stopped in front of me, bowing. "Fox Wesley, Your Highness."

I tilted my head in greeting. "A pleasure."

He took in a breath. "You are so beautiful."

"So I've been told. You can go now." I swept my arm across my body, pointing to the Men's Parlor.

Fox furrowed his eyebrows before giving me another bow and leaving.

The next boy was in front of me, tipping his head to greet me.

"Hale Garner, Your Highness."

"Welcome, sir."

"Thank you so much for letting us into your home. I hope to prove myself worthy of your hand more and more each day."

I cocked my head curiously. "Really? And how will you do that today?"

He smiled. "Well, today I would let you know I come from an excellent family. My father used to be a Two."

"Is that all?"

Undeterred, he went on. "I think it's pretty impressive."

"Not as impressive as having a father who used to be a One."

His face faltered.

"You may go."

He bowed and started to walk away. After a few steps he looked back. "I'm sorry to have offended you, Your Highness."

And his face was so sad that I nearly told him he hadn't. But that wouldn't fall in line with my plan for the day.

A parade of endlessly unmemorable boys crossed my path. A little past the halfway point, Kile came through the line, stopping in front of me. For once his hair was styled in such a way that I could actually see his eyes.

"Your Highness," he greeted.

"It's 'Royal Pain in the Ass' to you, sir."

He chuckled.

"So, how have they been treating you? Your mom says the papers spilled that you lived at the palace."

He shook his head in shock. "I thought that it would be an immediate invitation to be pummeled by a bunch of jealous meatheads, but it turns out, most of them see me as an asset."

"Oh?"

"They assume I know everything about you already. I've been bombarded with questions all morning."

"And what are you telling them, exactly?"

He smirked, his smile slightly crooked. "What a pleasure you are, of course."

"Right." I rolled my eyes, not believing him for a second. "You can go ahead—"

"Listen, I want to tell you I'm sorry again. For calling you bratty."

I shrugged. "You were upset."

He nodded, accepting that excuse. "Still, it's unfair all the same. I mean, don't get me wrong, you are exceedingly spoiled." He shook his head. "But you're tough because you have to be. You're going to be queen, and while I've seen things unfold in the palace, I've never actually had the weight of your work on me. It's not fair for me to judge."

I sighed. The polite thing would be to thank him. So, fine, I would be polite. "Thank you."

"Sure."

There was a long pause.

"Umm, the Men's Parlor is that way," I said, pointing.

"Right. See you later, I guess."

I smiled to myself, noticing as he left that he held a notebook in the hand he'd kept behind his back. Kile looked better than usual thanks to the mandatory makeover, but he was still an annoying little bookworm.

It was clear that the gentleman after him was anything but.

His caramel-colored hair was brushed back, and he walked with his hands in his pockets, as if he'd strolled down these halls before. His demeanor actually threw me for a second. Was he here to meet me, or was I here to meet him?

"Your Majesty," he greeted silkily as he sank into a bow.

"Highness," I corrected.

"No, no. It's just Ean."

He cocked one cheek up into a smile.

"That was awful," I said with a laugh.

"It was a risk I had to take. There are thirty-four other guys here. How else was I supposed to get you to remember me?"

His gaze was intent, and if I hadn't dealt with so many politicians in my life, I might have been charmed.

"Very nice to meet you, sir."

"And you, Your Highness. Hope to see you soon."

He was followed by a boy with a drawl so thick I had to really focus to catch his words. Another asked when he was going to be paid. There was one who was sweating so much I had to call over a butler to give me a towel for my hand once he left, and the one after him blatantly stared at my chest for the entirety of our meeting. It was an ongoing pageant of disasters.

General Leger came to my side. "In case you've lost count, this is the last one."

I threw back my head in relief. "Thank. Goodness!"

"I don't think your parents will want to ask you for a follow-up, but you should go to them when you're done."

I gave him a look. "If you insist."

He chuckled. "Go easy on them. Your father has a lot to deal with right now."

"*He's* got a lot to deal with? Did you see that one guy sweat?!"

"Can you blame him? You're the princess. You have the capacity to sentence him to death, if you wanted."

General Leger had these sparkling green eyes that shimmered with mischief, one of those men who grew even more handsome as he aged. I knew it for a fact because Miss Lucy once showed me a picture of their wedding day, and he seriously only got better looking. Sometimes, if he was tired or if the weather was bad, he walked with a limp, but it never slowed him. Maybe it was because I knew how much Miss Lucy loved him, but he always seemed like a safe place. If I hadn't been nervous about him siding with Mom and Dad, I would have asked for his advice on how to get these boys to plead to go home. Something in his eyes made me think he'd know exactly how to do it.

"A few of them make me uneasy," I confessed. The smooth words, the leering eyes. Even though I grew up knowing I was special, I didn't like being looked at as a prize.

His expression grew sympathetic. "It's a strange situation, I know. But you never have to be alone with anyone you don't like, you're free to dismiss someone for nothing more than a feeling, and even the dumbest of them wouldn't be stupid enough to hurt you," he promised. "Trust me; if someone did, I'd make sure they never walked again."

He gave me a wink before moving away and signaling for the final contestant to be brought out.

I was a bit confused when it wasn't one person but two. The first was dressed in a crisp suit, but the second wore only a button-up shirt. The slightly drabber one walked a few steps behind the other, his eyes trained on the floor. The first was nothing but smiles, and it looked like someone had tried to tame his hair and failed.

"Hello, Highness," he greeted, his voice thick with an accent I couldn't identify. "How are you?"

Confused but disarmed by his incredibly warm smile, I answered, "I'm well. It's been a long day. I'm sure it has been for you, too."

Behind him, the other boy leaned forward and whispered

something in garbled words I couldn't understand.

The first nodded. "Oh, yes, yes, but . . . eets nice to meeting you." He used his hands as he spoke, trying to get the words across with his gestures.

I leaned in, not understanding, and somehow hoping a closer proximity would clear up his accent. "Excuse me?"

The boy behind him spoke up. "He says it's a pleasure to meet you."

I squinted, still confused.

"My name ees Henri." He bowed in greeting, and I could see in his face that he meant to do this earlier and forgot.

I didn't want to be rude, so I nodded my head in acknowledgment. "Hello, Henri."

He lit up at the sound of his name, and he stood there, looking back and forth between the gentleman behind him and me.

"I can't help but notice your accent," I remarked in what I hoped was a friendly tone. "Where do you come from?"

"Umm, Swend—?" he began, but turned to the guest with him.

He nodded, carrying on in Henri's place. "Sir Henri was born in Swendway, so he has a very strong Finnish accent."

"Oh," I replied. "And does he speak much English?"

Henri piped up. "English, no, no." He didn't seem embarrassed though. Instead he laughed it off.

"How are we supposed to get to know each other?"

The translator turned to Henri. "*Miten saat tuntemaan toisensa*?"

Henri pointed to the translator, who answered, "Through me, it seems."

"Okay. Well. Umm." I wasn't prepared for this. Was it rude for me to dismiss him? Interacting with these people one-on-one was going to be awkward enough. I wasn't prepared for a third person.

In that instant Henri's application popped back into my mind. That was why some of the words were spelled wrong. He was guessing at them.

"Thank you. It's very nice to meet you, too, Henri."

He smiled at his name, and I got the feeling the rest of the words didn't even matter. I couldn't send him away.

"The Men's Parlor is over here."

Henri bowed as his translator mumbled the instructions, and they walked away together.

"General Leger," I called, burying my face in my hands.

"Yes, Your Highness."

"Tell Dad I'll update him in an hour. I need to take a walk."

CHAPTER 10

WE MADE IT THROUGH THE first day, the first dinner, and the first evening without further incident. As the cameras circled the dining hall, I could hear the men working them sigh in boredom. I didn't address anyone in the group, and the boys themselves seemed too nervous even to speak to one another.

I could hear Dad's thoughts as clearly as if they were my own.

This is dull! No one will want to see this! How will this buy us a single second let alone three months?

He glanced over at me a few times, begging me with his eyes to do something, anything, to make this worth enduring. I was at war with myself. I didn't want to fail him, but any warmth on my part today would set a bad precedent. They needed to know that I wasn't going to fawn over them.

I told myself not to worry. In the morning everything would change.

The following day the boys were dressed in their best, ready for the parade. An army of people swarmed on the front lawn, ready to prep us to go beyond the gates.

Dad was proud of this idea, my biggest contribution to the Selection so far. I thought it would be exciting to have a short parade, something never done before. I felt certain this would give everyone something to talk about.

"Good morning, Your Highness," one of the boys greeted. I remembered Ean in an instant, and after yesterday it was no surprise he was the first one to speak to me.

"And to you." I walked on, not slowing, though many of the others bowed or called my name. I only stopped to be briefed by one of the guards heading up the process.

"It's a short loop, Your Highness. At under ten miles an hour, it should take twenty to thirty minutes to make our way around. Guards are lining the route for good measure, but everyone is so excited, it should be a very fun event."

I clasped my hands calmly in front of me. "Thank you, officer. I appreciate your work to make this happen."

He pressed his lips together, attempting to hide his proud smile. "Anything for you, Your Highness."

He went to walk away, but I called him back. The officer puffed out his chest, so pleased to be needed again. I looked around at the swarm of young men, dazed by their number, trying to make the smartest choice.

I saw Henri's wild hair blowing in the wind and smiled to myself. He stood on the outside of a group, listening to what they were saying and nodding, though I was sure he couldn't understand anything going on around him. I didn't see his translator and wondered if Henri had banished him for the day.

I searched again, hunting . . . and found one boy who really knew how to wear a suit. It wasn't that he looked like a model but more like he understood the fine art of tailoring and had set his butler to work immediately on his choice for the day. Also, I couldn't get over his two-toned shoes. Thank goodness I remembered his name.

"When I'm up there, I'd like Mr. Garner on one side and Mr. Jaakoppi on the other, please."

"Certainly, Your Highness. I'll take care of it."

I turned and looked at the float. They'd taken the frame of one of the Christmas floats and adorned it with thousands of summer blooms. It was festive and beautiful, and the scent of the flowers permeated the air. I inhaled, and the clean, sweet smell soothed every piece of me.

Over the walls I could hear the shouts of people who had lined up for this moment. Whatever ways I'd failed last night would be more than forgotten today.

"All right, gentlemen." General Leger's voice boomed over the din. "I need you all to line up along the path, and we'll get you up safely."

Mom was in the back with Dad, who had picked up a few stray flowers that had blown off the float and stuck them in her hair. She looked at him with absolute adoration as he stepped away with his camera.

He circled the group, snapping pictures. He got plenty of the boys, some of the fountain, and a couple of me.

"Dad!" I whispered, a little embarrassed.

He winked and backed away, still taking shots but in a less obvious way.

"Your Highness," General Leger said, placing a hand on my back. "We're going to send you up last. I heard you wanted Henri and Hale beside you, is that right?"

"Yes."

"Good picks. They're polite ones. Okay, we'll be ready to go in a moment."

He walked over to my mother and relayed something to her. She seemed uneasy, but General Leger made motions with his hands, attempting to reassure her. Dad was a little harder to read from here. Either he wasn't bothered at all, or he was hiding it very well.

The boys were led up the hidden ladder, and I paced as I waited for my turn. Along the wall, mixed in with a few guards and guests, I noticed Henri's translator standing, arms crossed, watching the scene. He bit at a fingernail, and I shook my head, walking over.

"Don't do that," I started, trying to be firm without being rude. "You don't want the cameras to catch you with your fingers in your mouth, do you?"

He whipped his hand down immediately. "I'm sorry, Your Highness."

"Not going up there?" I nodded toward the massive float.

He smiled. "No, Your Highness. I think Henri can wave without interpretation." Still, I felt the nerves buzzing around him.

"He'll be right beside me," I assured him. "I'll try to make sure he knows what's going on."

The translator let out a massive sigh. "That makes this far less distressing. And he's going to be so excited. He talks about you every waking moment."

I laughed. "Well, it's hardly been a day. I'm sure it'll pass."

"I don't think so. He's in awe of you, of everything, really. The experience alone is big for him. His family has worked hard to establish themselves, and that he finds himself in a place where he can have even a second of your attention . . . he's so happy."

I looked up at Henri, straightening his tie as he waited on the front of the float. "Is that what he told you?"

"Not in so many words. He's aware of how fortunate he is, and he sees so many good things in you. He goes on and on."

I smiled sadly. It would have been nice if he could say as much to me. "Were you born in Swendway, too?"

He shook his head. "No. First generation to be born in Illéa. But my parents are trying to hold on to our old customs and things, so we live in a small Swendish community in Kent."

"Like Henri?"

"Yes. They're becoming more and more common. When Henri was Selected, his family put out a call for a reliable translator, and I submitted my résumé, flew to Sota, and now I have a new job."

"So you've only known Henri for . . . ?"

"A week. But we've already spent so much time together and get along so well, I feel like I've known him for years." He spoke with a sweet affection, brotherly in a way.

"I feel so rude—I don't even know your name."

He bowed. "I'm Erik."

"Erik?"

"Yes."

"Huh. I expected something a bit different."

He shrugged. "Well, that's the closest translation."

"Your Highness?" General Leger called, and that was my cue.

"I'll watch out for him," I promised, scurrying over to the float.

The ladder was a challenge. I had to conquer it while wearing heels and holding my dress with one hand, which meant I had to let go of one rung before grabbing the next, and I was particularly proud of myself for managing that on my own.

I brushed back my hair as I went to take my place. Henri turned to me immediately.

"Hello today, Your Highness." His blond curls were lifted by the breeze, and he smiled brightly.

I touched his shoulder. "Good morning, Henri. Call me Eadlyn."

He scrunched his face, a little confused. "Say to you Eadlyn?"

"Yes."

He gave me a thumbs-up, and I patted myself on the back for putting him beside me. In seconds he left me smiling. I leaned behind Henri, looking between the others to find Erik on the ground and gave him a thumbs-up, too. He smiled and put a hand over his heart like he was relieved.

I faced Hale. "How are you today?"

"Good," he said tentatively. "Listen, I wanted to apologize again for yesterday. I didn't mean to—"

I waved my hand, stopping him. "No, no. As I'm sure you can imagine, this is a bit stressful for me."

"Yes. I wouldn't want to be in your shoes."

"I *would* want to be in yours!" I exclaimed, looking down. "I love these!"

"Thank you. Do they work all right with the tie? I like to experiment, but I'm starting to second-guess."

"No. You make it all work."

Hale beamed, thrilled to be past his first impression and on to the second.

"So, it was you who said you'd prove yourself to me each day, yes?"

"Indeed it was." He seemed pleased I remembered.

"And how will you do that today?"

He considered. "If you feel the slightest bit unsteady, my hand is here for you. And I promise not to let you fall."

"I like that one. You think you've got it bad, try this in heels."

"We're opening the gates!" someone called. "Hold on!"

I waved good-bye to Mom and Dad, then grabbed on to the bar surrounding the top of the float. It wasn't too far of a drop if someone fell, but for the five of us across the front, there was a chance we'd get flattened by the float if we did. Hale and Henri were steady, just as I'd hoped, but plenty of the others clapped or shouted out self-encouragements. Burke, for one, kept yelling "We've got this!" even though all he really had to do was stand and wave.

The moment the gates opened, the cheering erupted. As we rounded the corner, I could see the first camp of cameras filming every second. Some people had signs supporting their favorite Selected boy or were waving the Illéan flag.

"Henri, look!" I said, leaning into him and pointing to a sign with his name on it.

He took a moment to understand. Then when he finally saw his name, he gasped. "Hey!" He was so excited, he lifted my hand off his shoulder and kissed it. Had anyone else done that it might have been unwelcome, but from him, the gesture felt so innocent, I wasn't bothered at all.

"We love you, Princess Eadlyn," someone called, and I waved in the direction of the sound.

"Long live the king!"

"Bless you, Princess!"

I mouthed my thanks to them for their support, and I felt encouraged. It wasn't every day that I saw my people face-to-face, heard their voices, and sensed how they needed us. I knew they loved me, of course. I was going to be their queen. But typically, when I did leave the palace, the focus was on Mom or Dad. It felt amazing to have so much of the affection finally centered on me. Maybe I could be as beloved as my father.

The parade went on, with people calling our names and throwing flowers. It was turning out to be the spectacle I'd hoped. I couldn't have asked for anything better, until we reached the final stretch of the route.

Something hit me that was clearly not a flower. I looked to see a runny egg dripping down my dress and onto my bare legs. After that, half a tomato hit me, then something else I couldn't identify.

I dropped down, covering myself with my arms.

"We need jobs!" someone shrieked.

"The castes still live!"

I peeked out and saw a cluster of people protesting and hurling their rotten food at the float. Some held angry signs they must have hidden from the guards until now, and others threw disgusting words at me, calling me things that I'd never imagined even the worst of people saying.

Hale dropped down and lay in front of me, wrapping an arm around my shoulder. "Don't worry, I've got you."

"I don't understand," I mumbled.

Henri got down on one knee, trying to hit anything that came near us, and Hale guarded me without wavering, even though I heard him grunt and felt him clench up when he was hit with something heavy.

I recognized General Leger's voice shouting at the Selected to get down. As soon as everyone was low and secure, the float sped up, moving faster than it was probably designed to. People who actually cared about the parade booed as we hurtled past them, stealing their opportunity to catch a glimpse of the whole entourage.

I heard the float hit the gravel of the palace driveway, and the instant we came to a stop I pulled back from Hale and jumped to my feet. I hurried to the ladder and worked my way down.

"Eadlyn!" Mom cried.

"I'm fine."

Dad stood in shock. "Love, what happened?"

"Hell if I know." I stormed off, humiliated. As if the whole thing wasn't embarrassing enough, the sad eyes of everyone around me made it even worse.

Poor thing, their expressions seemed to say. And I hated their pity more than I hated the people who thought this was acceptable.

I scurried through the palace, head down, hoping no one would stop me. It wasn't my lucky day, of course, because as I rounded onto the landing of the second floor, Josie was there.

"Ew! What happened to you?"

I didn't answer, moving even faster. Why? What had I done to deserve this?

Neena was cleaning when I walked in. "Miss?"

"Help," I whimpered before bursting into tears.

She came over and embraced me, getting my mess all over her pristine uniform. "Hush now. We'll clean you up. You get undressed, and I'll start the bath."

"Why would they do this to me?"

"Who did it?"

"My people!" I answered in pain. "My subjects. Why would they do this?"

Neena swallowed, disappointed for my sake. "I don't know."

I wiped at my face and makeup, and something green came off on my hand. The tears fell again.

"Let me start that bath."

She scurried away, and I stood there, helpless.

I knew the water would get rid of the mess, and I knew it would take away the smell, but no amount of scrubbing would ever wash away this memory.

Hours later I was scrunched up on a chair in Dad's sitting room, bundled in my coziest sweater. Despite the heat, my clothes were my only armor at the moment, and the layers made me feel safe. Mom and Dad were both drinking something a little stronger than wine—a rare occasion—though it didn't appear to be doing much for their nerves.

Ahren knocked but came in before anyone answered the door. Our eyes met, and I rushed across the room, throwing my arms around him.

"Sorry, Eady," he said, kissing my hair.

"Thanks."

"Glad you could come, Ahren." Dad was looking at some of the stills from the parade that the photographers had provided him, stacking them on top of several of today's papers.

"Of course." He put his arm around my shoulder and walked me to my seat, going to stand with Dad while I curled back up into a ball.

"I still can't believe this happened," Mom said, reaching the bottom of her glass. I could see her weighing in her head whether or not to have another. She decided against it.

"Me either," I mumbled, still suffering under the surge of hatred those people felt for me. "What did I do?"

"Nothing," Mom assured me, coming to sit beside me. "They're mad at the monarchy, not you. Today your face was the one they could see, and that's the one they attacked. It could have been any of us."

"I felt so certain a Selection would lift their mood. I thought they would delight in this." Dad stared at the pictures, still shocked.

We sat silent for a while. He'd been so wrong.

"Well," Ahren started. "They might have if it wasn't Eadlyn."

We all gaped at him.

"Excuse me?" I nearly started crying all over again, pained by his cruel words. "Mom just said it could have been you or her or anyone. So why are you blaming me?"

He pursed his lips, looking around the room. "Fine. We'll talk about this. If Eadlyn was a typical girl, one who wasn't raised to be in control all the time, this would probably look different. But pick up any of those papers," he said, gesturing to the pile. Dad did. "In general she comes across as distant, and every picture from last night's dinner is uncomfortable to look at. You're nearly scowling in some of them."

"If you were in my shoes, you'd know how hard this is."

Ahren rolled his eyes at me. More than anyone, he knew I wasn't intending to pick a mate in the next few months.

Mom left me and peeked over Dad's shoulder. "He's right. On your own, you look like an island, and with the Selected there's no chemistry, no romance."

"Listen, I'm not performing for anyone. I refuse to act all dopey over a bunch of boys to entertain people." I crossed my arms, determined.

Two days in and this was already a disaster. I knew it wouldn't work, and now I was stuck in this humiliating situation. Could they dare ask me to sink further into shame for the sake of something that clearly wasn't going to help?

The room went silent, and, foolishly, I thought for a moment that I'd won.

"Eadlyn." I looked at Dad, trying not to be moved by the pleading in his eyes. "You promised me three months. We're trying hard to brainstorm on our end, but we can't extinguish that fire if we're dealing with new ones. I need you to try."

In that moment I saw something I hadn't really noticed before: his age. Dad wasn't old by any stretch of the word, but he had done more in his lifetime than most people twice his age could even hope for. He was in a constant state of sacrifice—for Mom, for us, for his people—and he was exhausted.

I swallowed, knowing that I'd need to find a way to look like I cared about the Selection, if only for his sake. "I assume you know how to get in touch with the press?"

Dad nodded. "Yes. We have trusted photographers and journalists on call."

"Get a few cameras in the Men's Parlor tomorrow morning. I'll take care of this."

CHAPTER 11

THE NEXT MORNING I SKIPPED breakfast with my family so I could compose myself. I didn't want anyone seeing how rattled yesterday had left me, and I felt like I was building a shield around myself, one steady breath at a time.

Neena was humming as she tidied my room, and it was one of the best things. Not only was she gentle with me after I came in yesterday, she didn't ask a single question or bring up the topic again. I didn't have to worry about her, which was why she couldn't leave the palace one day. What about me?

"I think it's a pants day, Neena," I called.

She stopped humming. "More black?"

"At least a little." We shared a smile as she handed me my tight black pants, which I paired with heels that would kill me by noon. I pulled on a flowy shirt and a vest, and found a tiara with jewels that matched the shirt. I was ready.

I decided that I was going to do exactly what Dad had done with his Selection. On his first day he sent home at least six girls. I was planning to eliminate nearly twice as many. Certainly weeding out all the unlikely candidates would show how seriously I was taking this process, that the outcome was important to me.

I wished there was a way to do this without the cameras, but they were a necessary evil. I had a mental list prepared, and I knew vaguely what I wanted to say; but if I made a mistake with reporters present, it would be just as bad as yesterday . . . meaning I needed to be perfect.

Because the Women's Room was considered the property of the queen, any male had to ask permission before entering. The Men's Parlor had been thrown together for my convenience, so no such formality stood, and I was able to complete a rather dazzling entrance by pulling the double doors open and letting the rush of wind blow back my hair.

The Selected all hurried to face me, some jumping to their feet or pulling themselves away from the reporters accompanying the cameras.

I passed Paisley Fisher, noticing that he audibly gulped as I stopped. Smiling, I placed a hand on his shoulder.

"You can go."

He glanced at the people beside him. "Go?"

"Yes, go. As in, thank you for your participation, but your presence at the palace is no longer required."

When he lingered, I leaned in, breathing my instructions.

"The longer you stay, the more embarrassing it becomes. You should leave."

I pulled back, noting the marked anger in his eyes as he slowly left the room.

I couldn't figure out why he was so vexed. It wasn't as if I'd kicked him or shouted. I internally praised myself for getting rid of someone so childish and tried to remember my list. Who was next? Oh . . . this one was well deserved.

"Blakely, isn't it?"

"Ye—" His voice squeaked and he started again. "Yes, Your Highness."

"When we met, you couldn't stop staring at my breasts." His face went pale, as if he seriously thought he was so subtle no one would notice. "Make sure you get an equally satisfactory look at my backside as you leave."

I made sure to address him loud enough that the cameras and the other boys would hear. Hopefully his humiliation would prevent others from thinking they could behave similarly. He ducked his head and left the room.

I stopped in front of Jamal. "You can leave." Next to him, Connor was breaking out into a sweat again. "You can join him."

They shared a confused look and left together, shaking their heads.

I came upon Kile next. Unlike most of the others, he didn't avert his eyes. On the contrary, he stared into mine, and I could see him pleading for me to end his misery and get him out of here.

I might have if I didn't think his mother would kill me—as I would surely have to make him leave the palace—and if I hadn't seen his name on the most signs yesterday. Of course, Kile was the hometown pick, so maybe the crowd was biased. Still, I couldn't get rid of him. Not yet.

Beside him, Hale swallowed. I remembered how he'd protected me during the parade, knowing he'd taken hits that were intended for me, some of which had seemed rather painful.

I came near and spoke softly. "Thank you for yesterday. You were very brave."

"It was nothing," he assured me. "Though the suit couldn't be saved."

He said it jokingly, trying to make the whole thing seem like less of an issue than it was.

"Shame."

I lowered my eyes and continued walking. I didn't think the cameras would have picked up the conversation, but I knew they'd see our smiles. I wondered what would be made of that.

"Issir," I said to a slick-haired, gangly young man. "No. Thank you."

He didn't even question it. He blushed and fled as quickly as he could.

I heard a mumbling and wondered who would dare to speak right now. As I whipped my head around, I saw Henri's translator relaying the scene in Henri's ear as quickly and quietly as he could. Henri's eyes were stressed, but when he finished listening, he looked up at me and smiled. He had such a goofy little grin and his hair curled in a way that he looked like he was playing a game while standing still.

Ugh. I had intended to end his suffering and send him home, but he looked far too pleased to be here. Some of them had to stay anyway, and Henri was harmless.

I simply flicked my hand as I passed Nolan and announced to Jamie that his request for a payout was the most offensive way to introduce himself.

I continued to stalk around the room, checking to make sure I covered everyone I wanted gone. The reactions of the spared boys ranged from interesting to bizarre. Holden kept swallowing, waiting for the bomb to drop, while Jack smiled in a strange way, almost as if he found this all entertaining or exciting. I finally came up to Ean, who didn't look away but chose to wink at me.

I noticed he was sitting alone, with only a leather-bound journal and pen to keep him company. Not here to make friends it seemed.

"A wink is a bit bold, don't you think?" I asked quietly.

"What princess would want a man by her side who wasn't bold?"

I raised an eyebrow, amused. "You're not at all worried about being overconfident, are you?"

"No. It's who I am. And I don't intend to hide anything from you."

There was something almost frightening about his presence, but I liked that he had the nerve to be real. I noted the camera coming to hover behind him, trying to capture my expression, and I shook my head at him, suppressing a smirk. I moved on, adding Arizona, Brady, Pauly, and MacKendrick to the ranks of the evicted. If I'd counted correctly, that was eleven gone.

Once the eliminated had all left, I went to the door, turning to face the remaining candidates. "If you're still here, that means you've done something between our first meeting and now to impress me or have at least had the common sense not to offend me." Some smiled, probably thinking of Blakely, while others stood there stunned. "I want to encourage you all to be deliberate, because I take this very seriously. This isn't a game, gentlemen. This is my life."

I pulled the doors shut behind me and heard the flurry of activity pick up in my wake. Some laughed or sighed, while someone simply repeated "Oh, my goodness, oh, my goodness" again and again. The reporters' voices rose above them all, encouraging them to recount their feelings on the first elimination. Letting out a long breath, I walked away feeling confident. I'd taken a decisive step, and Dad could rest easy now, knowing the Selection was properly under way and that I wouldn't let him down.

To make up for the lackluster first evening and the complete absence of interaction after the parade yesterday, the boys were invited that night to a predinner tea to meet the household and, of course, speak with me, their beloved would-be bride. Mom and Dad were there, along with Ahren, Kaden, and Osten. Josie came with the Woodworks—who were working very hard not to hover over their son—and Miss Lucy was circling the room, not really speaking to anyone but looking lovely. She never seemed to care for crowds.

I'd changed into a gown for dinner and put on another pair of toe-destroying heels. I was still riding my post-elimination buzz, so pleased to be making steps to help Dad. It dwindled quickly though as Ahren walked toward me with a warning glare in his eyes.

"What in the world did you do to them?" he asked accusingly.

"Nothing," I vowed. "I held an elimination. I wanted to show everyone that this was important to me. Like Dad."

Ahren pressed his palm into his forehead. "Have you had your nose buried in reports all day?"

"Of course I have," I replied. "You might not have noticed, but that's kind of my job."

Ahren leaned in. "The clips on the news have painted you to be a black widow. Your face was smug as you kicked them out. And you got rid of a third of them, Eadlyn. That doesn't make the candidates look important. It makes them look disposable." I could feel the blood draining from my face as Ahren continued in a whisper. "Two of them have asked in the most circumspect and quiet ways possible if there was a chance that you prefer women."

I let out a sound that wasn't quite a laugh. "Of course, because the only way I could possibly like men is if I bowed down at their feet?"

"This isn't the time to make a stand, Eadlyn. You need to be gracious."

"Pardon me, Your Highness?"

Ahren and I both turned at the sound of our title, and I found myself with a reporter in my face, her eyes and smile bordering on manic.

"I hate to interrupt, but I was wondering if I could have a brief interview with the princess before my deadline." The reporter showed her teeth again, and I couldn't stop myself from feeling I was about to be eaten alive either figuratively or literally.

"She'd be happy to," Ahren offered, kissing my forehead as he disappeared.

My pulse sped. I hadn't prepared myself for this. But of all the things that could happen right now, I refused to let the public see me sweat.

"Your Highness, you eliminated eleven suitors today. Do you think this cut was a bit drastic?"

I squared my shoulders and gave her a sweet grin. "I can certainly see why some might think that," I answered generously, "but this is a very important decision. I don't think it would be wise to spend time on young men who are rude or unimpressive. I'm hoping with a smaller pool, I'll be able to get to know these gentlemen much better."

I scanned the words in my head. Nothing humiliating or incriminating in there.

"Yes, but why were you so harsh? For a few you simply said 'no' or flicked your hand."

I tried not to let the worry show on my face. At the time those things had seemed kind of funny.

"When my father is stern, no one chastises him. I don't think it's fair that when I act similarly, I'm seen as cruel. I'm making a huge decision, and I'm trying to be wise about it." While I wanted to scream those words, I said them with the voice I'd been trained to use in interviews, and I even managed to smile through most of it.

"But one of them cried after you left the room," she informed me.

"What?" I asked, worrying that my face was growing paler by the second.

"One of the Selected cried when the elimination ended. Do you think that's a normal response or that you maybe elicited it by being severe with them?"

I swallowed, scrambling for anything to say. "I have three brothers. They all cry, and I can assure you, the reasons rarely make sense to me."

She chuckled. "So you don't think you were too hard on them?"

I knew what she was doing, digging at the same question until I snapped. She was very close to getting the better of me.

"I can't imagine what it would be like on the other end of the Selection process and to be removed so early on. But, besides my father, no one here knows what it's like to be on this side of it either. I'm going to do my best to find a worthy husband. And if that man can't handle a harsh word or two, he definitely wouldn't make it as a prince. Trust me on that!" I reached out and touched her arm, as if this was gossip or a joke. It was a disarming technique.

"Speaking of suitors, I hope you'll excuse me. I need to go spend some time with them."

She opened her mouth to ask another question, but I turned away, holding my head high. I didn't know what to do. I couldn't go straight to the drinks, I couldn't unleash every swear word I knew into the air, and I couldn't run into the arms of my parents. I had to look content, so I walked around the room, smiling and batting my lashes at the boys as I passed them.

I noticed those small things alone made them grin at me or change their posture. Instead of retreating, their expressions softened, and I could see these tiny moments of gentleness were erasing their memories of this morning in the Men's Parlor already. I wished with everything I had that the public would let it slide as quickly as the boys did.

I figured eventually one of them would be brave enough to speak to me. And it turned out that person was Hale.

"So, we're at a tea party," he said, falling into step beside me. "What kind of tea does the princess like best?"

He sipped from his own cup, smiling shyly.

Hale had an effortless warmth about him, similar to Miss Marlee, and it was easy to hold a conversation with him. At the moment, I was more grateful he was the first one to approach me than he could have ever guessed. He'd rescued me twice now.

"It depends on my mood. Or the season. Like I can't seem to enjoy a white tea during the winter. But black tea is a good staple."

"Agreed." Hale stood there, nodding.

"I heard someone cried after I left today. Is that true?"

Hale's eyes widened and he let out a whistle. "Yeah, it was Leeland. I thought he'd broken a bone or something. Took us nearly an hour to calm him down."

"What happened?"

"You happened! You come in, prowling around the room, eliminating people at random. I guess he has a timid disposition, and you really shook him."

I spotted Leeland standing alone in a corner. If I was sincerely looking for a husband, he'd be gone already. I was a little surprised he hadn't asked to leave.

"I think it came out more callously than I'd intended."

Hale laughed once. "You don't have to be callous at all. We all know who you are and what you can do. We respect that."

"Tell that to the guy who asked when he was getting paid," I muttered.

He didn't have a response for that, and I felt bad for bringing our conversation to a halt.

"So, what is it today?" I asked, trying to regain my composure.

"I'm sorry?"

"How are you proving yourself to me today?"

He smiled. "Today it's my promise never to bring you white tea in the winter." He didn't say good-bye or bow but walked away, seeming hopeful.

Over his shoulder, Baden caught my eye. My first impression of him had nothing to do with our initial conversation. I only saw him as the boy Aunt May thought had promise.

I could tell he was debating whether or not to walk over. I looked down at the floor and peeked his way from under my lashes. I felt foolish trying to play this part, but it worked and he started to cross the floor. I thought back to the interviewer, musing over how funny it was that I'd been taught plenty of disarming techniques for interviews or negotiations, but when it came to boys, I was left to figure it out alone.

Baden looked eager to speak to me, but we were both shocked when another boy coming from a different direction arrived at us at the exact same moment.

"Gunner," Baden greeted. "How are you enjoying the party?"

"It's excellent. I was just coming to thank Her Highness for hosting it. It's been a pleasure to meet your younger brothers."

"Oh, dear. What did they do?"

Baden laughed, and Gunner tried to suppress a smile. "Osten is awfully . . . energetic."

I sighed. "I blame my parents. It seems that by the time you get to your fourth child, your desire to instill certain values goes out the window."

"I like him though. Hope he'll be around."

"It's hard to say. Osten's the hardest to keep tabs on. Even his nanny—whom he *despises*, by the way—can't keep up with him. Either he's causing chaos or he's hiding."

Baden jumped in. I wondered if he was trying to flirt or just seem brave. "Those two moods are so different! Is everyone in your family like that?"

I knew what he was asking: Was I the kind of girl who aimed to find solace or cause a stir with no in between? "Unquestionably."

Baden nodded. "Good to know. I'll buy a shield and some binoculars."

And, darn it, I giggled. I didn't mean to, but I did. I tried not to be upset for letting my guard down. Hopefully it would make for some good pictures. I curtsied and continued around the space.

I saw Henri across the room, Erik shadowing his every step. When our eyes met, he began walking my way immediately, grinning from ear to ear.

"Hello! *Hyvää iltaa*!" He kissed my cheek, which, again, would have been shocking from anyone else.

"He says 'Good evening.'"

"Oh um . . . *heevat eelah*?" I mumbled, attempting to duplicate his words.

He chuckled as I butchered his language. "Good, good!" Was he always this cheerful?

I turned to Erik. "How bad was it really?"

His tone was kind, but he wasn't going to lie. "I'm sorry to say, there is no way I could have even guessed at what that was."

I smiled, genuinely. The pair of them were so unassuming,

and considering how alienated Henri must have felt, that was saying something.

Before I could continue the conversation, Josie was beside me. "Great party, Eadlyn. You're Henri, right? I've seen your picture," she said in a rush, sticking her hand out to greet him.

He must have been confused, but he accepted the gesture all the same.

"I'm Josie. Eadlyn and I are practically sisters," she gushed.

"Except that we're not related at all," I added.

Erik tried to convey everything to Henri quickly and quietly, which distracted Josie.

"Who are you?" she asked. "I don't remember seeing your picture."

"I'm Sir Henri's translator. He only speaks Finnish."

Josie looked incredibly disappointed. I realized then that she must have come over because she found Henri attractive. He certainly seemed younger than most of the others and did have that happy-go-lucky air about him, which she must have thought suited her better than me.

"So . . . ," she began, "how does he, like, even live?"

Without even checking with Henri, Erik spoke up. "If you're practically Her Highness's sister, then I'm sure the palace has afforded you an excellent education. So, of course you know the relations between Illéa and Swendway are old and strong, drawing many Swendish people to settle here, making small communities, and vice versa. It's not difficult at all."

I pressed my lips together, trying not to grin at how articulately he put Josie in her place.

Josie nodded. "Oh, of course. Umm . . ." And that was as hard as she was willing to try. "Excuse me."

"I'm sorry," I whispered once she was out of earshot. "It has nothing to do with you two. She's just terrible."

"No offense taken," Erik replied honestly. He conversed back and forth for a moment with Henri in Finnish, presumably catching him up on what just happened.

"Pardon me. I need to speak with someone, but I'll see you at dinner." I curtsied and left them, searching for any sort of retreat.

I'd been totally thrown off by that interview earlier, and I was proud that I pulled myself back together in the aftermath. But Josie had the ability to ruffle me without fail.

I saw Mom alone and rushed over to her, hoping for some solace. Instead I was greeted by a glare similar to Ahren's when I'd first come in.

"Why didn't you tell us that was what you were going to do?" she asked quietly, holding a smile as if nothing was wrong.

I did the same as I answered. "I thought it would be good. That's what Dad did."

"Yes, but he did it on a much smaller scale and privately. You put their shame on display. No one will admire you for that."

I huffed. "I'm sorry. Really. I didn't realize."

She put an arm around me. "I don't mean to be hard on

you. We know you're trying." Just then a photographer came up to get a candid photo of us talking. I wondered what the headline for that one would be? Something about the Selected teaching the Selector maybe.

"What am I supposed to do now?"

She looked around the room, double-checking that no one could hear. "Just . . . consider a little romance. Nothing scandalous, for goodness' sake," she added quickly. "But watching you fall in love . . . that's what the people want to see."

"I can't *make* that happen. I can't—"

"America, dear," Dad called. It looked like Osten had spilled something on himself, and Mom rushed over to lead him away.

I would have bet money that whatever just happened was a deliberate attempt on Osten's part to get out of the room.

I stood there alone, trying to be inconspicuous as I scanned the room. Too many strangers. Too many eyes watching and waiting for me to perform. I was ready for the Selection to be over about four hours ago. I took a deep breath. Three months would buy me freedom. I could do this. I had to.

I walked across the room deliberately, knowing who I needed to speak to. Once I found him, I leaned in and spoke in his ear.

"Come to my room. Eight o'clock sharp. Tell no one."

CHAPTER 12

I PACED AS I WAITED for the knock to come. Kile was really the only person I could trust with this task, though I was loath to ask him. I was prepared to strike a bargain, but I wasn't sure what I could offer him yet. I felt confident he'd have his own ideas.

The raps on the door were quiet, and I could almost hear the question in them: *What am I doing here?*

I pulled the door open and there, right on time, was Kile.

"Your Highness," he said with a comical bow. "I've come to sweep you off your feet."

"Hardy har. Get in here."

Kile walked in and surveyed my shelves. "Last time I was in your room, you had a collection of wooden ponies."

"Outgrew that."

"But not being a bossy tyrant?"

"Nope. Just like you didn't outgrow being an insufferable bookworm."

"Is this how you win over all your dates?"

I smirked. "More or less. Sit down. I have a proposition for you."

He spotted the wine I'd provided and wasted no time in pouring himself a glass. "You want some?"

I sighed. "Please. We'll both need it."

He paused, eyeing me before continuing. "Now I'm nervous. What do you want?"

I took my glass, trying to remember how I wanted to explain this to him. "You know me, Kile. You've known me my whole life."

"True. In fact, I was thinking yesterday that I have a vague recollection of you running around in nothing but a diaper. It was a good look."

I rolled my eyes and tried not to laugh. "Anyway. You, to some degree, understand my personality, who I am when the cameras aren't rolling."

He sipped, contemplating my words. "I think I understand you when they're on as well, but please continue."

I hadn't thought about that, how he'd seen me go through the many phases of growing up, both on and off screen. There was a switch I had to flip when I was on display, and he knew it. "The Selection wasn't my idea, but it's something I need to put my best effort into. I think I am, personally. But the public expects me to be a giddy little girl next to all of you, and I don't think I can do that. I can't act stupid."

"Actually—"

"Don't!"

He smiled wickedly and took another sip of his wine.

"You're such a pain. Why am I even bothering?"

"No, go on, you don't want to act stupid." He set down his glass and leaned forward.

I took a breath, hunting for the words again. "They want romance, but I'm not prepared to behave like that publicly, at least not when I haven't truly connected with someone. Still, I need to give them something."

I ducked my head and peeked up at him from under my lashes.

"Like what exactly?"

"A kiss."

"A kiss?"

"Just a little one. And you're the only person I can ask, because you'd know it wasn't real and things wouldn't get complicated. And I'm willing to give you something in return."

He raised his eyebrows. "What?"

I shrugged. "Whatever you want, really. Within reason. I can't offer you a country or anything."

"Could you talk to my mom? Help get me out of here?"

"And go where, exactly?"

"Anywhere." He sighed desperately. "My mom . . . I don't know what happened that made her so crazy loyal to your parents, but she's got it in her head that this is our home forever. Do you know how much work it took for me to get out of here and take that one accelerated course?

"I want to travel, I want to build, I want to do more than read about things. Sometimes I think one more day behind these walls might kill me."

"I get that," I whispered, not thinking. I straightened up. "I can make it happen. As soon as an opportunity becomes available, I will help convince your parents that you need to leave the palace."

He paused a second, then threw back the rest of his wine. "One kiss?"

"Just one."

"When?"

"Tonight. There will be a photographer waiting down the hall at nine. Hopefully very well hidden, because I'd like to pretend he isn't there."

Kile nodded. "Fine. One kiss."

"Thank you."

We sat in silence, watching the hands on the clock. After three minutes I couldn't take it anymore.

"What do you mean you want to build things?"

He lit up. "That's what I study. Architecture and design. I like dreaming up structures, figuring out how to make them and, sometimes, how to make them particularly beautiful."

"That's . . . actually really interesting, Kile."

"I know." He gave one of his crooked smiles, just like his dad's, and it was fun to see how excited he was about it. "Do you want to see?"

"See what?"

"Some of my designs. I have them in my room. My old one, not my Selected one, so they're just down the hall."

"Sure." I took one last sip of wine and followed him out. Except for a guard or two, the hallway was empty as Kile and I made our way to his room.

He opened the door and flicked on the lights, and I had to stop myself from gasping.

He. Was. A. Mess!

His bed wasn't made, there were clothes amassed in a corner, and several dirty plates were piled on his side table.

"I know what you're thinking. How does he keep it so immaculate?"

"You read my mind," I said, trying not to appear completely repulsed. At least it didn't smell bad.

"About a year ago I asked the staff to stop cleaning for me. I do it myself. But the Selection kind of caught me off guard, so I just left it how it was."

He started kicking objects under his bed and trying to pull the things within his reach a little straighter.

"Why don't you let them clean?"

"I'm a grown man. I can take care of myself."

I didn't think he meant that as a dig at me, but it stung all the same.

"Anyway, this is my work space."

In the far corner of the room the walls were covered in pictures and posters of everything from skyscrapers to mud huts. His desk was overflowing with prints he'd drawn up, and models built from wooden scraps and thin strips of metal.

"Did you make all these?" I asked, gently touching a structure that slightly twisted as it went upward.

"Yep. Concept, design. I'd love to create real buildings one day. I'm studying, but there's only so much I can learn without getting my hands on things, you know?"

"Kile . . ." I took in all of it: the colors and lines, the amount of time and thought that must have gone into each of them. "This is amazing."

"It's just me fooling around."

"No, don't do that. Don't make it seem like less than it is. I could never do something like this."

"Sure you could." He went over and pulled out a ruler shaped like a *T* and laid it over something he was already working on. "See, it's just a matter of looking at the lines and doing the math."

"Ugh, more math. I do enough of that as it is."

He laughed. "But this is fun math."

"Fun math is an oxymoron."

Kile and I moved to his couch, and we went through a few books of his favorite architects, studying their styles. He seemed particularly interested in how some worked with the land around them and others worked against it. "I mean, look at that!" he said enthusiastically after nearly every page.

I couldn't believe it had taken me all these years to see this side of him. He tucked himself inside a shell, shutting himself away from others here because the palace had trapped *him*. Behind the books and the snippy remarks there was a curious, engaging, and sometimes very charming person.

I felt like I'd been lied to. Was someone going to pop around the corner and tell me Josie was really a saint?

Eventually Kile looked down to his watch. "It's ten after nine."

"Oh. We should go then." But I didn't want to get up. Kile's messy room was one of the most comfortable places I'd ever been.

"Yeah." Kile closed the book and put it back on the shelf. Even though that corner was as haphazard as the rest of the room, I could see the care he took with it.

I waited for him by the door, suddenly nervous.

"Here," he said, offering his hand. "It's the end of a date, right?"

I placed my hand in his. "Thanks. For showing me your work, and for doing this. I promise to pay you back."

"I know."

He opened the door and walked me down the hall. "When do you think we last held hands?" I wondered out loud.

"Probably a game of red rover or something."

"Probably."

We were quiet as we headed toward my room. When we reached it, I turned back to Kile and watched as he swallowed.

"Nervous?" I whispered.

"Nah." He smiled, but he also fidgeted. "So . . . goodnight."

Kile leaned down, lips meeting mine, holding them there. Then his lips parted and closed and parted again. I drew a breath in the moment between kisses, sensing he would come back again. He did, and thank goodness, because I hadn't been kissed like this before and I needed more.

The few times I'd kissed boys were rushed, sloppy moments hiding in a coatroom or behind a statue. But this, with so much air around us and no one coming to check on me . . . it was different.

I leaned into Kile, still holding him, and he brought up his free hand and cupped my cheek. He held my lips to his for what felt like forever before pulling back.

And even when he did pull away, his nose stayed right against mine, so close that when he whispered, I could smell what was left of the wine on his breath.

"Do you think that was enough?"

"I . . . um . . . I don't know."

"Just to be sure."

He pressed his mouth to mine again, and I was so surprised to get another kiss like that, it felt like my bones were turning into mush. I wrapped my fingers up into his hair, shocked at myself for having the urge to hold him in that pose all night.

He pulled back again, looking into my eyes, and there was something different. Was he feeling that funny warmth creep into his arms and chest and head, too?

"Thank you," I murmured.

"Any time. I mean"—he shook his head, laughing at himself—"you know what I mean."

"Goodnight, Kile."

"Goodnight, Eadlyn." He gave me a quick kiss on the cheek before heading toward the stairs that led back to his temporary quarters.

I watched him go and told myself that the only reason I was smiling like that was because the cameras were hidden somewhere, not because of anything Kile Woodwork had done.

CHAPTER 13

"So, I THINK I MANAGED to distract everyone for a while." I held on to Ahren's arm as we walked through the garden.

"I'll say." Ahren made a smart little face at me, and I fought the urge to hit him. "How was it?"

At that I really did hit him. "You pig! A lady never tells."

"Well, is a real lady meant to be photographed kissing her suitor in the dark?"

I shrugged. "Either way, it worked."

The pictures of Kile and me were gobbled up like food, just as predicted. It felt a little strange that this was what people were hungry for, but it didn't really matter as long as they were satisfied. The reactions to the kiss ranged though. A handful of the papers thought it was sweet, but the majority of them were displeased that I was so willing to give up a kiss this early in the competition.

One of the gossip magazines even had a back and forth with two of their biggest reporters over whether I was loose for giving such a kiss or if it was sweet because I'd known Kile since birth. I tried to shrug it off. There would be other things to talk about soon enough.

"I dug a few pages in," I said, turning back to Ahren. "Not a single report of post-caste discrimination."

"So, what are your plans for today? Going to make the boys cry again?"

I rolled my eyes. "It was only one. And, I don't know. Maybe I won't visit them today."

"Nope," Ahren blurted, moving us to a new path. "So help me, Eadlyn, if I have to drag you by your hair through this I will, but you've actually got to participate in the Selection."

I let my arm slip away from his. "I can't help feeling there's no way it was this hard for Dad."

"Have you asked him?"

"No, and I don't think I can. Just recently both he and Mom have been giving me more details, thinking it might be helpful. I feel like they must have held those things close to them for a reason, and it seems rude to ask. Besides, I don't know that any two people in this situation would handle it the exact same way, and I really don't want to know if Dad cared about anyone besides Mom."

"Isn't that a strange thought?" He sat on a nearby stone bench. "Some other woman could have been our mother!"

"No," I countered, joining him. "We only exist because

they found each other. Any other combination would not have created the two of us."

"You're messing with my head, Eady."

"Sorry. This situation is throwing me off." I traced my finger around the stone. "I mean, I get why the concept sounds appealing. That somewhere out there, my perfect match could be waiting for me, and by chance I could pull his name and meet him and fall madly in love. But then there's the feeling of being a prize horse, that I'm being judged more so than usual. And when I look at all these boys, they seem foreign in comparison to the type of people I generally encounter, and I don't think I like it. The whole thing makes me feel unsettled."

Ahren was quiet for a while, and I could see he was carefully choosing words, which made me nervous.

I wasn't sure if that was a twin thing or a bond exclusive to Ahren and me, but it was almost physical when we were at odds. It felt like a rubber band pulling tight between us.

"Listen, Eady, I know this might have been the wrong way to go about it, but I do think it's good for you to have someone in your life. I've been with Camille a long time, and even if everything ended tomorrow, I'd be a better person because of her. There are some things you don't learn about yourself until you let someone else into the most intimate places of your heart."

"How can you two even manage to do that? You spend almost all of your time apart."

He grinned. "She's my soul mate. I know it."

"I don't think soul mates are real," I said, examining my shoes. "You happened to meet a French princess because you only ever meet royalty, and you like her more than anyone else. Your true soul mate could be milking a cow right now, and you'd never know."

"You're always so down on her." His tone made the invisible rubber band stretch again.

"I'm simply discussing possibilities."

"In the meantime, you have dozens of possibilities in front of you and refuse to look at them."

I snorted. "Did Dad put you up to this?"

"No! I think you should look at this with an open mind. You're one of the most isolated people in the country, but that doesn't mean your walls have to be up all the time. You need to experience a romantic relationship at least once in your life."

"Hey! I've experienced romantic relationships!"

"A picture in the paper does not count as a relationship," he said heatedly. "Neither does making out with Leron Troyes at that Christmas ball in Paris."

I gasped. "How do you know about that?"

"Everyone knows about that."

"Even Mom and Dad?"

"Dad doesn't know. Well, unless Mom told him, because I'm positive she does."

I buried my face and made some screechy sound that encapsulated my complete humiliation.

"All I'm saying is, this could be good for you."

That line pushed all the shame out of my body and replaced it with rage.

"Everyone keeps saying that: it might be good for me. What does that even mean? I'm smart and beautiful and strong. I don't need to be rescued."

Ahren shrugged. "Maybe not. But you never know if one of them might need to be."

I stared at the grass, considering that. I shook my head. "What are you doing, Ahren? What's with the sudden change of heart? I thought you were on my side."

I saw a flicker of something in his eyes before he pushed it away and put an arm around me. "I am, Eadlyn. You, Mom, and Camille are the most important women in my life. So please understand me when I say that sometimes I wonder how happy you are."

"I'm happy, Ahren. I'm the princess. I have everything."

"I think you're mistaking comfort for joy."

His words vaguely reminded me of my recent chat with Mom.

Ahren rubbed my arm and stood, brushing off his suit. "I promised Kaden I'd help with his French lesson. Just think about all this, okay? Maybe I'm wrong. It certainly wouldn't be the first time." We shared a smile.

I nodded. "I'll think about it."

He gave me a wink. "Go on a date or something. You need to get a life."

I stood outside the door to the Men's Parlor pacing, worrying I was wasting time. After my talk with Ahren, I really should have gone straight to the office. Truthfully, I was looking forward to getting back to the normal monotony of shuffling papers. But his words, above anyone else's, made me wonder if I should at least try. And not the fake trying I was planning for the cameras, but genuine effort.

I told myself that I would have to date them eventually anyway. It was the bare minimum of what I'd need to do. It didn't mean I was choosing anyone; I was just keeping my promise to Dad and doing what the people expected.

Sighing, I handed the envelope to the butler. "Okay, go ahead."

He bowed before he left, and I waited outside.

I'd decided I wasn't going to barge into the Men's Parlor again. I wanted the Selected to be on their toes, but everyone needed a retreat now and then. I knew that better than anybody.

A moment later the butler returned, holding the door as Hale stepped out. Two things passed through my head as he approached. First, I wondered what Kile would think, which, admittedly, was odd. Second, it was obvious Hale still didn't know what to make of me, because he was very cautious as he came to a stop about two feet away and bowed. "Your Highness."

I clasped my hands in front of me. "You may call me Eadlyn."

There was a hint of a smile in his eyes. "Eadlyn."

No one in the world is as powerful as you.

"I was wondering if you'd like to join me for dessert tonight after dinner."

"Just you and me?"

I sighed. "Was there someone else you wanted to invite? Do you need a translator as well?"

"No, no!" he said, a real smile coming across his face. "I'm just . . . pleasantly surprised, I guess."

"Oh." It was a pathetic response to such a sweet admission, but I simply wasn't prepared.

Hale stood there, his hands jammed in his pockets, beaming, and it was hard to think of him as another person I'd just send home.

"Umm, anyway, I'll come by your room about twenty minutes after dinner, and we'll go to one of the parlors upstairs."

"Sounds great. See you tonight."

I started walking. "See you tonight."

I was a little bothered because I was looking forward to it now. His anticipation was kind of cute. But worse than the feeling that the Selection was getting to me was the triumphant look on Hale's face when he caught me peeking back at him.

CHAPTER 14

WOULD IT BE STRANGE IF I changed dresses between dinner and dessert? Was he going to change clothes? I'd been wearing tiaras for the last few days, but was it inappropriate if I wore one on a date?

On a date.

This was too far out of my comfort zone. I felt so vulnerable, which I couldn't understand. I had interacted with plenty of young men. I did have that spectacular interlude with Leron at that Christmas party, and Jamison Akers fed me a strawberry lip-to-lip hidden behind a tree at a picnic. I'd even made it through last night with Kile, though that was nothing close to a real date.

I had met all thirty-five of the Selected candidates and stood tall through every minute. Not to mention, I helped run an entire country. Why was one date with one boy making me so anxious?

I decided that, yes, I would change, and I put on a yellow dress that was longer in the back than in the front, which I paired with a navy belt so it looked a little less I'm-ready-for-the-garden-party and a little more let's-go-out. And no tiara. Why had I even considered it?

I gave my reflection a once-over and reminded myself that *he* was trying to win *me* over, not the other way around.

I jumped at the knock on the door. I still had five minutes! And I was supposed to go to him! He was throwing off my entire preparation strategy, and so help me, I'd send him away and start all over again if I had to.

Without waiting for an answer, Aunt May poked her head in, Mom smiling right behind her.

"Aunt May!" I ran over and crushed her in a hug. "What are you doing here?"

"I figured you could use some extra support, so I came back."

"And I'm here to make this whole thing more awkward than it has to be," Mom promised with a smile.

I laughed nervously. "I'm not used to this. I don't know what to do."

Aunt May cocked an eyebrow. "According to the papers, you're doing very well."

I blushed. "That was different. It wasn't an actual date. It didn't mean anything."

"But this does?" she asked, her voice gentle.

I shrugged. "It's not the same."

"I know everyone says this," Mom began, pushing back my hair, "but it's the best advice I can give you: be yourself."

That was easier said than done. Because, who was I really? One half of a set of twins. The heir to a throne. One of the most powerful people in the world. The biggest distraction in the country.

Never just daughter. Never just girl.

"Don't take any of this too seriously." Aunt May fixed her own hair in the mirror before turning back to me. "You should just enjoy yourself."

I nodded.

"She makes a good point," Mom agreed. "It's not as if we want you to choose someone today. You have time here, so have fun meeting some new people. Goodness knows, that's a rarity for you."

"True. It just feels awkward. I'm going to be alone with him, and then he'll tell all the other guys about it, and then we'll have to talk about it on TV."

"It sounds harder than it is. Most of the time it's funny," Mom insisted.

I tried to imagine teenage her, blushing and talking about her dates with Dad. "So you didn't mind it?"

She pursed her lips together, studying the ceiling as she thought. "Well, it was harder in the beginning. I was very hesitant to be the center of attention. But you're brilliant at that, so treat this like any other party or event you'd give an interview about."

May looked at her. "It's not exactly like a post–Grateful Feast recap," she pointed out before focusing on me, "but your mother is right about you being better in the spotlight.

She was embarrassing at your age."

"Thanks, May." Mom rolled her eyes.

"Any time."

I chuckled, wishing briefly that I had just one sister. Mom's other sister, Aunt Kenna, died years ago of a heart condition. Uncle James was a simple man, so he didn't want to raise Astra and Leo in the palace even though we offered several times. We kept in touch, of course, but Astra and I were very different girls. Still, I remembered all too clearly the way Mom had spent a week in bed holding May and Grandma Singer after Kenna passed away. More and more I wondered if losing a sister was like Mom losing part of herself. I knew it would feel like that for me if anything happened to Ahren.

Aunt May elbowed Mom, and they shared a smile. They never really fought, not over anything that truly mattered, and the two of them soothed my worries.

They were right. This was nothing.

"You're going to do great," Mom said. "You don't know how to fail." She gave me a wink, and I felt myself stand taller.

I checked the clock. "I should go. Thanks for coming," I said, taking Aunt May's hand.

"No problem." I hugged her at the door, and then headed downstairs.

When I got to Hale's room, I paused and drew in a deep breath before I knocked. He answered, not his butler, and he seemed thrilled to see me.

"You look fantastic," he said.

"Thank you," I answered, smiling in spite of myself. "So do you."

He'd changed, too, which made me feel much more comfortable, and I liked what he'd done with himself. His tie was gone, and he had his top button undone. Between that and the vest, he looked . . . well, he looked cute.

Hale tucked his hands into his pockets. "So where are we going?"

I pointed down the hall. "This way, up to the fourth floor."

He rocked on his feet a few times then hesitantly held out his arm for me. "Lead the way."

"All right," I began as we walked toward the stairs. "I know the basic facts. Hale Garner, nineteen years old, Belcourt. But those entry forms are a little cut and dried, so what's your story?"

He chuckled. "Well, I too am the oldest in my family."

"Really?"

"Yes. Three boys."

"Ugh, I feel bad for your mother."

He smiled. "Eh, she doesn't mind. We remind her of Dad, so when one of us is a little too loud or laughs at something he would have, she'll sigh and say we're just like him."

I was afraid to ask, but I wanted to be clear. "Are your parents divorced?" I asked, doubting that was the case.

"No. He passed away."

"I'm sorry," I said, feeling mortified that I'd indirectly insulted his memory.

"It's okay. Not one of those things you know without being told."

"Can I ask when he died?"

"About seven years ago. I know this will sound weird, but sometimes I'm jealous of my youngest brother. Beau was about six when it happened, and he remembers Dad, but not the way I do, you know? Sometimes I wish I didn't have so much to miss."

"I'd be willing to bet he's jealous of you for the opposite reason."

He gave me a sad smile. "I never thought about that."

We turned up the main stairs, focusing on our steps. When we got to the landing on the fourth floor, I started again.

"What does your mother do?"

Hale swallowed. "Right now she's working as a secretary at the local university. She . . . well, it's been hard for her to hold down a good job, but she likes this one, and she's had it for a long time. I just realized I began that sentence with 'right now' because I was used to her switching a lot, but she hasn't done that for a while.

"Like I said when we met, my dad was a Two. He was an athlete. Went in for a surgery on his knee, but there was a clot and it made its way to his heart. Mom had never worked a day in her life—between her parents and Dad she was taken care of. After we lost him, all she was good at was being a basketball player's wife."

"Oh, no."

"Yeah."

I was so grateful when we came upon the parlor. How had

Dad managed this? How did he sift through all those girls, testing them to find his wife? Getting to know one person was already wearing me out, and we weren't even five minutes into our first date.

"Wow," Hale whispered, admiring the setup.

From the fourth-floor parlors at the front of the palace you could just barely look out over the walls. Angeles in the evening let out a beautiful glow, and I'd asked for the parlor lights to be dimmed so we could really see it.

There was a small table in the middle of the room that had various cakes on it, and a dessert wine was waiting on the side. I'd never tried to set up a romantic evening before, but I thought I did a good job for my first try.

Hale pulled out my chair before joining me at the table.

"I didn't know what you liked, so I got several. These are chocolate, obviously," I said, pointing to the dozens of tiny cakes. "Then lemon, vanilla, and cinnamon."

Hale stared at the piles of treats in front of us like I'd actually given him something huge. "Listen, I don't want to be rude," he said, "but if there's anything you want, you should grab it now, because there's a serious chance I will demolish these."

I laughed. "Help yourself."

He picked up one of the chocolate cakes and popped the whole thing into his mouth. "Mmmmmmm."

"Try the cinnamon. It'll change your life."

We kept eating for a while, and I thought maybe this would be enough for one night. We'd moved into very safe territory; I could talk about desserts for hours! But then, without warning, he started talking about his life again.

"So my mom works at the university, but I work with a tailor in town."

"Oh?"

"Yeah, I'm very interested in clothes. Well, I am now anyway. Right after Dad died it was harder to get new things, so I learned to hide the rips in my brothers' shirts or let out a hem as they grew. Then Mom had a pile of dresses she was hoping to sell to get some money, and I took two pieces and combined them to make something new for her. It wasn't perfect, but I was good enough at it that I could probably get a job.

"So I read a lot and study what Lawrence does—he's my boss. Every now and then he'll let me take projects on my own. I guess that's what I'll do down the line."

I smirked. "You're definitely one of the more put-together guys in the group."

He smiled bashfully. "It's easy when I've got so much to work with. My butler is great, so he's helped me with making sure the fit on everything is impeccable. I don't think he appreciates all my pairings, but I want to look like a gentleman while still looking like myself, if that makes any sense."

I nodded enthusiastically as I swallowed a bit of cake. "Do you know how hard it is when you love jeans but you're a princess?"

He chuckled. "But you balance it so well! I mean, they plaster your outfits across every magazine, so I've seen plenty.

Your style is very individual."

"You think so?" I felt encouraged. Criticism was heavy these days, and that one scrap of praise was like water in the desert.

"Definitely!" he gushed. "I mean, you dress like a princess but then kind of not. I wouldn't be surprised if you were actually the ringleader of an all-girl mafia."

I spit out my wine all over the table, which made Hale burst into laughter.

"I'm so sorry!" I felt my cheeks burning. "If Mom saw that, I'd get the worst lecture."

Hale wiped the tears from his eyes and leaned forward. "Do they really lecture you? I mean, aren't you basically running the country?"

I shrugged. "Not really. Dad does most of the work. I just shadow him."

"But that's a formality at this point, right?"

"How do you mean?" My words must have come out harsher than I meant, because the laughter in his eyes disappeared instantly.

"I'm not trying to insult him or anything, but lots of people say he looks tired. I've heard some people speculate all the time on when you'll be ascending."

I looked down. Did people really talk about Dad being tired?

"Hey," Hale said, grabbing my attention again. "I'm really sorry. I was only trying to talk. I didn't mean to make you upset."

I shook my head. "No, you're fine. I'm not sure what got

to me. Maybe thinking about doing this without Dad."

"It's so funny to hear you call the king 'Dad.'"

"But that's who he is!" I found myself smiling again. Something about the way Hale talked made everything feel calmer, brighter. I liked that.

"I know, I know. Okay, so back to you. Besides being the most powerful woman in the world, what do you do for fun?"

I ate another piece of cake to hide how big my grin was. "It may or may not surprise you that I am also very into fashion."

"Oh, really?" he replied sarcastically.

"I sketch. A lot, actually. I've tried my hand at the things my parents like as well. I know a bit about photography, and I can play the piano a little. But I always come back to my sketchbook."

I knew I was smiling. Those pages with their scribbles of colored pencils were one of my safest places in the world.

"Could I see them?"

"What?" I crossed my ankles and sat up straighter.

"Your sketches. Could I see them sometime?"

No one saw my sketches. I only ever showed designs to my maids when I had to since I didn't do any of the construction. But for every one I shared, there were a dozen I hid, things I knew I could never wear. I thought about those pieces, each of them stored in my head or on paper, as if keeping them secret was the only way they could possibly be mine.

I knew he didn't understand my sudden silence or why I

held tightly to the arms of my chair. Hale asking that question, assuming he was welcome in that world, made me feel like he had somehow seen me—really seen me—and I didn't like it.

"Excuse me," I said, standing. "I think I had a little too much wine."

"Do you need help?" he asked, standing as well.

"No, please stay and enjoy yourself." I moved as quickly as I could.

"Your Highness!"

"Goodnight."

"Eadlyn, wait!"

In the hallway I moved much faster, unable to express my relief when he didn't follow me.

CHAPTER 15

I FULLY BELIEVED MY CURRENT state was not my fault, not even in the slightest. I knew who to point the finger at, and they were all other Schreaves. I blamed Mom and Dad for not being able to get the country under control and forcing me into this situation, and I blamed Ahren for trying to get me to consider these boys in the first place.

I was going to be queen, and a queen could be many things . . . but vulnerable wasn't one of them.

Last night's interlude with Hale made me sure of several things. First, I was right about the Selection. There was no way I could possibly find a companion under these circumstances, and I considered it miraculous that anyone had in the past. Forced openness with scores of strangers could not be good for one's soul.

Second, if I ever did get married, the chances of me

having a passionate, enduring love for that person were slim. Love did nothing but break down defenses, and I could not afford that. I already gave so much affection to my family that I knew they were my weakness, Dad and Ahren in particular. It was hard to imagine doing that to myself on purpose.

Ahren knew his words could sway me, knew how much I loved him. That was why, above the others, I wanted to throttle him after my date.

I went down to breakfast, walking with determined steps as if nothing had changed. I was still in control, and a bunch of silly boys were not going to take over my world. My plan for today was to get back to work. There had been far too many distractions lately, and I needed to focus. Dad talked about me finding someone to help me do my job, but so far all they were managing to do was make it harder.

Ahren and Osten sat next to Mom, and I took my place between Dad and Kaden. Even from the opposite side of the table I could hear Osten chewing.

"You all right, sis?" Kaden asked, pausing between heaping spoonfuls of oatmeal.

"Of course."

"You look a little stressed."

"You would, too, if you were going to run the country," I teased.

"Sometimes I think about that," he said, getting all serious. "Like, what if a disease swept over all of Illéa, and you and Mom and Dad and Ahren got sick and died. Then I'd be in charge and have to figure out everything on my own."

In my periphery I saw Dad lean forward, listening to his son. "That's a little morbid, Kaden."

Kaden shrugged. "It's always good to plan ahead."

I propped my chin on my hand. "So what would be King Kaden's first order of business?"

"Vaccinations, obviously."

I chuckled. "Good call. And after that?"

He considered. "I think I'd try to meet people. Nonsick people, so I could know what they need me to do. It probably looks a little different out there than it does in here."

Dad nodded. "That's pretty smart, Kaden."

"I know." And Kaden went back to eating, his imaginary rule at an end. Lucky him.

I picked at my food, surreptitiously looking over at Dad. Yes, I'd noticed him looking tired the other night, but that was a one-time thing. Sure, he needed glasses these days, and he had laugh lines surrounding his eyes, but that didn't translate into being worn-out. What did Hale know?

I peeked around the room. The boys were speaking to one another in hushed tones. I saw Ean chatting with Baden. Burke had spilled something on his tie and was trying to remove it discreetly and failing. My eyes passed over Hale, happy he wasn't looking in my direction at the moment.

At the back of the far table I saw Henri and Kile. Erik was translating patiently, and based on all three of their expressions, they were having a pretty good conversation.

I was engrossed. I tried for a minute to figure out what

they were talking about but to no avail. I sat there staring at Kile, watching his hands. It was funny to see the way they gestured to others and gripped a fork when I knew how well they held a pencil for sketching. Or—even better—pulled back hair for a kiss.

Eventually Kile caught me staring and gave me a little nod and a smile. Henri noticed him looking, and he turned in his chair to give me a wave. I bowed my head in acknowledgment, hoping no one noticed my blush. Henri turned back immediately to say something to Erik, who passed it on to Kile, who raised his eyebrows and nodded. I knew they were talking about me, and I couldn't help but wonder if Kile had shared certain details of our kiss.

Aunt May might be the only person I could spill all the little details of that kiss to without being completely horrified. I'd be lying if I said that moment in the hall hadn't crossed my mind several times since it happened.

Ahren stood, kissing Mom on her cheek before he turned to leave.

"Wait, Ahren, I need to talk to you," I said, standing as well.

"See you in a bit, sweetie?" Dad asked, glancing at me.

"I'll be up shortly. I promise."

Ahren held out his arm for me, and we walked together from the room. I could feel how we drew attention. It was like an energy that followed me nearly everywhere I went. I often reveled in that feeling.

"What do you want to talk about?"

I spoke through my smile. "I'll tell you once we're in the hall."

His step faltered. "Uh-oh."

When we rounded the corner, I pulled back and whacked him on the shoulder.

"Ow!"

"I went on a date last night, and it was awful, and I blame you personally."

Ahren rubbed his arm. "What happened? Was he mean?"

"No."

"Did he . . ." He lowered his voice. "Did he try to take advantage of you?"

"No." I crossed my arms.

"Was he rude?"

I sighed. "Not exactly, but it was . . . awkward."

He threw both of his arms up in exasperation. "Well, of course it was. If you saw him again, it would be better. That's the point. It takes time to get to know someone."

"I don't want him to get to know me! I don't want any of them to get to know me!"

His face fell into a confused scowl. "I always thought that you were the one person in the world I would understand no matter what. I thought you'd always understand me, too. But you tease me for being in love, and when the opportunity to find someone falls into your lap, you hate it."

I pointed a finger at his chest. "Wasn't it you who said this made no sense for me? Weren't you looking forward to how I'd make them squirm? I thought you and I both agreed this was a joke. And now, suddenly, you're the Selection's biggest cheerleader."

The hallway was painfully silent. I waited for Ahren to argue with me, or at least to explain.

"Sorry I let you down. But I think this is about more than a date. You need to figure out why you're so scared."

I raised myself to my full height. "I'm the next queen of Illéa. I'm scared of nothing."

He backed away. "Keep saying that, Eadlyn. See if it fixes the problem."

Ahren didn't get too far down the hall though. Josie had friends over this morning, and the whole lot of them basically melted at the sight of his face. I recognized one of them from the day in the garden and only remembered her because she had addressed me correctly.

I watched as they gave shy grins and ducked their heads. Ahren, to his credit, was polite as always.

"Josie has said your mastery of literature is very impressive," one of the girls said.

Ahren looked away. "She's exaggerating. I do love to read, and I write a little, but nothing worth sharing."

Another girl stepped forward. "I doubt that's true. I bet our tutor would be happy to have you come teach us sometime. I'd love to hear your thoughts on a few of the books we've been reading."

Josie clasped her hands together. "Oh, yes, please, Ahren. Won't you come teach us?"

Her friends giggled at her casually using his first name, a

habit from growing up beside him.

"I'm afraid I have far too much to do at the present. Perhaps another time. You ladies have a wonderful day." He bowed kindly and continued down the hall, and the girls didn't even wait until he was out of earshot to start giggling like idiots.

"He's so handsome," one said, ready to burst with adoration.

Josie sighed. "I know. He's so sweet to me, too. We took a walk together the other day, and he was saying that he thinks I'm one of the prettiest girls he's ever met."

I couldn't take it anymore. I barged past them, not slowing down. "You're too young for him, and he has a girlfriend, Josie. Let it go."

I rounded up the stairs to go to the office. I knew I'd feel better once I did something manageable, something I could check off a list.

"See," Josie said, not bothering to lower her voice. "I told you she was awful."

CHAPTER 16

WORK DIDN'T MAKE ME FEEL better. I was still very unsettled about last night with Hale, and any time Ahren and I fought, it was like I lost my equilibrium. The whole planet was off its axis. Adding Josie's ridiculous comments to the mix was the cherry on top.

My head was swarming with other people's words and my own questions, and I was positive the day was going to end up being a waste.

"You know," Dad said, peeking up from his work. "I got distracted early on, too. It gets easier to manage as the group gets smaller."

I smiled. Fine, let him think I had a crush. "Sorry, Dad."

"Not at all. Do you need me to cover your work for you today? Take the afternoon off?"

I straightened my papers. "No, that's not happening. I'm perfectly capable."

"I wasn't doubting you, love. I just—"

"I've already taken so much time away from work for this. I don't want to neglect my duties. I'm fine."

I didn't mean to sound so snippy with him.

"All right." He adjusted his glasses and started reading again. I tried to do the same.

What did Ahren mean, it was more than the date that upset me? I knew why I was mad. And since when had I given him a hard time about Camille? Sure, I didn't talk to her very much, but that was because we didn't have a lot in common. I didn't dislike the girl.

I shook my head, focusing on the papers.

"It would be fine if you needed to clear your head," Dad offered again. "You could go spend some time with one of the Selected and come back after lunch. Besides, you'll want to have something to talk about on the *Report*."

I felt a flurry of emotions, trying to figure out how I would discuss how exposed I'd felt after my date with Hale . . . or how stunned I felt after my kiss with Kile. Trying to balance the conflicting feelings around those two moments was dizzying without adding anything else.

"I went on a date last night, Dad. Isn't that enough?"

He swallowed as he thought. "Eventually you need to start alerting us when you have dates. A few pictures from some of them would be good for everyone. And I think you need at least one more date before Friday."

"Really?" I whined.

"Do something you enjoy. You're treating it like work."

"That's because it is!" I protested with an incredulous laugh.

"It can be fun, Eadlyn. Give it a chance." He looked at me over his glasses, almost like he was daring me.

"Fine. One date. That's all you get, old man," I teased.

He chuckled. "Old man is right."

Dad went back to his papers, satisfied. I sat there, peeking furtively at him from my desk. He stretched often, rubbing the back of his neck, and even though there weren't any urgent tasks today, he ran his hands through his hair as if he was troubled.

Now that Hale had put it in my head, I was going to be watching him often.

I decided to make Baden my next target. Maybe Aunt May knew something, because Baden didn't come in brashly or, conversely, like he was trying to hide. When someone else stole a moment that should have been solely his at the tea party, he didn't make a fuss. And when I approached him for time alone, he turned the focus back to me.

"You play the piano, right?" Baden asked when I invited him on a date.

"I do. Not as well as my mother, but I'm pretty proficient."

"I play the guitar. Maybe we could make some music."

It wasn't anything I would have thought of. Perhaps music would mean less talking, though, and I was all up for that.

"Sure. I'll secure the Women's Room for us."

"Am I even allowed in there?" he asked skeptically.

"When you're with me, yes. And I'll make sure it's empty.

My favorite piano in the palace is there. Do you need a guitar?"

He smirked. "Nah. I brought my own."

Baden ran a hand over his cropped hair, seeming very relaxed. I was still attempting to come across as distant and impenetrable, but I could tell there were a handful of guys who weren't bothered by my attitude at all, and Baden was one of them.

"What are the chances of the room being empty now?" he asked.

I smiled at his enthusiasm. "High, actually, but I have work to do."

He bent down, his eyes devilish. "But don't you always have work to do? I bet you could stay up till three in the morning if you had to."

"True, but—"

"And it'll all still be there when you get back."

I clasped my hands and considered it. "I'm really not supposed to . . ."

He started chanting slowly. "Skip it, skip it, skip it!"

My lips were pressed together, trying to hide my smile. Really, I ought to tell someone. I was going to have yet another undocumented date . . . but maybe I deserved one more. *Next week,* I bargained with myself. *After this* Report, *I'll worry about the cameras.*

"Go get your guitar," I said, caving.

"Two minutes!" He bolted down the hall, and I shook my head. I hoped he wouldn't tell everyone I was an utter pushover.

I walked to the Women's Room, expecting to find it empty. Except for Miss Marlee sitting alone in a corner reading, I was right.

"Your Highness," she greeted. It was one of those funny things. Plenty of people called me that, but when Mom's friends said it, they might as well have been calling me pumpkin or kiddo or baby. I didn't mind it, but it was always kind of strange.

"Where's Mom?"

She closed her book. "Migraine. I went to see her, and she made me leave. Any sound was excruciating."

"Oh. I was supposed to be having a date right now, but maybe I should go check on her."

"No," she insisted. "She needed rest, and both your parents would be pleased for you to have a date."

I considered. If she was really feeling that bad, maybe it would be better to wait.

"Umm, all right. Well, would it be okay if I used the room? Baden and I are going to make music." I squinted. "I mean that literally, by the way."

She giggled and stood. "That's no problem at all."

"Is it weird for you?" I asked suddenly. "That Kile is a part of this? That you know I'm about to go on a date with someone who isn't him? Is it, you know, okay?"

"It was quite a shock to see you two on the front page of every paper," she said, shaking her head like she couldn't fathom how it had happened. Then she came close, as if we were trying to keep a secret. "But you forget your parents aren't the only ones here who've been through a Selection."

I felt like a downright idiot. Why hadn't I thought of that?

"I remember watching your father scramble to find time for everyone, trying to please those around him while searching for someone who'd be a good partner. And it's even harder for you, because it's bigger than that. You're making history while trying to divert attention. Saying it's tough is an understatement."

"True," I admitted, my shoulders sagging under the weight of it all.

"I don't know how you and Kile ended up . . . umm . . . in that position, but I'd be surprised if he made it to the top of your list. All the same, I'm thankful to you."

I was taken aback. "Why? I haven't done anything."

"You have," she contradicted. "You're giving your parents time, which is very generous of you. But you're giving me time, too. I'm not sure how much longer I can keep him here."

A knock came at the door.

I turned. "That'll be Baden."

She placed a hand on my shoulder. "You stay put. I'll let him in."

"Oh!" Baden exclaimed when Miss Marlee opened the door for him.

She chuckled. "Don't worry, I'm on my way out. She's waiting for you."

Baden looked past her to find me, smiling the entire time. He looked so triumphant, so pleased to be alone together.

"Is that it?" he asked, pointing just behind me.

I spun, taking in the piano. "Yes. The tone on this one is wonderful, and this room has great acoustics."

He followed me, and I could hear his guitar case bump into his leg or a couch as he navigated through the maze of seats.

Without asking, he found an armless chair and pulled it up beside the piano. I trilled my fingers over the keys, doing a quick scale.

Baden tuned his guitar, which was dark and worn. "How long have you been playing?"

"As long as I can remember. I think Mom sat me down next to her as a toddler, and I just went along with whatever she did."

"People have always said your mother was a fantastic musician. I think I heard her play on TV once, for a Christmas program or something."

"She always plays a lot at Christmastime."

"Her favorite time of the year?" he guessed.

"In a way, sure, but in others, no. And she usually plays when she's worried or sad."

"How do you mean?" He tightened a string, finishing his preparations.

"Oh, you know," I hedged. "Holidays can be stressful." I didn't feel right exposing Mom's memories, losing her father and sister during the same time of year, not to mention a horrific attack that nearly stole my father.

"I can't imagine being sad at Christmastime here. If she

was poor, I could see why she'd be anxious."

"Why?"

He smiled to himself. "Because it's hard to watch all your friends getting piles of gifts when you don't get any."

"Oh."

He took the stab at our social differences in stride, not getting mad or calling me a snob, which some might have done. I examined Baden, trying to learn more. The guitar was old, but it was hard to make a call about his financial status while he wore palace-issued clothes. I remembered what Aunt May said about his last name.

"You're in college, right?" I asked.

He nodded. "Well, it's on hold for now. Some of my professors were thrown off, but most of them are letting me send assignments back to finish the semester from here."

"That's really impressive."

He shrugged. "I know what I want. So I'm willing to do whatever it takes to get it."

I gave him a curious smirk. "How does the Selection fit into that?"

"Wow, no holding back there." Again, no anger. He almost treated it as a joke.

"It's a fair question, I think." I started playing one of the classics Mom had taught me. Baden knew the song and joined in. I'd never considered how it would sound with strings.

The music won, and we dropped the conversation. But we didn't stop communicating. He watched my eyes, and

I studied his fingers. I'd never played with anyone before other than Mom, and I was engaged in a way I didn't know I could be.

We played on with no more than two or three missteps across the entire song. Baden was beaming as we finished.

"I only know a handful of classics. Some Beethoven and Debussy, mostly."

"You're so talented! I've never imagined songs like that on a guitar."

"Thanks." He was only the slightest bit bashful. "To answer your question, I'm here because I want to get married. I haven't dated much, but when this opportunity came up, I thought it might be worth a try. Am I in love with you? Well, not today. I'd like to know if I could be though."

Something about his tone made me trust he was being completely transparent. He was trying to find a mate, and I was someone he would never have met if he hadn't put his name in for the drawing.

"I'd like to make you a promise, if that's okay," he offered.

"What kind of promise?"

He plucked at a few strings. "A promise about us."

"If you're vowing to give me your unwavering devotion, it's still too soon."

Baden shook his head. "No, that's not in my plan."

"Okay, then. I'm listening." His fingers outlined a slightly familiar melody, not a classic, but something I knew. . . . I couldn't pinpoint it.

"If you found that I wasn't a reasonable choice for you, you'd send me home so you could focus on your other options. What I want to promise you is this: if I can tell that you're not the right one for me, I'll tell you. I don't want either of us to waste our time."

I nodded. "I'd appreciate that."

"Good," he said smartly, then began bellowing: "Well she walks up in the room with that smile, smile, smile and those legs that go on for a mile, mile, mile! Eyes searching the room for a little fun!"

I laughed, finally recognizing the tune he was playing. It was a Choosing Yesterday song that I sang in the bath more often than I cared to admit.

"I can't look away from her face, face, face until she starts dancing to that bass, bass, bass! I can't help it, that girl is number one!"

I joined in on the piano, giggling a little too hard to get all the notes right for the chorus. But we both sang along, botching up the melody and having too much fun to care.

"Oh, she can't be more than seventeen, but she's all grown up if you know what I mean. She's the prettiest thing that I've ever seen, yeah, she's my"—*BAM BAM!*—"she's my, she's my queen!"

I kept up with Baden through most of the song, even though I really only had experience with classical music.

"Why are you bothering with college? You should be touring," I cheered.

"That's my backup plan if the prince thing doesn't pan out." He was so candid, so real. "Thanks for playing hooky for me."

"No problem. I should get back to work though."

"That was the shortest date in history!" he complained.

I shrugged. "You would have had more time if you waited until tonight."

He huffed. "Fine. Lesson learned."

I pulled the cover back over the keys as he placed his guitar in its case. "You should take that to the others," I said. "I bet they'd get a kick out of trying to play."

"What, my guitar? No, no, no. This is my baby!" I watched as he gently petted the shabby case. "If someone broke this, I'd be devastated. My dad got it for me, and it was hard earned. I try to take good care of it."

"I'm like that with my tiaras."

"*Pffff!*" Baden laughed outright at me.

"What?"

He took his time, covering his eyes and shaking his head. "Tiaras!" he finally said. "You really are a princess, huh?"

"Did you think the last eighteen years were a clever trick?"

"I like that, you know? That you protect your tiaras like I do my guitar. I like that that's your thing."

I pushed the door open, leading us into the hallway. "Good. Because they're beautiful."

He smiled. "Thanks for spending some time with me."

"Thank *you*. It was a pleasure."

There was a pause. "So do we shake or hug or what?"

"You may kiss my hand," I replied, extending an arm.

He took it. "Until next time."

Baden kissed me quickly, bowed, and headed toward his room. I walked away thinking of how Aunt May would say she told me so as soon as I saw her again.

* * *

I knew I'd be the focal point of the *Report*. Typically, I didn't mind giving speeches or updates. But tonight was going to be different. One, this would be the first time I faced the public since the parade, and two, I knew they'd want to hear about Kile.

I wore red. I felt strong in red. And I pulled my hair up, hoping I'd come across as mature.

Aunt May hovered in the background, winking at me, while Mom helped Dad with his tie. I heard one of the boys yelp and turned to see Alex holding something sharp in his hand. He was rubbing his backside like he'd sat on it. I hunted, finding Osten in a corner trying desperately not to laugh aloud.

With all the company, the room felt crowded, adding to my discomfort, which was why I jumped when someone called my name, even though it was hardly above a whisper.

"I'm sorry, Your Highness," Erik said.

"No, I'm just a little on edge. How can I help you?"

"I hate to bother you, but I wasn't sure who to ask. Where is it most convenient for me to sit so I can translate for Henri?"

I shook my head. "How rude, I didn't even think about that. Um, here, follow me."

I escorted Erik to the stage manager, and we placed Henri in the back row of the stadium-style chairs. Erik was given a seat behind him that was low enough so he wouldn't be seen but close enough that Henri would be able to hear him.

I stayed by them until they were settled. Henri gave a

thumbs-up, and Erik turned to thank me.

"I'll make sure to go to the stage manager next time so I won't bother you. I apologize."

"It's fine, really. I want you to be comfortable, the both of you."

Erik bowed his head and smiled shyly. "You don't need to worry about my comfort, Your Highness. I'm no suitor."

"Eadlyn! Eadlyn, where are you?" Mom called.

I turned from Erik, running around to the front. "Here, Mom."

She placed a hand on her heart like it had been racing. "I couldn't find you. I thought maybe you were backing out on us," she said quietly as I approached.

"Calm down, Mom," I replied, grabbing her hand. "I'm not perfect, but I'm no coward."

Tonight's *Report* centered around the women. Mom gave an update on province-run aid systems, encouraging others to follow the example set by three northern provinces that were helping the homeless by donating food as well as free classes on topics like managing finances and interviewing skills. Lady Brice spoke about a drilling proposal that would affect a large chunk of central Illéa. It would benefit the country as a whole, but those six provinces would have to approve it by a vote first. And then, of course, all eyes went to the boys.

Gavril stepped onto the stage, looking as dashing as ever, and I could see a bit of a spring in his step. This was the fifth Selection Illéa had witnessed, and he had overseen three of them. We all knew he'd find a replacement once this was over, but he seemed so pleased that this would be his final role for the royal family.

"Of course, ladies and gentlemen, we will be dedicating a lot of airtime to the charming young men of the Selection. For now, how about we say hello to a few of them?"

Gavril strode across the floor, looking for someone in particular. I wondered if he was having as hard a time memorizing their names as I was.

"Sir Harrison," he began, stopping in front of a sweet-faced boy with dirty-blond hair and dimples.

"A pleasure," Harrison greeted.

"How are you enjoying the palace?"

He beamed. "It's beautiful here. I've always wanted to come up to Angeles, so that alone has been a real treat."

"Any challenges so far?" Gavril prodded.

Harrison shrugged. "I was worried that it would be all-out fistfights from dawn till dusk with the princess on the line," he said, gesturing over to me. I instantly arranged a smile on my face, knowing a camera would zoom in on me at any second. "But the other guys have been great."

Gavril slid the microphone to the boy next to him. "What about you? And can you remind us of your name?"

"It's Fox. Fox Wesley," he answered. Fox had a bit of a tan, but, unlike me, I could see that he wasn't born with it. He must spend a lot of time outside. "Honestly, and I hope I'm not alone here, so far the biggest challenge is mealtimes. They set out at least a dozen forks for each of us."

A few people chuckled, and Gavril nodded. "You have

to wonder where we could possibly store so much cutlery."

"It's crazy," mumbled the boy behind Fox.

"Oh, Sir Ivan, yes?" Gavril stretched to put the mic in front of him.

"Yes, sir. Happy to meet you."

"And you as well. How are you managing at mealtimes?"

Ivan held both hands in front of him as if this was very serious. "My current approach is using one fork for each bite and then making a pile of them in the middle of the table. It's working so far."

The room laughed even more at Ivan's ridiculous answer, and Gavril stepped away from the group, turning to the cameras.

"Clearly, we have an extremely entertaining pool of candidates here. So why don't we take a moment to speak with the young lady who somehow has to narrow it down to only one? Ladies and gentlemen, Her Royal Highness, Princess Eadlyn Schreave."

"Go get 'em," Ahren whispered as I pushed myself out of my seat and crossed the floor, embracing dear Gavril.

"Always nice to see you, Your Highness," he said as I sat in the chair opposite him center stage.

"And you, Gavril."

"So here we are, one week into the first-ever female-led Selection. How would you say it's going?"

I gave an award-winning smile. "I think it's going well. Of course, I still have work to do each day, so we're off to a fairly slow start."

Gavril glanced back over his shoulder. "Judging by the thinning crowd, I wouldn't say it's that slow."

Batting my eyes, I giggled. "Yes, about a third of the gentlemen invited to the palace have been eliminated. I have to trust my gut, and between our initial meetings and the information I've been given, I feel very confident about my choices."

Gavril inclined his head. "It sounds like you're using more of your head than your heart at the moment."

I fought the blush. I couldn't tell how well I'd done, but I refused to touch my face to check.

"Would you suggest that I fall in love with thirty-five young men at once?"

He raised his eyebrows. "Well, when you put it that way . . ."

"Exactly. I only have one heart, and I'm saving it."

I heard sighs around the room, and I felt I'd gotten away with something. How many more lines could I dream up over the following months to keep everyone entertained and at bay? Then I realized, I hadn't planned those words. I really felt them, and they escaped under pressure.

"It seems you may have let your heart lead the way at least once," he said knowingly. "I have a picture to prove it."

I watched as a huge picture of me and Kile was displayed, and the room erupted with hoots and claps.

"Could we get him down here for a moment? Where's Sir Kile?"

He hopped up from his place and sat on a chair next to me.

"Now, this is a very unique position for me," Gavril began, "because I've known both of you your entire lives."

Kile laughed. "I was thinking about this the other day. My mom said I crawled on set once as a baby, and you held me for the closing of the *Report*."

Gavril's eyes widened. "That's true! I'd forgotten all about that!"

I looked at Kile, giggling at this new story. That must have happened before I was born.

"So, from the pictures, it looks like perhaps a childhood friendship is growing into something more?"

Kile stared at me, and I shook my head. No way was I going first on this.

He finally caved. "Honestly, I don't think either of us ever thought about the other as a possibility until we were forced to."

Our families laughed boisterously.

"Although, if he had gotten a haircut years ago, I might have considered it," I teased.

Gavril shook his head at us. "Everyone's dying to know: how was this infamous kiss?"

I knew it was coming, but I was mortified. This was much worse than I imagined it would be, having my private life on display.

Mercifully, Kile addressed it. "I think I can speak for both of us when I say it was a surprise. And while it was special, I don't think we're going to put too much stock in it. I mean, I've been spending time with these other guys, and so many of them would make a wonderful prince."

"Really? And would you agree with that, Princess? Have you had one-on-one time with anyone else this week?"

It felt like Gavril's words were on a delay. I didn't hear them until I'd processed everything Kile had just said. Did he mean that? Did he not feel anything at all? Or was he only saying that to maintain some level of privacy?

I snapped back into the moment and nodded enthusiastically. "Yes, a few."

Gavril eyed me. "And?"

"And they were very nice." I wasn't really in the mood for this in the first place, and Kile had made me doubt sharing anything at all.

"Hmm," Gavril said, turning to the group of the Selected. "Maybe we'll get some more information out of the gentlemen in question. Sir Kile, you may head back to your seat. Now, who were the lucky men?"

Baden raised his hand, followed by Hale.

"Come on down, gentlemen."

Gavril started applauding and the room joined in as Hale and Baden approached and yet another chair was brought in. I considered myself pretty intelligent, but I could not think of a way to beg them to keep their mouths shut without actually using words.

Only then did I realize how easily Kile managed to do just that. I supposed there was something to be said for knowing each other forever.

"Now, what's your name again, sir?" Gavril asked.

"Hale Garner." He pressed down his tie, though it was already in place.

"Oh, yes. So, what can you tell us about your date with the princess?"

Hale gave me a shy smile, then turned back to Gavril. "Well, I can tell you that our princess is as smart and gracious as I always believed she was. Umm, and that we do have a few things in common. We're both the oldest children in our families, and it was fun to talk about my work as a tailor with such a well-dressed young lady. I mean, she looks like a million bucks."

I ducked my head, trying to take the compliment playfully while staying on my toes.

"But beyond that, I hope you'll forgive me if I keep most of the details to myself," Hale added.

Gavril made a face. "You're not going to tell us anything?"

"Well, dating and falling in love are typically private things. It's kind of weird to talk about at this stage."

"Perhaps we'll get more out of the next gentleman," Gavril said impishly to the cameras. "Remind us of your name again?"

"Baden Trains."

"And what did you and the princess do?"

"We played music. Princess Eadlyn is as talented as her mother."

I heard Mom's "aww" in the background.

"And?"

"And she's a lovely dancer, even when she's sitting down. Just so everyone knows, the princess is very up-to-date on current music." Baden laughed and a few people joined in.

"And?" Gavril pressed.

"And I kissed her hand . . . and I'm hoping for more kisses in the future."

I wanted to die. For some reason Baden's request for a kiss was much more embarrassing than talking about one that had already happened with Kile.

The room made encouraging noises again, and I could see Gavril was trying to milk this. Unfortunately for him, there really weren't any more juicy details. Kile was the only one with anything remotely shocking to share, and that had already been soaked up.

"You look so disappointed, Gavril," I remarked quickly.

He made a little pout. "I'm simply excited for you, Your Highness, and want to know everything that's happening. And if we could ask our millions of viewers, I'm sure they'd agree."

"Well, don't worry. You, and all of Illéa, will be happy to know that tomorrow I will be hosting a small party for the Selected and members of the palace household. Cameras will be there for the entire event, so everyone will get to peek inside the Selection process."

The room burst into applause again. I could see Josie practically floating out of her chair, she was so excited.

Gavril sent Hale and Baden back to their seats with the others before launching into questions again.

"What kind of party can we expect tomorrow, Your Highness?"

"We'll be out in the gardens, enjoying the sun and

spending time getting to know one another."

"That sounds like a wonderful plan. Very relaxing."

"Well, it will be, except for one tiny detail," I added, pinching my fingers in the air.

"And what is that?"

"After the party there will be an elimination."

Murmurs filled the room, and I knew, regardless of how the public felt about me, meeting the boys tonight would make them curious about who stayed and who left.

I continued, hushing the crowd with my words. "It could be one person, it could be three. . . . I don't know. So, gentlemen," I said, turning back to the Selected, "come prepared."

"I can't wait to see how this all turns out, and I'm positive it will be a wonderful event. Now, one final question before we call it a night."

I sat up taller. "Go for it."

"What are you looking for in a husband?"

What was I looking for? My independence. Peace, freedom . . . a happiness I thought I had until Ahren questioned it.

I shrugged. "I'm not sure anyone knows what they're looking for until they find it."

CHAPTER 17

How did Josie get her hands on another one of my tiaras? I'd just about had it with her. She was going to parade around in front of the cameras in her best dress and my tiara pretending she was royal for the millionth time in her life.

I made eye contact and smiled at people as I passed, but I didn't stop to talk to anyone until I found Kile. He was standing with Henri again, sipping iced tea and watching a game of badminton. Henri bowed right away.

"Hello today, Your Highness," he said, his accent making the words sound brighter.

"Hello, Henri. Kile."

"Hi, Eadlyn."

I might have been imagining there was something different about Kile's voice, but for maybe the first time ever, I wanted to hear him speak. I shook my head, focusing.

"Kile, could you please go talk to your sister?"

The contentment in his eyes quickly turned to frustration. "Why? What'd she do this time?"

"She's taken yet another one of my tiaras."

"Don't you have, like, a thousand of those?"

I huffed. "That's hardly the point. It's mine, and she shouldn't be wearing it. When she walks around like that, she gives the impression that she's royal when she's not. It's inappropriate. Could you please talk to her about her behavior?"

"When did I become the person who did all these favors for you?"

My eyes darted over to Henri and Erik, who didn't know about the arrangement behind our kiss. They didn't seem to catch on.

"Please?" I asked in a hushed voice.

His eyes softened, and I saw a little of the person he showed me in his room, someone sweet and engaging. "Fine. But Josie just likes attention. I don't think she's doing it to be mean."

"Thank you."

"I'm going. Be right back."

He stomped off as Erik conveyed what was happening to Henri.

Henri cleared his throat before speaking, his words ending on strange pitches. "How are you today, Your Highness?"

I wasn't completely sure if I should try to go through Erik or not. . . . I went with Henri. "Very good. You?"

"Good, good," he replied cheerfully. "I to enjoy . . . umm." He turned and conveyed the rest of his comment to Erik.

"He thinks the party is great, and he likes the company."

I wasn't sure if he meant Kile or me, but either way, it was nice of him to say.

"So when did you move over from Swendway?"

Henri was nodding his head as if to confirm he was from Swendway but not actually answering the question. Erik whispered over to him quickly, and Henri gave him a lengthy reply that was translated for me.

"Henri emigrated to Illéa last year when he was seventeen. He comes from a family of cooks, which is what he does back home. They make food from their homeland and generally interact with others who also came from Swendway and only speak Finnish. He has a younger sister who is working very hard on her English, but it's a difficult language."

"Wow. That was a lot to keep up with," I said to Erik.

He waved his hand. "I try."

I could guess how hard Erik's work was, but I appreciated his modesty. I turned to Henri. "We'll have to spend some time together soon. Where we can talk easier."

Erik passed that on to Henri, who nodded vigorously. "Yes, yes!"

I giggled. "Until then."

The lawn was full of the Selected. General Leger had Miss Lucy on his arm as he spoke with a handful of boys by a fountain, and Dad was making his rounds, occasionally clapping someone on the back and saying hello before whisking off again. Mom was sitting in a chair under a parasol, and I wasn't sure if it was charming or unsettling that several of the Selected were buzzing around her.

It was a delightful party. People were playing games, there was lots of food, and a string quartet was performing under a canopy. The cameras zoomed around capturing it all, and I hoped this would be enough to calm the people. I had no idea whether Dad was closer to having a plan for how to soothe the country permanently.

In the meantime, I had to find a way to eliminate at least one person after today, and have a good enough reason to make it seem believable.

Kile sneaked up on me. "Here you go." He held my tiara in his hands.

"I can't believe she gave it up."

"It took some convincing, but I reminded her that if she made a scene at this event, Mom probably wouldn't let her come to another one. That was enough to get her to take it off. So here."

"I can't take it," I said, keeping my hands together.

"But you just asked for it," he complained.

"I don't want it on her, but I also can't carry it around. I have things to do."

He shifted his weight, clearly vexed. It was kind of nice to be on this side of the irritating.

"So, what, I have to hold on to it for the rest of the day?"

"Not the *whole* day. Just until we go inside, and then I can take it."

Kile shook his head. "You're really unbelievable."

"Hush. Go enjoy the party. But first, wait, we have to take off this tie."

He looked down as I started tugging. "What's wrong with my tie?"

"Everything," I said. "Everything in the universe is wrong with this tie. I bet we could find world peace if we burned it."

I got it unknotted and wrapped it up in my hand.

"That's so much better." I placed the wadded fabric in his palm, grabbed the tiara from his other hand, and placed it on his head. "That really works with your hair."

He smirked, his eyes staring into mine with amusement. "So, since you don't want your tiara now, maybe I could give it back to you tonight. I could come by your room, if you like." Kile bit his lip, and all I could think about was how soft they were.

I swallowed, understanding the unspoken question. "That would be fine," I answered, fighting a blush. "Maybe around nine?"

"Nine." Kile nodded and backed away.

So he was just being discreet on the *Report*! I furrowed my brow in thought. Or maybe he was simply planning to pass his time kissing me. Or maybe he'd been deeply in love with me since he was seven and was only now finding the courage to stop teasing me and say so. Or maybe—

Ean walked up and laced his arm through mine.

"Oh!" I gasped.

"You look upset. Whatever that little boy said to upset you, don't give it another thought."

"Sir Ean," I greeted, impressed with how calm he was around me. "How can I help you?"

"By taking a walk with me, of course. I still haven't gotten a chance to speak with you just the two of us."

Ean's caramel-colored hair looked almost golden in the sun, and while he didn't have the same cutting-edge style Hale did, he looked smarter in his suit than most of the others. Some men simply didn't look good in them.

"Well, you have me alone now. What would you like to talk about?"

He smirked. "Mostly, I'm curious about you. I've always thought of you as very independent, so I was surprised that you would start looking for a husband so young. Based on seeing you on the *Report* and all the specials on your family, I thought you'd take your time."

He knew. He was so calm in his assessment, I was sure he knew this was all for show.

"It's true; I'd planned to wait. But my parents are so blissfully in love, I thought this might be worth trying."

Ean examined me. "Do you feel like any one of these candidates truly has what it takes to be your partner?"

I raised my eyebrows. "Do you think so little of yourself?"

He stopped walking, and we faced each other. "No, but I think very highly of you. And I can't see you deigning to settle before you've really lived."

It seemed impossible that a stranger could see so much, especially considering the lengths I took to guard my thoughts and feelings. How closely had Ean been watching me all these years?

"People can change," I replied vaguely.

He nodded. "They can, I suppose. But if you ever find yourself feeling . . . lost in this competition, I'd be happy to help you in any way I could."

"And how exactly would you help me?"

Ean gently escorted me back toward the crowd. "I think that's a conversation for another day. But know that I am here for you, Your Highness."

He stared deep into my eyes, as if he thought that all my secrets would spill out if he held my gaze long enough. I found myself needing to take some deep breaths once we finally broke eye contact.

"It's a lovely day."

I looked up, and one of the Selected was standing there. I was completely blanking on his name.

"Yes, it is. Are you having a good time?" Oh, please, what was his name?

"I am." He had a very friendly face and a pleasant warmth to his voice. "I just won a round of croquet. Do you play?"

"A little." How was I going to figure this out? "Do you play a lot back home?"

"Nah. Not really. Up in Whites, it's mostly winter sports."

Whites! . . . Nope, still didn't have it.

"If I'm honest, I'm a bit more of an indoor girl."

"Well, then you'd love Whites," he said with a laugh. "I only get out when I have to."

"Excuse me."

Whites Boy and I turned to the newcomer. This one I knew.

"I'm sorry, Your Highness, but I was hoping I could steal you away for a moment."

"Certainly, Holden." I took his arm. "Nice talking to you," I said to Whites Boy, who looked a bit forlorn.

"I hope that wasn't too rude of me," Holden said as we wandered away.

"Not at all."

We moved slowly, and he seemed comfortable, like he'd walked with a princess dozens of times.

"I don't want to keep you. I only wanted to tell you that I admired the way you cut people last week."

I was taken aback. "Really?"

"Absolutely! I admire a woman who knows what she wants, and I like that you're assertive. My mother is the head of a lab back in Bankston. I know how hard it is to run something that small, so the pressure you must be under is hard for me to imagine. But you do it well, and I like that. I just wanted you to know."

I stepped back. "Thank you, Holden." He nodded, and I walked away, lost in thought.

This entire situation only confirmed what I knew to be true: If I came in sweet and gentle, no one would take me seriously. If I had kindly tapped people on the shoulder and hugged them on their way out, would Holden have admired me less? The whole thing was—

"Oh!" I fell to the side, only missing the ground because of a pair of steady arms.

"Your Highness." Hale clutched my arms, helping to pull me up. "I'm so sorry, I didn't see you."

I heard the click of a camera nearby and pushed my cheeks up into a smile.

"Laugh," I said through my teeth.

"Huh?"

"Help me up and laugh it off." I giggled, and after a moment Hale gave a few chuckles.

"What was that about?" He kept the smile on his face.

I straightened my dress as I explained. "The camera crews are watching."

He glanced to the side.

"Don't," I urged, and he faced me again.

"Yikes. Are you always on the lookout like that?"

This time my laugh was genuine. "Basically."

His smiled faded. "Is that why you ran away the other night?"

My face became serious as well. "I'm sorry. I wasn't feeling well."

"First you run, and then you lie." He shook his head, disappointed.

"No."

"Eadlyn," he whispered. "That wasn't easy for me. I don't

like talking about my dad dying or my mom having a hard time keeping a job or my family losing our status. That was difficult for me to share. And when we started really talking about you, you left me."

That prickling, naked feeling came over me again.

"I sincerely apologize, Hale."

He studied my face. "I don't think you mean that." I swallowed, nervous. "But I like you all the same."

I looked up at him, mesmerized by that possibility.

"When you're ready to talk—to really talk—I'll be here. Unless, of course, you come in and ninja eliminate me like you did those other guys."

I laughed awkwardly. "I don't think that'll happen again."

"I hope not." Hale stared, and I didn't like that his eyes felt like they could dig several layers beneath my skin. "Glad your dress didn't get stained. Would have been a pity."

He went to leave, but I grabbed his arm. "Hey. Thank you. For being reserved on the *Report*."

He grinned. "Something every day, remember?"

CHAPTER 18

"ALL RIGHT, YOUR HIGHNESS, WHENEVER you're ready."

The makeup girl did a last check, and I corrected my posture, reviewing the names in my head. I nodded, and the light on the camera turned red, telling me we were filming.

"You've seen the extravagant tea party, you heard about the delicious food, and you saw all the breathtaking fashion; but who did you think should be eliminated?

"Yes, Sir Kile looked somewhat less than manly in my tiara, and Sir Hale nearly swept me off my feet . . . in a bad way," I concluded with a grin. "But, after much deliberation, the two Selected leaving us today are Kesley Timber from Whites and Holden Messenger from Bankston.

"How is your favorite doing? Dying to learn more about the remaining contestants? Hungry for more Selection-related news? Tune in to the *Report* each Friday night for updates from me and the gentlemen themselves, and don't forget to look out for exclusive programs dedicated to the Selection exclusively on the Public Access Channel."

I held my smile a few seconds longer.

"Cut!" the director called. "Excellent. Sounded perfect to me, but let's do one more for good measure."

"Sure. When will this go out?"

"They'll edit all the footage from this afternoon's party tonight and get it on air tomorrow, so this should be out on Monday."

I nodded. "Great. One more time?"

"Yes, Your Highness, if you don't mind."

I swallowed and went over my speech again before pulling myself up into the exact same pose.

At ten past nine I heard the knock on my door, and I skipped over to answer it. Kile was there, leaning against the door-frame, tiara in hand.

"I heard you were missing this," he said jokingly.

"Come in, loser."

He passed through the doorway, looking around again as if I redecorated my room daily. "So am I getting cut yet?"

I grinned. "No, it's Kesley and Holden. Don't let that spill though. I can't send them away until after the garden party airs."

"That won't be a problem. Neither of them really speaks to me anyway."

"No?" I asked as he handed me my tiara.

"I've heard they thought me being a part of the Selection was unfair. And then seeing our kiss plastered everywhere sealed that opinion."

I placed the tiara on the shelf with the others. "Made a good call then, didn't I?"

He chuckled. "Oh, I brought you another present."

"I love presents!"

"You'll hate this one, trust me." He reached into his pocket and pulled out that spectacular disaster of a tie.

"I figured if you were having a bad day, you could take it to the garden and burn it. Get your aggression out on something that won't cry. Unlike Leeland."

"I wasn't *trying* to make him cry."

"Sure you weren't."

I smiled, taking the wound-up fabric from his hand. "I actually really like this present. It assures me that no human will be forced to wear it ever again."

Looking over at him, at his hitched-up smile, I was able to push away everything for a minute. It felt like the Selection wasn't even happening just then. I was a girl with a boy. And I knew what I wanted to do with that boy.

I dropped the tie on the floor and put a hand on his chest. "Kile Woodwork, do you want to kiss me?"

He let out a whistle. "Not shy at all, are you?"

"Stop it. Yes or no?"

He pursed his lips, pretending to think it over. "I wouldn't mind it."

"And you understand that me kissing you doesn't mean I actually like you and that I would never, ever marry you?"

"Thank goodness."

"Right answer."

I wrapped my hand around his head, pulling him to me, and an instant later his arms were around my waist. It was the perfect balm for a long day. Kile's kisses were direct and slow, and he made it impossible for me to think about much else.

We toppled onto the bed, holding each other as we laughed.

"Of all the things I thought would happen when my name was called, I never dreamed I'd ever kiss you."

"I never dreamed you'd be good at it."

"Hey," he said, "I've had a bit of practice."

I propped myself up on my elbow. "Who was your last kiss?"

"Caterina. When the Italian family visited in August, right before I left."

"That doesn't surprise me at all."

Kile shrugged, not ashamed in the slightest. "What can I say? They're very friendly."

"Friendly," I repeated, rolling my eyes. "That's one word for it."

He chuckled. "What about you?"

"Ask Ahren. Apparently everyone already knows."

"Leron Troyes?"

"How did *you* find out?"

We lay there, laughing so much we were nearly crying. I played with a button on his shirt, and he twirled a piece of my hair between kisses, and the world shrank to just the two of us.

"I've never seen you like this," he commented. "I didn't know it could be so easy to make you smile."

"It's not. You must be in rare form today."

Kile wrapped an arm around me and placed his face inches from mine. "How are you feeling? I know this has got to be a crazy time for you."

"Don't," I whispered.

"Don't what?"

"Don't ruin this. I like having you here, but I'm not in need of a soul mate. You can be quiet and go back to kissing me, or you can leave."

He rolled onto his back, silent for a few minutes. "Sorry. I just wanted to talk."

"And you can. But not about you, not about me, and definitely not about you and me together."

"But it seems like you must be lonely. How in the world do you deal with all this?"

I huffed, standing and pulling him to his feet. "If I need advice, I talk to my parents. If I need a friendly ear, I have Ahren. You were helping for a minute, and then you had to start with the questions."

I turned him around and pushed him toward the door. "Do you realize how unhealthy that is?" he asked

"Are you the model of adult behavior? You can't even get

your mother to cut the apron strings."

Kile rounded back, staring me down. I was sure his anger was reflected in my face. I waited for him to scold me again, as he'd done a thousand times growing up. But his eyes softened, and before I knew it, his hand was at the base of my neck, pulling me to him.

He crushed his lips to mine, and I simultaneously hated and adored him for it. All I could think of was the way his mouth moved and how I seemed so fragile in his hands. The passion slowed, until the kisses were so soft they tickled.

When Kile finally pulled away, he kept his fingers teasingly close to my hair, rubbing the skin absentmindedly.

"You are so spoiled, and you are so obnoxious . . . but I'm here." With a final kiss, he opened the door and left.

I gazed around my room, dizzy with confusion. Why was he trying to get me to open up when he clearly couldn't stand me? And I didn't like him either! Sometimes he could be just as bratty as Josie.

I went toward my closet to get ready for bed and saw his ugly tie on the floor. I'd be doing everyone a favor if I threw it away now.

Maybe I would set it on fire the next time I was having a particularly wretched day. For now I tucked it into a drawer.

My thoughts the next morning were a mess. I kept wondering what Kile's goal was last night. And I couldn't shake off how it made me feel similar to when Hale asked too many questions. They were such different people with vastly different understandings of me, yet they'd both quickly figured out how to make me back away. Would all the boys be like that? Was that something they all knew how to do?

"Neena?" I pulled the brush through my hair, trying to tame it as my maid walked behind me in the steam-filled bathroom, picking up the pajamas I'd left on the floor.

"Yes, Your Highness?" She caught my eyes in the mirror as we spoke.

"I feel like it's been a while since we've talked about your boyfriend. What's his name again?"

A smile crept up on her face. "Mark. Why do you ask?"

"I'm surrounded by a million boys. Just wondering how it is when you only have to deal with one."

She shook her head at me. "One boy on a string is a wonderful thing," she said, her happiness forcing me to smile along with her. "He's doing great. He finally got into a university, and he's studying all the time. I get a call from him maybe once or twice a week. It's not much, but we both have pretty full schedules."

"I do need constant supervision," I said with a wink.

"Amen."

"Does he mind much? That you're far away and busy?"

She straightened the clothes looped over her arm. "No. His program is very demanding, so for now it's actually helpful."

I leaned my head to one side, continuing to brush. "That's interesting. What's he studying?"

"Mark is a chemist. He's studying biochemistry, specifically."

My eyes widened. "Really? Such a range in your professions."

She frowned. "There's no caste system anymore, Your Highness. People can date and marry anyone they want to."

I turned away from the mirror to look at her directly. "That's not what I mean. It's simply intriguing to me the dynamic you must have. You have my laundry in your arms, and he might cure a disease. Those are two incredibly different roles in the world."

Neena swallowed and dropped everything on the ground. "I won't be doing your laundry forever. I made a choice to come here, and I can leave whenever I like."

"Neena!"

"I don't feel well," she said abruptly. "I'll send someone else up to help you."

She didn't even curtsy.

"Neena, I was simply talking!"

The door slammed, and I looked after her, shocked that she so shamelessly left without permission. I hadn't meant to offend her. I was merely curious, and that one observation didn't even begin to touch on the things I truly wanted to ask about.

I finished my hair and makeup on my own. When the substitute maid showed up, I sent her away. Just because Neena was in a bad mood didn't mean she could get out of her work. I could take care of myself, and she could clean tomorrow.

I picked up the applications for the remaining boys in

the Selection. Whether I liked it or not, I knew what was expected of me. All I needed was to find situations that kept things as close to the surface as possible.

Ean was certainly captivating, but his charisma was almost too overwhelming. I wasn't sure I was prepared to spend time alone with him. Edwin was harmless enough. I pulled out Apsel's sheet and looked it over. Nothing extraordinary there. I was tempted to send him home for being so bland, but after the reaction over the first elimination, I didn't think I could get away with that. Kile's form came up next, but he was a no at the moment. Winslow was, I hated to say it, considerably unattractive. The more and more I looked at him, the easier it was to see. I didn't think I had a type, but he made me wonder if I had an anti-type. Ivan . . . was this the guy who smelled vaguely of chlorine?

Near the bottom of the pile, Jack Ranger's picture jumped out at me. I had caught him staring at me a few times at the party, but we hadn't spoken. I took that to mean he might still be intimidated enough for me to get through an evening together without him leaving me feeling as unpleasant as some of the others had.

I wrote a note out on my stationery inviting him to watch a movie with me tonight. That was an easy enough date. No unnecessary talking. I'd have a butler deliver it to him once Jack had joined the others. I was planning always to announce dates by sending a letter into or drawing the boys out of the room. That should make things interesting.

I sped through breakfast, ready to work. Looking at these

endless requests and bills and budgets and proposals wasn't exactly my favorite thing, but it kept me busy, and I liked having my mind occupied all day. My nights and weekends for the next three months would belong to those boys, but the rest of the time I had a different job to do.

"Eadlyn, dear," Dad said, taking a break for some tea. "I didn't get to tell you, but I thought the garden party was a success. I saw some of the stories in the papers this morning, and it was very well covered."

"I glanced at a few myself. And I caught a little of the special they did, and it all looked nicely done." I stretched in my chair, achy from sitting still.

He smiled. "Indeed. I think you should try to do another event like that soon—something with the group that people can see."

"Something that might have an elimination afterward?"

"If you think that would help."

I walked over to his desk, pouring myself some of his tea. "I think it adds something. Like people might be more interested if their favorite might be on the line."

He considered that. "Interesting. Any thoughts on how it would be structured?"

"No, but I thought, since we're supposed to be looking for a prince here, it might be good to test them on the things they would need to know as a prince. History or policy. I think there's a way to make it playful, kind of like a game show maybe?"

He laughed. "The public would eat that up."

I sipped my tea. "See, I have great ideas. I don't need a prince."

"Eadlyn, you could run the world on your own if you needed to. That's not the point," he said with a chuckle.

"We'll see."

CHAPTER 19

I STOPPED BY JACK'S ROOM after dinner, and he was waiting for me outside the door. That was kind of strange, but I figured his nerves had gotten the best of him.

"Good evening, Jack," I said, approaching.

"Your Highness," he replied with a bow.

"You can call me Eadlyn."

He smiled. "Great. Eadlyn."

There was an awkward silence as I waited for him to offer his arm. He simply stood there, his smile tight but his eyes animated. When I finally gave up on him figuring it out, I pointed toward the stairs. "It's this way."

"Super." Then he started walking ahead of me, even though he didn't know the way.

"No, Jack. We need to turn here." I said the same thing maybe three or four times as we traveled, and he never apologized. He simply went where I told him as if he'd been planning to go that way all along. I did my best to let his missteps slide. With a handful of boys already mentally lined up for the next elimination, I didn't want a reason to add Jack to that list.

The palace went up four stories, but it went down much farther. The *Report* was filmed on the sub-one floor, and there was a storage area as well as the theater. The staff and guards also had rooms on the first and second sublevels, but their quarters weren't connected to the theater wing. There was also a monstrous safe room beneath all of that. I'd only had to go there twice that I remembered: once during a drill when I was three and once when the last string of rebels attacked us shortly after.

It was strange to think about it. The rebels were gone, but now we were faced with different pockets of people fighting the monarchy. I almost wished the rebels still existed. At least we could put a name to that. At least back then we knew exactly who we were fighting.

I shook my head, coming back to the situation at hand. I was on a date. As I remembered that fact, I chided myself. Dad would have wanted a camera here for this. Oh, well. Next time.

"So, I hope you like movies."

"I do," Jack replied enthusiastically.

"Good. I do as well, but it's not always possible for me to go out to the theater. We have access to a few new films downstairs, though our options are limited. Chances are we'll have something good."

"That's great." It was strange, this fine line he was walking between being rude and polite. I wondered if he simply didn't know how many mistakes he was making.

A butler had already made us popcorn, and I used the remote to scroll through our options.

"How about *Eye of the Beholder*?" I suggested. The brief description hinted at romance and drama, as did the poster image.

"That sounds okay. Any action in that one?"

"I don't think so. There is in *Black Diamonds*." The picture was dark and brooding, with the silhouette of a man with a gun off to one side. It wasn't something I'd have seen of my own volition.

"Yeah! That sounds good."

"We have other choices," I said, trying to make my way back to the menu.

"But this is what I want to watch. It won't be too scary. And if it is, you can snuggle up next to me."

I made a face, wondering if I should have given Apsel more consideration. The seats in our theater were wide and very soft. The only way I could snuggle up to anyone would be to squish myself into his seat, which was not going to happen. Also, I'd rather be scarred for life than admit to being afraid.

Then again, that wasn't what I was worried about with this movie. It simply didn't seem worth watching.

I sighed, feeling a little overrun. Again, it was as if he

wasn't aware of how foolish he was acting. I let it go, thinking I'd need to tell Dad that the boys as a whole required more etiquette training, and started the movie.

Long story short, Main Guy's dad was killed by Bad Guy. Main Guy spends his life tracking down Bad Guy, but Bad Guy slips from his grasp several times. Main Guy sleeps with Super Blonde. Super Blonde disappears. Main Guy kills Bad Guy, and Super Blonde shows up again. Oh, and some things explode.

Jack seemed to enjoy it, but I was bored. If Super Blonde had killed someone, I might have cared a little more.

But at least we didn't have to talk.

When the credits rolled, I used the remote to raise the lights.

"So, what did you think?" he asked, his eyes bright with excitement.

"It was okay. Definitely seen better."

The movie seemed to leave him hyperanimated. "But the effects were incredible!"

"Sure, but the story was tired."

He squinted his eyes. "I liked it."

"All right."

"Does that make you upset?"

I made a face. "No. It just means you have bad taste."

He laughed, a dark sound that was more foreboding than friendly. "I love it when you do that."

"Do what?" I stood and took my popcorn bowl to the counter, leaving it for the staff.

"I've been waiting all night for a little of your attitude."

"Excuse me?"

"I've been hoping you'd get mad or snippy." He brought his bowl over, too. "When you cleared out the Men's Parlor the day after the parade? That was great. I mean, I don't want to go home, but I wouldn't be devastated if you yelled at me."

I stared at him. "Jack, you do realize we've hardly spoken to each other, and in the first conversation we have, you reveal that my anger turns you on. Do you see how this might be a lapse in judgment on your part?"

He broke into a smile, undeterred. "I thought you'd appreciate my honesty. I have the feeling you get irritated easily, and I want you to know that doesn't bother me. I actually like it."

Jack reached for my hand, and I ripped it away. "You thought wrong. This date is over. Goodnight."

He caught up to me, grabbing me again. I didn't want to admit how scared I was, but I could feel the icy strands of fear pulsing through my veins. He was bigger than me, and he seemed to enjoy a fight.

"Don't run off," he said silkily. "I'm only trying to tell you that I think I could be a good fit for you, an easy match." He ran his fingers down my cheek and under my jaw. His breathing was speeding up, and I knew I couldn't waste time. I had to get out of here now.

I squinted my eyes. "And I'm only trying to tell you that if you don't remove your hand, you will be dead before you could be a match for anyone."

"Hot." He smirked, seeming to think I was enjoying this. "This is a fun little game."

"Let. Me. Go."

He loosened his hand, but I could still see the wild excitement in his eyes. "This was fun. Let's do it again soon."

I went for the stairs, praying he wouldn't chase me. From this second forward, there would be cameras on every. Single. Date.

When I made my way breathlessly to the first floor, I found a pair of officers and ran straight to them.

"Your Highness," the first gasped as I fell into his arms.

"Get him out of here!" I insisted, pointing toward the stairs. "Jack! Get him out of my house!"

The guards let me go, sprinting to capture him, and I cowered on the floor, petrified.

"Eadlyn?"

Just behind me, Ahren was approaching. I let out a cry and bolted into his embrace.

"What happened? Are you hurt?"

"It was Jack," I stammered. "He grabbed my arm. He touched me." I shook my head, trying to understand how it escalated so quickly, only then seeing it hadn't been fast at all.

He was often watching me, never approaching, quietly biding his time. Even tonight his moves were slow, watching my rising frustration with a reserved thrill of energy, enjoying the building tension until the moment of release.

"He kept saying strange things, and the way he looked at me . . . Ahren, I've never been so scared."

We both turned at the uproar coming up the stairs. The two guards were wrestling with Jack, getting him up to the landing. Once his eyes fell on me, he began snarling.

"You liked it!" he insisted. "You were coming on to me!"

Grabbing my hand, Ahren pulled me over to Jack, though my instinct was to run in the other direction. He planted me right in front of Jack's face.

"Knock his lights out, Eadlyn," Ahren commanded. I stared up at him, thinking it was a joke. But the rage in his eyes told me otherwise.

I was tempted. I couldn't retaliate when people called me names or criticized my clothes. I couldn't go back to the parade and tell all those people how foolishly they'd acted. But here, for once, I could take revenge on someone who'd truly wronged me.

I might have done it if it wasn't for Jack's wicked grin, like he hoped I would, like he'd dream about the touch later. Sex and violence were connected in his head, and to give him one was close to giving the other.

"I can't," I whispered.

Jack gave a fake pout. "You sure, sweetie? I wouldn't mi—"

I'd never seen Ahren throw a punch before. It was almost as shocking as Jack's limp body after my brother's fist forced his head to whip back at an awkward angle.

Ahren grunted, holding his hand. "That hurts! Ow, that really hurts!"

"Let's get you to the hospital wing," I urged, pointing Ahren down the hall.

"Your Highness, should we take him with you?"

I looked at Jack's limp form, noting the rise and fall of his chest.

"No. Get him on a plane, conscious or not."

I piled into Ahren's bed with him on one side and Kaden on the other. Ahren was flexing his wrapped fingers, which were badly bruised.

"Does it hurt?" Kaden asked, seeming more excited than worried.

"A little, but I'd do it all over again in a second."

I smiled up at my twin, so grateful for him.

"If I had been there," Kaden started, "I'd have challenged him to a duel."

I giggled as Ahren reached across me to ruffle his hair. "Sorry, buddy, it all happened too quickly for me to think of that."

Kaden shook his head. "All those years of sword-fighting lessons for nothing."

"You were always better than me anyway," Ahren said as Osten came in without knocking, a phone to his ear.

"If you had only practiced more!" Kaden chastised.

Osten landed on the bed chatting into the phone. "Yeah, yeah. Okay, hold on." He turned the receiver away and looked to me. "Eady, where was that Jack guy from anyway?"

I tried to remember his form. "Paloma, I think."

Kaden nodded. "It was Paloma."

"Awesome." Osten spoke into the phone again. "Did you hear that? I'll be in touch."

He hung up and slid the phone into his pocket as we all stared at him.

I laughed. "I'd usually try to stop whatever you're doing, but I'm not even going to ask."

"I think that's for the best."

I looked around at all my brothers, so caring and smart and puckish. So many times I'd hated them for not being older than me, for forcing me into a role I never wanted. Tonight, maybe for the first time, I loved them for exactly who they were. Kaden was distracting, Ahren had defended me, and Osten . . . well, he'd help in his own way.

Osten had left the door open, and Mom and Dad walked in to find all their children together.

Mom seemed happy to see her family safe, but Dad was shaken.

He put one hand on his hip and gestured with the other. "Everyone okay?"

"Slightly spooked," I admitted.

"And a little bruised," Ahren added.

Dad swallowed, taking us all in. "Eadlyn, I'm so sorry. I don't know how he slipped through the cracks. I thought the applications were vetted, and I had no idea . . ."

He stopped, looking as though he was close to tears.

"I'm all right, Daddy."

He nodded but didn't speak.

Mom stepped forward, taking over. "We'd like to put some guidelines in place. Perhaps have a guard nearby on any dates from here on out, or have all dates in a public area."

"That or have photographers. I think that would help, too." I cursed myself again for not remembering earlier.

"Excellent idea, sweetie. We want to keep this safe."

"Which reminds me," Dad said, under control again. "How do you want to proceed with Jack? Should we cover this up? Press formal charges? Personally, I'd like to tear him limb from limb, but that's really up to you."

I smiled. "No charges, but let's not cover it up. Let everyone know exactly what kind of man he is. That will be punishment enough."

"Very wise," Ahren agreed.

Dad folded his arms, considering. "If that's what you want, that's what we'll do. I've been told he's on his way home now, and that will be the end of it."

"Thank you."

Dad put his arm around Mom, and they turned to leave, Mom taking one last look at all of us.

"By the way," Dad said, glancing over his shoulder, "while I agree with the sentiment behind throwing him out without seeing if he regained consciousness, if he *had* died, that would have looked really bad."

I pressed my lips together, but I knew my eyes were smiling. "Fine. No more carelessly tossing people out through the gates."

"And more sword fights!" Kaden yelled.

While Ahren and I laughed, our parents shook their heads. "Goodnight. Don't stay up too late," Mom warned.

And we didn't mean to, but we did end up talking for a long time. I eventually fell asleep with Kaden's back pressed against mine, Ahren's arm under my head, and Osten holding on to one of my feet.

I woke early the next morning, well before the others, and smiled at my brothers, my protectors. The sister in me wanted to stay. But the princess in me got up and went to prepare for the new day.

CHAPTER 20

While we sat at the breakfast table the next morning, I found myself looking over the boys, searching for signs that anyone else might be like Jack. I kept thinking that if I'd paid more attention those first few days, I'd have been able to see there was something off about him.

Then my eyes passed over some of the others I'd gotten to know, like Hale and Henri. Even Erik's presence was a welcome one. After meeting them, I couldn't let one boy make me fearful of all the others. And in truth, I really didn't have the privilege of being fearful.

So I pulled myself together, remembering who I was. I couldn't run scared.

As the meal drew to a close, I stood, commanding their attention. "Gentlemen, I have a surprise for you. In fifteen minutes, please come meet me in the studio for a little game."

Some laughed and others clapped, but they didn't know what was waiting for them. I almost felt bad. I left the room before them, going to make sure my dress and hair looked right for filming.

Shortly thereafter, the boys filed in, all of them seeming a little stunned by the set.

I sat in front, a bit like a schoolteacher, while they each had a stool with a paper and marker and a large, cartoonish name tag like the ones I'd seen on TV game shows.

"Welcome, gentlemen!" I sang. "Please come find your seat."

The cameras were already rolling, capturing the nervous smiles and confused head shaking as they found their places and stuck on their tags.

"Today we're having a pop quiz on all things Illéa. We'll be discussing history, foreign affairs, and domestic policies. When you get an answer right, one of the maids standing by," I said, motioning to the ladies waiting in the wings, "will come and put a gold check mark sticker on you. Get one wrong, and they'll bring a black X."

The boys chuckled with excitement and anxiety, looking at the baskets of stickers.

"Don't worry, this is all for fun. But I will be using this information to help decide my next elimination. If you get the most wrong, it doesn't mean you're automatically out . . . but I'm watching," I teased, pointing a finger at them.

"First question," I announced. "This is an important one! When is my birthday?"

There were several laughs as the boys bent their heads,

scribbling answers and peeking at their neighbors' answers.

"Okay, hold up your signs," I ordered, and gawked humorously at the range of dates.

Kile, of course, knew it was April 16, and he had plenty of company, but there were only a few who knew the year as well.

"You know what, I'm going to go ahead and give this to anyone who got April at all."

"All right!" Fox called enthusiastically, and Lodge and Calvin high-fived in the back. The maids crossed the stage, and boys who got an X wailed comically but took the stickers without sulking.

"Here's one with lots of potential answers. Who would you consider Illéa's greatest allies?"

Some correctly guessed France, Italy, and New Asia, while Henri held up Swendway, followed by several exclamation points.

Julian's sign had several arrows drawn up to his face and had *ME* written in large letters.

I pointed at him. "Wait, wait, wait! What does that even mean?" I asked, trying to suppress a smile.

His grin was huge as he shrugged. "I just think I'd be a really great friend."

I shook my head. "Ridiculous." But I didn't think I came off sounding as reproachful as I meant to.

A maid raised her hand on the side of the stage. "So does he still get an X or . . . ?"

"Oh, that's an X!" I assured her, and the boys chuckled, even Julian.

Most correctly named August Illéa as Dad's partner in eradicating the rebel forces, and they all knew the history of the Fourth World War. By the time we got to the end, I was pleased that the majority of them were so well-informed.

"Let me see. Who has the most checks?" The maids helped me count across the rows, which was very efficient since they had handed out the points. "Hale has six. So do Raoul and Ean. Bravo, gentlemen!"

I clapped, and the others joined in before realizing what was next.

"Okay, and now, who has the most X marks?"

The maids quickly pointed to the back corner, where poor Henri was covered with black.

"Oh, no, Henri!" I yelled with a laugh, trying to communicate how little stock I took in the game.

I really had hoped to weed out someone this way, but I knew Henri's lack of information came from living in the country for only a year or a misunderstanding of the questions in translation.

"Who else do we have? Burke and Ivan . . . not too terrible." They had each done pretty badly but still had three correct answers over Henri. At least it confirmed my lack of excitement over Ivan.

"Thank you all for indulging me this morning, and I will keep this information in mind as I continue to narrow down suitors in the next few weeks. Congratulations on being so intelligent!" I applauded them, and they patted one another on the back as the cameras powered down.

"Before you go, gentlemen, I have one last question; and it comes from some very recent history, so you all had best get it right."

They nervously murmured among themselves, ready for the challenge.

"If you know the answer, feel free to just shout it out. Ready? When is it acceptable to put your hands on me without my permission?"

I stared at them all, stone-faced, daring a single one of them to laugh. They exchanged glances with one another, but it was only Hale who was brave enough to answer.

"Never," he called out.

"That is correct. You'd all do well to remember that. Jack Ranger was let off easy, with nothing more than a punch to his face from my brother and the shame of his ejection. If another one of you attempts to touch me without my consent, you will be caned or worse. Are we clear?"

The room was still.

"I'll take that as a yes."

I walked away, hoping my words would linger after me. The game was over, and they couldn't be left doubting that.

After lunch Dad was a little late getting into the office, which was rare. So I was alone when Lady Brice came knocking on the door.

"Your Highness," she greeted. "Is your father not here yet?"

"No. Not sure what's holding him up."

"Hmm." She tidied the stack of papers in her arms, thinking. "I really needed to speak with him."

Lady Brice looked so young sometimes. She was much older than me, of course, but not quite Dad's age. I never really knew what to make of her. Not that I disliked her or anything, but I always wondered why she was the only woman Dad worked with.

"Anything I could help you with?" I offered.

She looked down, thinking it over. "I'm not sure how widely he'd want to share this information, so I don't think so. Sorry."

I smiled, knowing she meant it. "No problem. Lady Brice, can I ask you a question? You're very smart and kind. Why haven't you ever married?"

She giggled a little. "I am married. To this job! It means a lot to me, and I'd rather do it well than seek out a spouse."

I rolled my eyes. "Amen to that."

"I know you understand. And the only people I ever get to see are the other advisers, and I don't think I'd want to be in a relationship with any of them. So I'll just keep working."

I nodded. "I respect that. I think people assume women aren't happy without a husband and children, but you seem quite satisfied."

She shrugged. "I think about it. I might adopt one day. I do think motherhood is an honor. And not everyone does it well."

The hint of bitterness in her tone made me think she was

referring to her own mother, but I didn't want to ask about specifics.

"I know. I'm fortunate to have such a wonderful one."

She sighed, melting a little. "Your mom is a natural. In a way, she was like a second mother to me when I was younger, and I learned a lot from her."

I squinted. "I didn't realize you'd been around the palace that long." I tried to remember if there was a time when I hadn't seen her in the hallways, though I'd never paid much attention to the advisers until I hit thirteen and started working with Dad in earnest. Perhaps I simply didn't notice.

"Yes, miss. I've been here almost as long as you," she replied with a laugh. "Your parents are far too generous."

Eighteen years was a long time to hold a position in the palace, especially as an adviser. Dad switched most people in and out every five to eight years based on recommendations and the mood of the country. What kept Lady Brice in her place for so long?

I studied her as she swept her hair over her shoulder and smiled. Had Dad let her stay because she was attractive? No. I felt guilty for even thinking Dad could be capable of being that shallow or selfish.

"Well, I'm sorry I can't help you, but I'll tell Dad you came by."

"Thanks, Your Highness. It's not terribly urgent, so there's no rush. You have a good day."

"You, too."

She curtsied and left, and I watched the door long after she was gone, curious about this woman I'd apparently known all my life without realizing it. I shrugged it away, turning back to my papers. Between the Selection and work, there was no room in my head for Lady Brice.

CHAPTER 21

DINNER THAT NIGHT WAS PLEASANT because I could tell the boys had learned from Jack's mistake. They all sat a little taller as I entered, nodding their heads as I passed, and I sensed that, once again, I'd regained control.

Dad looked a little calmer as well, though I could tell he hadn't quite let go of all his worry. Ahren leaned across the table to give me a conspiratorial wink, and it was almost like this terrible thing had made life a little better.

Dad had suggested that I try to make conversation with the boys at dinner, but calling out over all those people felt rude. I didn't think I could do that, at least not in a way that felt natural. I knew that, even with what I'd gone through, I was expected to get back out there. Instead of talking, I looked at my options. . . .

Of all the boys left, Ean struck me as the most intimidating.

Not because he seemed violent in any way, but because of that constant pride and calmness that hung around him, like an earthquake couldn't make him move if he didn't want it to.

So maybe going out with him next would conquer a fear in some way. There was no way he was as impervious as he seemed. We'd simply need to do something in the open and make sure the photographers came.

As if he could read my thoughts, Ean looked up at me at that very second, and I turned away, pretending to be engrossed with my brother.

I noticed Kaden was reading a newspaper beneath the table.

"What's that article about?" I asked.

He answered without looking away, like he was trying to finish his day's work before the end of dinner. "A collection going around in an area in Midston. They're raising money for a girl to go to art school. She's talented, but she can't afford to study on her own. She says . . . hold on. Here it is. 'I come from a line of Threes. My family thinks it's beneath me to study art, even though the castes no longer exist. It's hard. I remind them that the queen was born a Five, and she's brilliant. They won't pay for my schooling, so I'm asking for help to pursue my dreams.'

"Look at the picture of her paintings. They aren't bad."

I grew up with a deep appreciation for art, and while her work wasn't an aesthetic I particularly cared for, I could see she was talented.

"They're good. It's so silly. The point of getting rid of the castes was so people could have the choice of whatever profession they wanted, and they're not even using it. It's almost like they don't want it to work."

"Setting up a system to allow something doesn't mean people will do it."

"Obviously," I commented coldly, sipping my drink.

"The key is to make them understand that. Do you remember Mom showing us those old history books and how the United States had that paper"—he paused to think of the name—"the Declaration of Independence? And it said the people were allowed to pursue happiness. But no person making that document could actually hand over happiness."

I smiled. "You're too smart."

"I'd take that as a compliment, but last week you were caught kissing Kile in the dark."

"Oh, ha ha ha," I said, tempted to stick out my tongue at him. "It's not like my opinion ever mattered much anyway."

"Are you going to marry Kile?"

I nearly choked. "No!"

Kaden laughed wildly, making most of the room look our way.

"I take it back," I said, dabbing my lips. "You are a singularly gifted idiot!"

I stood, flicking Kaden's ear as I passed. "Hey!"

"Thanks for being there for me, Kaden. You're a great brother."

He rubbed at his ear, still grinning. "I try."

Marry Kile, I thought, doing my best not to burst out laughing again. If he could continue to be discreet, the chances of me kissing Kile again were very, *very* high . . . but I couldn't imagine actually being married to him.

I wasn't sure I could imagine being married to any of these boys.

I wasn't sure I could imagine being married at all. . . .

I slowed, looking at some of their faces as I passed. What would it be like to fall asleep next to Hale? Or to have Baden slip a ring on my finger?

I tried to picture it and couldn't. I remembered Ahren mentioning that some of the Selected asked him if it was possible I liked girls, but even thinking about that made me laugh. I knew that wasn't what was stopping me from genuinely being able to connect with a boy . . . but I sensed now that something was. It wasn't simply a desire to be independent; there was a wall around me, and I wasn't completely sure why.

But wall or no wall, I'd made a promise.

When I got to Ean, I paused.

"Mr. Cabel?"

He stood and bowed. "Yes, Your Highness."

"Do you ride horses?"

"I do."

"Would you like to accompany me on a ride tomorrow?"

A wicked glint came into his eye. "I would."

"Excellent. See you then."

★ ★ ★

I chose to wear a dress and do the whole thing sidesaddle. It wasn't my favorite way to ride, but I thought a touch of femininity would add to the purpose of the afternoon.

When I walked out to the stables, Ean was waiting for me, saddling his horse.

"Ean!" I called as I approached.

He lifted his head and waved. He was very handsome, the kind of person I thought people expected to see next to me. Every action of his was controlled, and I was determined to match him and not let myself be anxious.

"Are you ready?" he asked.

"Almost. I need to grab my saddle." I walked past him into the stalls.

"Is that what you're going to wear?"

I whipped back around. "I can do more in ten minutes wearing this dress than most men can do all day wearing pants."

He laughed. "I don't doubt it."

Butterscotch was at the back, in a slightly wider stall than most of the others. A princess's horse deserved some space and a good view.

I prepped her and walked back to Ean. "If you don't mind, we're going to take some photos in the garden first."

"Oh. No, that's fine."

We took our horses by the reins and walked them around to the garden. A man with a camera was there, snapping shots of the sky or trees as he waited. When he saw us, he came over.

"Your Highness," he greeted, shaking my hand. "I'm Peter. I thought it'd be nice to get a few pictures of the two of you together."

"Thank you." I petted Butterscotch. "Where do you want us?"

Peter looked around. "If you can put the horses by a tree, I think a couple of shots in front of this fountain would look nice."

I let go of Butterscotch, knowing she wouldn't run. "Come on," I said warmly.

Once he had tied his horse to a branch, I took his hands. Peter wasted no time. Ean and I smiled and looked shyly away from each other, and this little walk was documented in pictures. We stood in front of the fountain, sat against a shrub, and even took a couple of pictures in front of the horses.

When Peter announced that would be plenty, I nearly threw my arms up in celebration. He walked off rather quickly, grabbing his bags and double-checking his camera. I looked around, and as promised, we weren't completely alone. Guards lined the palace walls, and a few workers moved around the grounds, tending the grass and paths.

"Here, Butterscotch!" I walked up to her, and she flicked her tail.

Ean masterfully mounted his horse, and I was happy that he was as competent as he'd led me to believe.

"Forgive me, but that seemed a bit staged," Ean said as we trotted toward the edge of the lawn.

"I know. But allowing them to capture staged moments means that I get to keep the candid moments private."

"Interesting. So, was that scene with Kile staged or private, then?"

I smirked. Wow, he was quick.

"Last time we spoke, it sounded like you had something you wanted to talk about," I reminded him.

"I do. I want to be honest with you. But that will require you being completely honest with me. Can you do that?"

Looking into his face, I wasn't sure I could give him what he asked for. Not today.

"That depends."

"On?"

"Many things. I don't tend to divulge my soul to people I've only known two weeks."

We trotted on for a few minutes in silence.

"Favorite food?" he asked, a satisfied smile on his face.

"Do mimosas count?"

He chuckled. "Sure. What else . . . favorite place you've ever visited?"

"Italy. Partly for the food and partly for the company. If they come here, you have to meet the royal family. They're too much fun."

"I'd like that. Okay, favorite color?"

"Red."

"Power color. Nice."

He stopped quizzing me for a moment, and we continued on our path around the palace. It was kind of peaceful. We passed the front gates, and the gardeners stopped their work and bowed as we went by. Once we were out of their hearing, Ean brought his horse closer to mine.

"I could be very wrong, but I'm going to take a guess at some things about you."

"Go ahead," I dared.

He hesitated. "Hold on. Let's stop over here."

Along the palace wall there was a lone bench, and we pulled up to it.

I hopped off Butterscotch and sat on the small space with Ean.

"Your Highness."

"Eadlyn."

"Eadlyn." He swallowed, showing the first chink in his super-confident armor. "I get the feeling that the Selection isn't something you truly wanted to do."

I said nothing.

"If it was, perhaps it's not what you thought it would be, and now you're in a situation you don't particularly like. Most women would die to have dozens of men at their beck and call, but you come across as distant."

I smiled kindly. "I told you. I don't open up to people I just met."

He shook his head. "I've seen you on the *Report* for years. You seem above something like this."

I inhaled deeply, unsure what to say.

"I come to you with an offer. You may not need it at all, but I want to present the option all the same."

"What could you, sir, offer to your future queen?"

He smiled, seeming sure of himself again. "A way out."

It was risky to ask what he meant, but I couldn't help being curious. "How?"

"I would never hold you down. I would never hold you back. I wouldn't even ask you to love me. If you choose me, you can have a marriage free of conventional restraints. Make me your king, and you would be free to reign however you see fit."

I brushed out my dress. "You would never be king."

He tilted his head comically. "Not your type?"

I rolled my eyes. "That's neither here nor there. Any man who married me would never be king. He would be a prince consort, as no one can hold a title higher than mine."

"I'd take that."

I leaned on the arm of the bench. "Out of curiosity, why make such an offer? You're very charismatic, quite handsome. I'd assume you could have a marriage filled with happiness, which makes me wonder why you would commit yourself to one you just admitted would be loveless."

He nodded. "That's a fair question. Personally, I believe love to be overrated."

I couldn't help but smile.

"I come from a large family. Six children. I've managed to scrape by, but I don't want to live that life forever. The chance at a comfortable life with an agreeable woman is better than anything else I can hope for."

"Agreeable?" I raised an eyebrow. "Is that it?"

He chuckled. "I like you. You are yourself at all costs. I certainly don't consider marrying a clever, beautiful, powerful woman settling. And I can offer you the means to an end if you find no one suitable in this group. Honestly, I can tell you, the majority of these guys are jokes. And you can give me something I've never had."

I considered. So far the Selection hadn't been anything I'd expected. It had opened with people assaulting me with food, complaining about my first elimination, and judging my kiss with Kile. Even though I was just figuring out that, for me, there was something inherently unappealing about getting married, I couldn't help but wonder if I'd take someone simply for the sake of making Dad happy. Every time I looked into his eyes, I was more and more aware of how tired he seemed.

I loved my dad.

But I also loved myself.

And I would have to live with me much longer.

"You don't have to say yes or no," Ean said, drawing me back to the moment. "I'm simply saying that I'm here if you need me."

I nodded. "I can't say if I'll even consider it." I stood. "For now let's continue our ride. I don't get to see my Butterscotch nearly enough."

And we did ride for quite a while longer, but Ean didn't speak much. It was comfortable in a way not to be burdened with the need to make conversation. Ean would take my silence gratefully. I wondered if that could last, if he would eventually tire of that kind of life.

For the time being I studied him. Handsome, proud, straightforward. His confidence didn't hinge on my approval, and I knew I wouldn't worry about receiving his. I could possibly be married without actually *feeling* like I was. . . .

He might be a very attractive suitor, indeed.

CHAPTER 22

I SENT EAN IN SHORTLY thereafter, and he didn't protest at all, maybe proving right away that he would be as compliant as I needed him to be. It was certainly an interesting proposition, though I'd have to get much further along in this process before I could know if I'd need to use it or not.

Too soon, I had to get ready for dinner, so I put Butterscotch away and took a brush to my boots. I wasn't terribly dirty. "Night, night," I whispered to my horse, slipping her a piece of sugar before heading back to the palace.

"Eadlyn!" someone called as I entered the palace.

It was Kile. He was talking with Henri, Erik, Fox, and Burke. He gave the others a sign to wait for him and jogged down the hall to me.

"Hey," he said, his crooked smile settling on his face. He looked a little nervous.

"How are you?"

"Good. I was talking with some of the guys, and we have a proposal for you."

I sighed. "Another one?"

"Huh?"

"Nothing." I shook my head to clear it. "Should I come speak to them now?"

"Well, yeah, but I wanted to ask you something first."

"Sure."

Kile stuffed his hands in his pockets. "Are we okay?"

I squinted. "Kile, you realize you're not actually my boyfriend, right?"

He chuckled. "Yeah, I do. But, I don't know, I liked having someone to show my designs to and laugh with, and I wanted to come check on you after I heard about Jack, but I was afraid you wouldn't want to talk about it. Then I was afraid that staying away would make you upset, too. Do you know how difficult you are?"

"I'd forget, but you keep reminding me!" I teased.

Kile fidgeted. "I'll ease up. But seriously, are we okay?"

I watched as he bit his lip, and I had to fight myself from daydreaming about them. He said he was here for me, so I hoped, maybe, I'd get to feel those lips again.

"Yes, Kile. We're okay. Don't worry so much."

"All right. Come over here. I think you're going to like this idea."

We turned and walked down to the cluster of boys waiting. Henri immediately kissed my hand.

"Hello today," he greeted, making me laugh.

"Hello, Henri. Burke, Fox. Hi, Erik."

"Your Highness," Burke began. "Maybe this is a little out of line, but we were thinking that the Selection is a very challenging time for you."

I chuckled. "You have no idea."

Fox smiled. He and Burke looked a little comical next to each other. Burke was so burly, and he was so lean. "It has to be crazy. You have your work to do, and then you need to find time to do solo dates or try to get around to everyone at a party. It seems exhausting."

"So we had an idea," Kile said. "Could the four of us do something with you this week?"

This was completely brilliant. "Yes!" I exclaimed. "That would be great. Any ideas on what to do?"

"We were thinking about cooking together." Burke's face was so happy, I couldn't say no, even though that was exactly what I wanted to do.

"Cooking?" I said, a fake smile plastered on my face.

"Come on," Kile urged. "It'll be fun."

I exhaled nervously. "All right. Cooking. How about tomorrow night?"

"Perfect!" Fox said quickly, like he was worried I'd change my mind.

"Okay. Thursday, six o'clock. I'll meet you in the foyer, and we can walk to the kitchens together." This was going to be a nightmare. "If you'll excuse me, I have to get ready for dinner."

I headed upstairs wondering if there was any way to make this better. I doubted it.

"Neena," I called, walking into my room.

"Yes, miss?"

"Can you start a bath? I need one before dinner."

"Certainly."

I wrestled with my boots and flung off my dress. Besides the simple giving and responding to orders, we hadn't spoken much lately, and I had to admit, it was hard on me. My room was my retreat, the place I rested and sketched and hid from the world. Neena was a part of that, and her being upset with me set everything off-kilter.

I walked into the bathroom, happy to find that she was dropping pieces of lavender into the tub without me asking.

"Neena, you're a mind reader."

"I try," she said slyly.

I moved cautiously, not wanting to anger her again. "Have you heard from Mark recently?"

It seemed she couldn't help her smile. "Yes, just yesterday."

"What did you say he studied again?" I slipped into the warm water, already feeling better.

"Biochemistry." She looked down. "I admit, he uses plenty of words I don't understand when he tells me about it, but I get the idea of what he means."

"I wasn't trying to imply I thought you were stupid, Neena. I was curious. I thought that was obvious." Biochemistry. Something about that rang a bell.

She sighed and dropped more lavender into the bath. "It

came out much harsher than that."

"There are boys here from very different walks of life than mine. I can hardly stand to be in the same room with some of them. It was intriguing that the two of you do such varied jobs and still manage to share common ground."

She shook her head. "We work. It's not something you can figure out on paper. Some people are meant to be together."

I leaned back in the tub. If there was no way to explain anything, then why bother? I thought again of Ean's offer and Kile's worry and Hale's questions. I couldn't believe how murky everything had become. I barely understood my own feelings anymore. I knew I wanted my independence, and the idea of any man coming up behind me trying to fix my work or do it for me was unacceptable. Then I thought of Dad's gray hairs, slowly mixing in with the blond, and wondered how far I'd go to make his life easier.

It was strange. Basically, every boy downstairs was an option, if I really had to choose one. And each of them could easily hurl my world into a new trajectory. I didn't like that. I wanted to be in charge of my path. I wondered if that was the reason for putting a fence around myself, if it was the worry that anyone who crossed it would take away my control.

But maybe that control was an illusion. Even if I passed on all the Selected boys, would someone eventually come along and make me not even care about control? Would he cause me to hand it over willingly?

It seemed impossible, something I certainly couldn't have

imagined happening a few weeks ago.

There were still plenty of reasons to keep my guard up, and I knew I would. Still, I didn't think I'd be able to ignore the way these boys were affecting me much longer.

CHAPTER 23

I WAITED NERVOUSLY IN THE palace foyer. I wasn't sure about what I was wearing—what did people wear to cook?—or how to fake expertise in the kitchen or how to disperse attention evenly among four suitors.

And while I knew having a photographer there was both good for publicity and personal safety, the idea of someone documenting this night did not make me feel any less jittery.

I pulled at my shirt, which was rather plain in case I got dirty, and touched my hair, making sure it was still in place. The clock showed the boys were four minutes late, and I was getting antsy.

Just as I was about to send a butler to fetch them, I heard the echo of voices in the hallway. Kile rounded the corner first. Burke was right beside him, clearly trying to buddy up to the alleged leader of the pack. Fox was with Henri, both smiling quietly. Not far behind, Erik walked with his hands tucked behind him. His presence was necessary, but I sensed he felt a little out of place as the sole nonparticipant in a group date.

Kile rubbed his hands together. "You ready to eat?"

"Eat, yes. Cook? We'll see how that goes." I tried to hide my worry with a smile, but I think Kile knew.

"So is it true you two have known each other your whole lives?" Burke asked. It was so abrupt, I didn't know how to respond.

"Trust me, you've got the better end of the deal," Kile replied smoothly, elbowing him in the ribs.

"It's true," I confirmed. "It's like Kile said on the *Report*: I never considered him boyfriend material until I was forced to. He's like family."

Everyone laughed, and I realized how true that was. It annoyed me whenever Josie told people she was like my sister, but I did know both her and Kile better than I knew my cousins.

"The kitchen is this way," I said, pointing past them to the dining hall. "The staff knows we're coming, so let's go cook."

Kile shook his head at my fake enthusiasm but said nothing.

We walked to the back of the dining hall and rounded a partition. There was a wide dumbwaiter the staff used to bring up carts of food next to a stairwell that led to the main kitchen. Burke rushed to my side quickly, offering his arm as we traveled down the wide steps.

"What do you want to cook tonight?" he asked.

I wondered if my face showed my shock. I really thought someone else would be providing the ideas.

"Oh, I'm kind of up for whatever," I hedged.

"Let's make courses," Kile suggested. "An appetizer, an entrée, and a dessert."

"That sounds good," Fox agreed.

Erik piped up from the back. "Henri and I will do dessert, if that's all right."

"Sure," Kile answered.

I could smell the dinner that was being prepared for the rest of the palace. I couldn't pinpoint everything, but there was a delicious hint of garlic in the air, and I suddenly had a new reason to hate this date: I had to postpone actually eating.

In a low-ceilinged room, a dozen people with their hair pulled back tightly or tucked under scarves were running around, tossing vegetables into pots of steaming water or double-checking the seasonings of the sauces. Despite the fact that there was still a meal to finish preparing for everyone in the palace, the staff had cleared half of the space for us to use.

A man in a tall chef's hat approached us. "Your Highness. Will this be enough room?"

"More than enough, thank you."

I remembered his face from a few weeks ago when he'd presented me with the sample ideas for the first dinner. I'd been so annoyed at the time, Mom did most of the choosing, and I hadn't even thought to thank him. Looking around and seeing how much work was going into a single meal, I felt ashamed of myself.

"*Missä pidät hiivaa*?" Henri asked politely.

My eyes went to Erik, who spoke up. "Pardon me, sir, but where do you keep your yeast?"

Fox and Burke giggled, but I remembered what Erik had told me once and what was crudely worded on Henri's own application: he was a cook.

The chef waved Henri down, and he and Erik followed him closely, trying to chat. The chef was clearly excited to have someone with some experience in the room. The other boys . . . not so much.

"Okay, so . . . let's go see what's in the fridge." Fox hesitantly led the way to one of several large refrigerators along the wall. I looked at the organized contents—parchment-wrapped meats labeled in pencil, the four different types of milk we used, and the various sauces or starters prepped and stored ahead of time—and knew I was way out of my league.

I heard a click and turned to see the photographer had arrived.

"Just pretend I'm not here!" she whispered cheerfully.

Kile grabbed some butter. "You always need butter," he assured me.

I nodded. "Good to know."

Burke found a pile of something on the counter. He turned to the chef. "What is this?"

"Phyllo paper. You can make dozens of things with that. Melt some of that butter, and I'll get you some recipes."

Kile gave me a face. "See?"

"How do we want to decide who works together?" Burke asked, obviously hoping I'd simply go with him.

"Rock, paper, scissors?" Fox suggested.

"That's fair," Kile agreed. He and Fox went up against each other first, and though no one said it one way or the other, they knew the losers would be stuck with each other.

Kile beat both Fox and Burke. Fox took it in stride, but Burke had no talent at masking his emotions. The two of them picked an appetizer to make together—asparagus wrapped with prosciutto and phyllo—while Kile and I were left staring at some chicken, trying to figure out what to do with it.

"So, what's step one?" I asked.

"I cooked plenty when I was away in Fennley, but I need a recipe at least. I bet those books would help." We walked over to a cupboard that contained dozens of cookbooks. Most of them had markers hanging in multiple places, and there were piles of note cards next to them with more ideas.

As Kile flipped through the pages, I played with the jars of herbs. The kitchen made me think of what a scientist's lab would look like, only with food. I opened some, inhaling them or feeling the texture.

"Smell this," I insisted, holding up a jar to Kile.

"What's that?"

"Saffron. Doesn't it smell delicious?"

He smiled at me and went straight to the back of the book he was holding. "Aha!" he said, turning forward to find his page. "Saffron chicken. Want to give that a try?"

"Sure." I clutched the jar in my hand like it was my big contribution to the night.

"All right. Saffron chicken . . . so, let's preheat the oven."

I stood next to him, staring at the buttons and dials. Probably the ovens in normal people's homes didn't look like this, but this massive, industrial setup seemed like it might launch a satellite if we touched the wrong thing. We looked at the stove like it might give us some instructions if we waited long enough.

"Should I get more butter?" I asked.

"Shut up, Eadlyn."

The chef walked past and mumbled, "Dial on the left, three fifty."

Kile reached over and turned it as if he knew what to do the whole time.

I glanced toward Fox and Burke. Burke was clearly acting as their leader and loudly giving orders. Fox didn't seem to mind at all, laughing and joking without being obnoxious. They peeked back over at us several times, Burke sneaking in a wink now and then. Past them, Erik and Henri were working quietly, with Erik doing a minimal amount of labor, only assisting when Henri asked for it.

Henri's sleeves were rolled up and he'd gotten some flour

on his pants, and I kind of loved that he didn't seem to care about it. Erik was a little messy himself, and he didn't bother wiping any of it off either.

I looked at Kile, who was buried in the cookbook. "I'll be right back."

"Sure." As I walked away, I heard him quietly try to get the chef's attention.

"Looking good, boys," I said, pausing by Fox.

"Thanks. This is actually kind of soothing. I never cooked much at home, nothing like this anyway. But I'm looking forward to trying it." Fox's hands stuttered for a moment, trying to find his rhythm again.

"This will be the best asparagus you've ever had," Burke promised.

"I can't wait," I replied, moving to the far end of the table.

Erik looked up, greeting me with a smile. "Your Highness. How's our dinner looking?"

"Very bad indeed," I promised. He chuckled and told Henri the state of our poor supper.

Their hands were covered in dough, and I could see bowls of cinnamon and sugar waiting to be used. "This looks promising though. Do you cook as well, Erik?"

"Oh, not professionally. But I live on my own, so I cook for myself, and I love all the traditional Swendish foods. This is a favorite."

Erik turned to Henri, and I could tell they were talking about food because Henri was alight with excitement.

"Oh, yeah! Henri was just saying there's this soup he has

when he's sick. It's got potatoes and fish, and, oh, I miss my mother just thinking about it."

I smiled, trying to imagine Erik alone trying to master his mother's meals and Henri in the back of a restaurant already having conquered every recipe in his family's memory. I kept worrying that Erik felt like an outcast. He certainly worked to separate himself from the Selected. He dressed differently, walked at a slower pace, and even carried himself a little lower. But watching him here, interacting with Henri, who was too kind for me to dismiss, I was so grateful for his presence. He brought a little piece of home to a situation twice removed from Henri's idea of normal.

I stepped away, allowing them to work, and went back to my station. Kile had collected some ingredients in my absence. He was dicing garlic on a wooden brick next to a bowl of something that looked like yogurt.

"There you are," he greeted. "Okay, crush those saffron threads and then mix them in the bowl."

After a moment of blank staring, I picked up the tiny bowl and mallet I assumed was meant for thread crushing and started pressing. It was a strangely satisfying exercise. Kile did most of the work, smothering the chicken with the yogurt mix and throwing it in the oven. The other teams were at various stages of prep as well, and in the end, the dessert was ready first, followed by the appetizer, and our entrée pulled up the rear.

Realizing belatedly that Kile and I should have made something to go with our chicken, we decided to use the wrapped asparagus as a side, all laughing at how poorly we'd planned this.

The whole lot of us crowded around one end of the long table. I was sandwiched between Burke and Kile, with Henri across from me and Fox at the head. Erik was slightly removed but still clearly enjoying the company.

Honestly, I was, too. Cooking made me nervous because it was totally foreign to me. I didn't know how to cut or sauté or anything, and I despised failing or looking foolish. But the majority of us had limited experience, and instead of it becoming a stressor, it became a joke, making this one of the most relaxed meals I'd ever had. No formal place settings, no assigned seats; and since nearly all the china was in use for our very full house, we were using plain plates that looked so old, the only reason they could possibly still be here was sentimentality.

"Okay, since they were supposed to be the appetizer, I think we should try the asparagus first," Kile insisted.

"Let's do it." Burke speared his asparagus and took a bite, and we all followed. It appeared the results were inconsistent. Henri nodded approvingly, but mine tasted awful. I could tell Fox's was bad as well based on his poorly concealed grimace.

"That . . . that is the worst thing I've ever tasted," Fox said, trying to chew.

"Mine's good!" Burke said defensively. "You're probably just not used to eating such quality food."

Fox ducked his head, and I gathered something I wouldn't

have known otherwise: Fox was poor.

"Can I try a bite of yours?" I whispered to Henri, using my hands and happy to find he understood without Erik's help.

"Do you mind?" Fox replied quietly, and I pretended to be too focused on the food to hear him. And Henri's piece actually was much better. "Who's to say it's not because of your cooking?"

"Well, maybe if I had a better partner," Burke snapped.

"Hey, hey, hey!" Kile insisted. "There's no way yours could be worse than ours."

I giggled, trying to break the tension. I could feel Burke's anger like an actual, physical thing hanging in the air, and I wanted nothing more than to return to the relaxed feeling we had when we'd sat down.

"All right," I said with a sigh. "I think the first thing we need to do is cut each piece of chicken in half to make sure it's cooked through. I seriously don't want to kill anyone."

"Are you doubting me?" Kile asked, offended.

"Definitely!"

I took a tentative bite . . . and it was pretty good. It wasn't undercooked; in fact, some of the edges were a little dry where the paste hadn't covered it all. But it was edible! Considering that I'd only done a fraction of the work, I was maybe a little too proud.

We ate, sharing pieces of the asparagus that hadn't turned out too bad, though I genuinely worried I might be sick later.

Finally, I'd had enough. "I'm ready for dessert!"

Henri chuckled in understanding and went over to where his pastries were cooling on a rack. With careful movements, only using the edges of his fingers even though the rolls seemed firm, he transferred them all to a plate and set them in front of us.

"Is *korvapuusti*," he said, giving the dish a name. Then, taking my hand, he gave me a very important speech; I could tell by the intensity in his eyes. I wished so badly that I could understand him on my own.

When he finished, Erik smiled and turned to me.

"*Korvapuusti* is one of Henri's favorite things to prepare as well as eat. He says that if you do not like it, you should send him home tonight, for he's sure your relationship could not survive if you aren't as in love with this as he is."

Fox laughed at my shocked face, but Henri nodded, assuring me he meant it.

I took a deep breath and picked up one of the delicately rolled pastries. "Here goes nothing."

Right away I could taste the cinnamon. There was something else in there that reminded me of grapefruit . . . but I knew that wasn't it. It was deliciously sweet, but more than it being a fantastic recipe, I could tell it was made by a fantastic *chef.* Henri had poured himself into this. And I was willing to bet part of that was for me . . . but I thought it was mostly for himself, that he couldn't allow himself to make it anything less than incredible.

I was blown away. "It's perfect, Henri."

The others grabbed pieces and shoved them into their mouths, grunting in approval.

"My mom would be dying right now. She has such a sweet tooth!" I said.

Kile was nodding with his eyes wide. He knew how she was about desserts. "This is great, Henri. Nice job to you, too, Erik."

Erik shook his head. "I barely helped."

"Was this rigged?" Burke asked, his mouth half full with the pastry.

We all looked at him, confused.

"I mean, I came up with this idea, and then Henri jumped in on it just to show the rest of us up."

His face was turning red, and that feeling of unease was filling the room again.

Fox put a hand on his shoulder. "Calm down, man. It's just a cinnamon roll."

Burke shrugged it off and threw the rest of his dessert across the room. "I would have done way better if you weren't there screwing me up the whole time!"

Fox made a face. "Hey, you were the one standing there talking about how hot she was when you should have been watch—"

Burke threw a punch that knocked Fox back several steps. I sucked in a breath, frozen. Fox came back at him, and I was pushed to the floor by Burke's arm pulling back for another punch.

"WHOA!" Kile jumped over me and started pulling at

Burke, while Henri was yelling at Fox in Finnish. After everything with Jack, my new instinct was to get back up and throw a punch. No one was going to hurt me and get away with it. And I might have tried if it wasn't for one thing.

Erik, the quiet observer, had launched himself over the table to pick me up.

"Come," he said.

I wasn't particularly a fan of obeying orders. But he said it so urgently, I followed.

CHAPTER 24

ERIK RUSHED ME UP THE stairs and into the dining hall. Everyone else in the palace was in the middle of their dinner, and the room felt too loud.

"Eadlyn?" Daddy called, but Erik kept me moving, somehow knowing that I couldn't bear to stay there. He only paused when we got to the end of the room, and just long enough to pass along the problem.

"Pardon me, officer, some of the Selected are in a fight in the kitchen. It's very physical, and it looked to be escalating."

"Thank you." The officer motioned to two other guards, and they followed him as he ran toward the fray.

I realized I was hugging myself, both frightened and enraged. Erik gently placed a hand on my back and ushered me away. My parents were calling after me, but I couldn't deal with that many people right now, surrounding me, asking questions.

He slowed and asked me quietly, "Where do you want to go?"

"My room."

"Lead the way."

He didn't touch me exactly, except for the occasional brush against my back, which made me realize he must have kept his hand there the whole time, inches away from me, just in case. I pushed open my door, and Neena was inside, polishing the table, filling the room with the scent of lemons.

"My lady?"

I held up a hand.

"Maybe go get her some tea?" Erik offered.

She nodded and rushed away.

I walked over to my bed and took a few deep breaths. Erik stood there, calm and silent.

"I've never seen anything like that," I confessed. He got down on a knee so he was level with me. "My father has never so much as swatted my hand, and he's always taught us to seek peaceful resolutions. Ahren and I gave up trying to fight each other before we could really talk."

I remembered this all with a laugh.

"When we were down there, all I could think about was how I ran from Jack. Burke knocked me to the ground, and this time I was going to fight back, but I just realized I'd have no idea how to do it."

Erik smiled. "Henri says, when you're upset, the look in your eyes is as strong as a punch. You're not powerless."

I ducked my head, thinking of how I told myself over and

over that no one in the world was as powerful as me. There was truth to it, sure. But if Jack had pinned me to the ground or Burke had turned his fists on me, my crown would have done me no good until after the fact. I could punish, but I couldn't prevent.

"You know, boy or girl, I think aggression is a sign of weakness. I'm always more impressed when people can end something with words." His eyes were seeing another place and time when he went on. "Maybe that's why language became so important to me. My father, he always used to say 'Eikko, words are weapons. They are all you need.'"

"Ayco?" I asked.

He grinned, a little embarrassed. "E-I-K-K-O. Like I said, Erik is the closest in English."

"I like it. Really."

He turned his attention back to me, looking at my arms. "Are you hurt?"

"Oh . . . umm, I don't think so." I felt a little sore from hitting the ground, but it was nothing serious. "I just can't believe how fast it happened."

"I don't want to excuse either of them at all—that was unacceptable—but I hear the guys talking, and they're stressed. They all want to impress you, but they have no idea how to do it, considering who you are. Some talk about trying to undermine others without getting caught. A few are working out at every turn to be physically superior. I understand that it's a lot of pressure, and that's probably why Burke snapped. But that will never make it okay."

"I'm so sorry you have to be around that."

He shrugged. "It's fine. Mostly I just stick with Henri and Kile, sometimes Hale, and they're good company. Not that I'd ever try to choose for you, but the three of them are a pretty safe place to start."

I smiled. "I think you're right." Though I hadn't spent one-on-one time with everyone yet, I already knew Hale was a good guy. And seeing Henri so excited about his food tonight, about this part of his life, gave me a glimpse of the person behind the barrier. And Kile . . . well, I didn't know what to make of Kile, but he was a better companion than I'd given him credit for.

"Would you tell Henri for me how wonderful his food was? I could tell how important it was to him, and I admire his passion."

"I will. Happily."

I extended my hand and he gave me his, resting them both on my knee. "Thank you so much for this. You really went above and beyond tonight, and I'm so thankful you were here."

"It's the least I could do."

I tilted my head, really looking at him. It felt like something had just happened, but I didn't know what it was.

Erik, without knowing me, had done so much right. He pulled me away before I made the situation worse, got me to solitude before I lost control of my emotions, and stayed with me, listening to my worries and making everything better with his words. There were scores of people on call, ready to do whatever I asked.

It was so funny to me that with him I didn't even have to ask.

"I won't forget this, Eikko. Not ever."

There was a tiny lift of a smile at the sound of his given name, and he squeezed my hand ever so slightly.

I remembered the feeling of my first date with Hale, how I felt when I was sure he'd peeled everything back and had seen the real me. This time, I felt like I was on the other side of that, looking past duty and worry and rank, seeing the true heart of a person.

And his was so beautiful.

Neena came back in carrying a tray, and Erik and I ripped our hands apart.

"Are you all right, my lady?"

"Yes, Neena," I promised her, standing. "There was a fight, but Erik got me away. I'm sure the guards will come with a report soon. In the meantime I just need to calm down."

"The tea will help. I got some chamomile, and we'll get you into something comfortable before you need to report anywhere," Neena said, already making my night easier by planning it.

I turned back to Erik, who was standing by the door. He bowed deeply.

"Goodnight, Your Highness."

"Goodnight."

He walked away quickly, and Neena came over, handing

me a cup of tea. The strange thing was, my hands were already so warm.

About an hour later I met Mom and Dad in the office to discuss what'd happened.

"Sir Fox looks pretty bad," a guard relayed. "Sir Henri tried to pull him away, but Sir Burke was practically unstoppable. Both Sir Henri and Sir Kile got some marks simply from trying to separate them."

"How bad?" I asked.

"Sir Henri has a bruise on his chest and a cut just above his eye. Sir Kile's lip was busted open, and there aren't any big scars besides that, but he feels sore from trying to contain Sir Burke."

"You can stop calling him 'Sir'!" Dad insisted. "Burke is leaving right now! The same for Fox!"

"Maxon, reconsider. Fox didn't do anything," Mom urged. "I agree it was inappropriate, but don't make that choice on Eadlyn's behalf."

"I will!" he yelled. "We did this to bring our people joy, to give our daughter a chance at the same happiness we have. And since it began, she's been assaulted twice! I will NOT have monsters like that under my roof!" He finished his speech, slamming his fist into a side table, knocking his tea onto the floor.

I stiffened, gripping the arms of my chair. "Daddy, stop," I pleaded, my words hushed with fear I might somehow make it worse.

He looked over his shoulder at me, as if he only now realized Mom and I were still in the room. His eyes instantly softened, and he turned away, shaking his head.

After a deep breath he straightened his suit and spoke to the guard. "Before anything continues, I expect thorough background checks on each of the Selected. Do it secretively and use whatever means possible. If anyone has so much as gotten into a squabble in grade school, I want them gone."

Calm again, he sat beside Mom. "I unconditionally insist that Burke leaves. That's not up for debate."

"But what about Fox?" Mom asked. "It sounds like he didn't really instigate anything."

Dad shook his head. "I don't know. The idea of letting anyone involved stay seems like very poor judgment."

Mom leaned her head on Dad's shoulder. "Once upon a time I was involved in a fight during the Selection, and you let me stay. Imagine how things would have been if you hadn't."

"Mom, you got into a fight?" I asked, dumbfounded.

"It's true," Dad confirmed, sighing.

Mom smiled. "I actually still think about the other girl often. She turned out to be quite lovely."

Dad huffed, his tone begrudging. "Fine. Fox can stay, but only if Eadlyn thinks he might be someone she'd have a chance at happiness with."

Their eyes settled on me, and I was confused about so many things at once, I felt positive it read on my face. I turned to the guard. "Thank you for your update. Have

Burke escorted from the premises and tell Fox I'll speak with him shortly. You can go now."

Once he left the room, I rose from my chair, trying to compose my thoughts.

"I'm not going to ask about that fight, though, for the life of me, I cannot figure out why you two have withheld so much about your Selection from me and have only decided to share some of the bigger bits and pieces now. And *after* I've faced something you've already experienced."

They sat there guiltily.

"Mom met you before she was supposed to," I accused, pointing to Dad. "Your candidates were all planted by your father. . . . Maybe you could have given me a heads-up about how to deal with a fight two weeks ago."

I crossed my arms, exhausted.

"I promised you three months, and I'm going to give you that," I said, taking in their worried expressions. "I'll go on dates and let people take pictures so we have something to print in the papers and to talk about on the *Report*. But you two seem to think that if I stick this out, I'm magically going to fall in love."

I stood there, shaking my head. "That's not going to happen. Not for me."

"It could," Mom whispered tenderly.

"I know I'm disappointing you, but it's not what I want. And these boys are fine, but . . . some of them make me uncomfortable, and I don't think they can handle the pressure of this position. I'm not going to handcuff myself to a weight for the sake of a distracting headline."

Dad stood. "Eadlyn, that's not what we want either."

"Then please"—I raised my hands in front of me, guarding myself—"stop pressuring me to fall for people I never wanted here in the first place."

I clasped my hands together. "This whole situation has been awful. I've had people throw food at me in public; others have judged me over a kiss. One boy touched me against my will, and another flung me to the ground. For all the effort I put in to make things right, the papers have had a field day with the constant shame."

They exchanged a concerned glance.

"When I said I'd help distract people, I didn't think it would be this degrading."

"Sweetheart, we were never trying to hurt you." Mom looked heartbroken, close to tears.

"I know, and I'm not mad. I just want my freedom. If this is what I have to do in order to get that, then I will. If you want your distraction, I'll deliver. But please don't place all those expectations on me. I don't want to let you down any more than I have already."

CHAPTER 25

I KNOCKED ON FOX'S DOOR, kind of hoping he wouldn't answer. It had been a draining night, and I wanted to go hide under my blankets.

Of course, his butler opened the door and pulled it so far back that Fox saw me before I could be announced.

He looked as bad as I'd been told. One eye was swollen and surrounded by varying shades of purple, and the opposite side of his head was covered in a bandage, as well as the knuckles across his right hand.

"Eadlyn!" he said, hopping up off his bed, then wincing and grabbing his ribs. "Sorry. I meant Your Highness."

"You can go," I said hurriedly to the butler as I rushed over to Fox.

"Sit," I urged. "Shouldn't you still be in the hospital wing?"

He shook his head as he settled down again. "I've been medicated, and they thought I'd rest better in my own room."

"How are you feeling?" I asked, though I could tell he was in pain.

"Besides the bruises?" he asked. "Humiliated."

"Can I join you?" I asked, pointing to the spot beside him on the edge of bed.

"Of course."

I sat, not sure where to start. I didn't want to send him home now, partly out of charity. I peeked at Burke's and Fox's applications before going to see Dad, and Fox had actually hinted at a lot about his home life on his form. Typically, I was looking for mutual interests or things we could talk about, so I'd missed some important details about him.

Living in Clermont, he worked as a lifeguard at the beach, which explained the sun-kissed skin and overly blond hair. I got the feeling that it wasn't paying enough to support the rest of his family, though that situation was a little unclear on paper. His mother wasn't living at home, but I didn't know if that meant she had passed or not. I also could see his father was terminally ill, so I doubted he was contributing to the finances.

Furthermore, if I'd paid attention at all, I would have noticed how much fuller his cheeks looked compared to the picture on his form now that he was getting fed properly.

I wanted him to stay. I wanted him to keep his stipend. I wanted him to steal some of the things from his room when he left and sell them when he got home.

But asking him to stay meant giving him hope.

"Listen," he started, "I understand if you have to send me home. I do. I don't want to leave, but I know the rules. I just . . . I don't want to leave with you thinking I'm like Burke or Jack. Try not to think poorly of me when I go, okay?"

"I won't. I don't."

Fox looked over and gave me a sad grin. "I never got to tell you so many things. Like how I wish I could command a room like you. It's so impressive. Or how your eyes sparkle when you make a joke. It's really pretty."

"Do they do that? Wait, do I make jokes?"

He chuckled. "Yeah. I mean, they're mostly subtle, but you give it away with your eyes. And I can see how pleased you are when you're teasing us. Like at the quiz the other day."

I smiled. "That was fun. Tonight was fun, too, up until the end."

"I'll never forget your face when you bit into that asparagus."

I pressed my lips together, pretty sure that his expression and mine had been similar. What made it better was that I knew how hard he'd tried, and he still wasn't upset over it. The only thing hurting him now was this worry that I'd remember him as something less than a gentleman.

"Fox, I'm going to ask you some questions, and I need you to be completely honest with me. If I think you're lying at all, that's it. You'll be gone within the hour."

He swallowed, the silliness of the last few moments fading from his face. "You have my word."

I nodded, believing him. "All right. Would you tell me about your dad?"

He huffed, clearly not expecting the conversation to head in this direction. "Umm, he's sick, which I guess you know. He's got cancer. He's still functioning pretty well. Like he's working, but it's only part-time right now. He needs a lot of sleep.

"When he got sick my mom left, so . . . I really don't want to talk about her, if that's okay."

"That's okay."

He looked at the floor as he continued. "I've got a brother and a sister, and they go on and on about her like she's coming back, but I know that's not happening. If she did, then *I'd* leave."

"We really don't have to talk about her, Fox."

"Sorry. You know, I thought the hardest part about coming here would be the distance, but what's so bad it almost hurts is seeing you with your family." He scratched at his hair with his good hand. "Your parents are still in love, and your brothers look at you like you're heaven on earth, and I wish I had that. I don't have anything close."

I put a hand on his back. "We're not perfect. I promise. And it sounds like you and your dad have something special."

"We do." He glanced over at me. "I didn't mean to get

like that. I don't talk about my family a lot."

"That's fine. I have other questions."

He sat up straight again, and I could see the pain of the action. I pulled my hand away and rolled my eyes. "Actually, I just realized this might be a hard one, too."

He smiled. "Go ahead anyway."

"Okay . . . did you come here for me or to get away from them?"

Fox paused, his eyes dead set on mine. "Both. I love my dad. I can't tell you how much he means to me, and I don't mind taking care of him, really. But it's also kind of tiring. It's been like a holiday here most of the time. I also think my brother and sister are starting to appreciate what I do, which is validating in a way.

"And then, there's you." He shook his head. "Look, you know I live paycheck to paycheck. And I come from a broken family. I realize I'm nothing special," he said, placing his hand on his chest. Then he suddenly got shy. "But, you know, I've watched you my whole life, and I've always thought you were so sharp and beautiful. I don't know if I stand the smallest chance of getting to be with you . . . but I had to at least put my name in. I don't know; I just thought if I could get here, I'd find a way to show you that I could be worth taking a chance on.

"And then I got in a fight." He shrugged. "So I guess that's how it ends."

I hated the disappointment in his voice. I didn't *want* to care. I knew that letting him get closer to me would end badly. I couldn't explain why I knew, but I was sure that if I allowed any of these boys to cross into a certain level of intimacy, it would be disastrous. So why—*why*—couldn't I keep them from getting closer?

"I have another question."

"Sure," he replied, defeated.

"What's it like to work on the beach all day?"

He didn't try to fight the smile. "It's wonderful. There's something kind of fascinating about the ocean. It's almost like it has different moods on different days. Like, sometimes the water is so still and other times it's wild. And I'm so glad Angeles is warm all the time, or I don't think I could have handled it."

"I love the weather here, too, but I don't get to go to the beach very often. Mom and Dad don't like it, and people end up swarming Ahren and me if we go just the two of us. It's kind of a pain."

He poked me gently. "If you ever come to Clermont, look me up. You can rent a private beach and swim and lounge to your heart's content."

I sighed dreamily. "That sounds perfect."

"I'm serious. It's the least I could do."

I looked at my hands and back to Fox's hopeful face. "How about this? If you make it to, say, the top three, we can go out there together and rent a beach, and maybe I could meet your dad."

His face froze in shock as he understood what that meant. "I'm not going home?"

"Tonight wasn't your fault. And I appreciate you being honest about your motivations. So, how about you stay a little longer, and we'll see how it goes?"

"I'd love that."

"All right then." I stood, feeling so many things. Before tonight Fox was hardly a draw for me, and now I was looking forward to seeing him around the palace. "Forgive me for dashing off, but there's a lot to take care of before the morning."

"I can imagine," he said, walking beside me to the door. "Thank you, Your Highness, for giving me a chance."

"That's all you wanted, right?" I smiled. "And you really can call me Eadlyn."

He grinned and used his good hand to pick up mine. He placed the gentlest kiss across the ridges of my fingers. "Goodnight, Eadlyn. And thank you again."

I gave him a quick nod before I scurried from the room. That was one issue taken care of . . . but tomorrow there would be a thousand more.

The photographer had done such a remarkable job of blending into the background, I didn't realize she was still there when the fight broke out. Burke and Fox were front-page news, and the headline proclaimed that the first was ejected while the second was spared. There were other pictures, too. Me, standing next to Kile, grinding saffron, and again beside Erik as he translated something to Henri. But they were all overshadowed by the animalistic rage on Burke's face as he threw himself at Fox.

I bypassed that photo for the smaller ones with the others, tearing them out to save. I wasn't sure why. I ended up tucking them into the drawer next to Kile's catastrophe of a tie.

I walked into breakfast feeling the weight of everyone's stares. Typically that wasn't an issue for me, but between all the boys being overcurious about the fight and my parents' worried eyes, I was buried beneath all the unspoken words.

I wondered if maybe I'd said too much last night, or if it had come off as me accusing them. I meant to explain how hurtful and draining this process had been, not to blame them for it. Still, as little as I wanted to participate, I knew I'd done what I'd promised. Burke's fists had overshadowed everything else in the country, at least for today.

"What happened?" Kaden whispered.

"Nothing."

"Liar. Mom and Dad have been messed up all morning."

I peeked over. Dad kept rubbing the spot over his eyebrow, and Mom was trying to fool everyone by moving the food around her plate.

I sighed. "It's grown-up stuff. You wouldn't understand."

He rolled his eyes. "Don't talk to me like that, Eadlyn. I'm fourteen, not four. I read all the papers, and I pay attention at the *Reports*. I speak more languages than you, and I'm learning all the things you have without anyone making me do it. Don't act like you're better than me. I'm a prince."

I sighed. "Yes, but I will be queen," I corrected, sipping my coffee. I really didn't need this right now.

"And your name will be in a history book one day, and some bored ten-year-old will memorize it for a test and then forget all about you. You have a job, just like everybody in the world. Stop acting like it makes you more or less than anyone else."

I was left speechless. Was that what Kaden really thought about me?

Was that what *everyone* thought about me?

I had intended to be strong today, to show Mom and Dad that I really was going to follow through and prove to the boys that things like last night could not break me. But Kaden's words made me—and all my efforts—seem worthless.

I stood up to leave, trying to think of what I'd need to grab from the office. I certainly couldn't work there today.

"Hey, Eadlyn, wait up."

It was Kile, jogging to catch up with me. I hadn't even looked at him when I went into the dining hall this morning. His lip was a little swollen, but he seemed okay otherwise.

"Are you all right?" he asked.

I nodded my head . . . then I shook it. "I really don't know."

He put his hands on my shoulders. "Everything's okay."

I was so overwhelmed, I pressed my lips into his, knowing that would make everything else stop for a minute.

"Ow!" he cried, backing away.

"Sorry! I just—"

He grabbed me by the wrist and swung me into the nearest

room, slammed the door, and pushed me against the wall. He kissed me harder than I'd kissed him, apparently not bothered by his lip so much if he knew what was coming.

"What's this all about?" he breathed.

"I don't want to think. Just kiss me."

Without a word, Kile drew me to him, his hands lost in my hair. I grabbed fistfuls of his shirt, holding on to him tightly.

And it worked. As we swayed together, everything else stopped mattering for a little while. His lips moved from my mouth and onto my neck. These kisses were different than before. They were aggressive and demanding, pulling all my focus. Without thinking about it, I dragged his shirt upward.

He laughed devilishly into my cheek. "Okay, if clothes are coming off, we really ought to go to a room. And you should probably know my middle name."

"Is it Ashton? Arthur? I feel like it starts with an *A*."

"Not even close."

I sighed, letting go of his clothes. "Fine."

He leaned back, his arms still around my waist, smirking at me. "Are you all right? I know last night was kind of scary."

"I just didn't expect it. It was asparagus. . . . He literally punched someone over a vegetable."

Kile laughed. "See, this is why you stick with butter."

"Oh, you and your stupid butter." I shook my head, tracing a finger down his chest. "I'm really sorry about your lip. Does anything else hurt?"

"My stomach. He elbowed me a few times trying to get free, but I'm surprised I didn't get it worse. Henri's eye looks painful. Glad he didn't get hit an inch lower."

I grimaced, thinking about how bad it could have been. "Kile, would you have kicked them both out? If you were in my position?"

"I think I would have even had to consider Henri and me if I were you," he replied.

"But you both tried to stop it."

He raised a finger. "True. You know that because you were there. But the others have seen the papers, and the pictures make it look like we were all involved."

"So keeping Fox, Henri, and you makes it seem as if you got away with something?"

"And that maybe others could, too."

"This day just gets worse." I sighed, running my fingers through my hair and propping myself up against the wall.

"Is my kissing that bad?"

I started laughing, thinking back to the other night in my room. It had seemed so alien when Kile wanted to talk to me, but I wasn't completely sure why I thought that now. I could have had a new outlet, a new perspective this whole time.

"Why haven't we really talked before? It's so easy."

He shrugged. "You're the one in charge here. What do you think?"

I looked down, embarrassed to say it. "I think I held Josie against you. The constant imitation drives me crazy."

"I think I held the palace against you. It's our parents' fault, not yours, but I lumped you in since you were going to be queen."

"I can understand that."

"And I know what you mean about Josie. But it's hard for her, growing up in your shadow."

I couldn't deal with adding Josie to the growing list of things I felt guilty about. I straightened my clothes, knowing that going to work would distract me. "Let's do something soon. Not a date, just spending some time together."

That crooked smile spread across his face. "I'd like that."

He started tucking his shirt back in, and I fought the blush that I could feel on my cheeks. How had I gotten so out of control?

"And, listen," he said. "Don't let this stuff get you down. You're bigger than the Selection."

"Thanks, Kile." I kissed his cheek and left, heading to my room.

I remembered how angry I was when I saw his name come up the day of the drawing, like I was being cheated somehow. Now I didn't care how that form ended up in the pile; I was just glad it did.

I hoped that he felt the same way.

CHAPTER 26

TONIGHT WAS GOING TO BE a challenge. Yes, the pictures with Ean looked fantastic in print, and yes, the little game show clips came off as charming, but I wondered if Gavril would feel obligated to ask about Jack's and Burke's dismissals instead of focusing on the remaining candidates.

What was worse was that I wasn't sure I had much to tell about the boys as it was. Dad was entering his security sweep, so unless the guards moved quickly, I wouldn't have any dates this week . . . meaning nothing to share on next week's *Report.* Tonight had to matter, and I wasn't sure how to do it.

I couldn't shake the feeling that something was off, like I was missing some key piece of information that would make the Selection process better.

It wasn't an absolute disaster in my eyes, if only because

I got to know Kile, Henri, Hale, and Fox. But as far as the public knew, nearly everything was going down in flames.

Even though I'd only glanced at the paper that day for a millisecond, I remembered the way I looked shrinking down on the parade float. Worse than that, I could still see people on the sidelines pointing and laughing. We'd kicked out two candidates this week alone for misconduct, and in their wake every romantic gesture had been completely overshadowed.

It looked so, so bad.

I sat in my room, sketching, trying to organize my thoughts. There had to be a way to spin this, to turn it into something good.

My pencil zipped across the page, and it felt like each time a line straightened out, so did a problem. I'd probably have to skip talking about my previous dates this week. Bringing up one would require me to bring up them all, and I didn't want to rehash Jack's hands on me.

But maybe, instead of events, I could talk about what I knew of the boys. There was enough to praise, and if I came across as enamored by their talents, it would make sense to be confused about who to choose. It wasn't that the Selection was falling apart; it was that there were too many good choices.

By the time I had a plan, I also had a beautiful design. The dress came up into a halter, was very fitted, and ended mid-thigh. Over it I drew a sheer, long bubble of a skirt that made it look modest. The colors I'd used—a burgundy for the dress and a golden brown for the overskirt—gave it a delicious autumnal feeling.

I could imagine how I'd style my hair with it. I even knew what jewelry would look best.

As I looked at it, though, I knew this gown was more suited for a starlet than a princess. In my eyes, it was gorgeous without end, but I worried about other people's opinions. More than any other season of my life, they really mattered now.

"Oh, miss!" Neena said, catching a glimpse of the drawing in passing.

"You like it?"

"It's the most glamorous thing I've ever seen."

I stared at the gown. "Do you think I could get away with wearing this on the *Report*?"

She made a face as if I should already know. "You're basically covered from head to toe, and as long as you don't plan on coating it in rhinestones, I don't see why not."

I petted the paper like I could almost really touch it.

"Should I get started?" Neena asked, a hint of excitement in her voice.

"Actually, could you take me down to the workroom? I think I'd like to help make this one. I want it for tonight."

"I'd be thrilled," Neena said. I grabbed my book and followed her into the hallway, more excited than I'd ever been.

It was worth the marathon of cutting and sewing when I walked in for the *Report* and the first thing I saw was the out-and-out envy in Josie's eyes. I'd worn a pair of golden heels and curled my hair so it fell loosely over my shoulders, and it was possibly the most beautiful I'd ever felt. The blatant stares from the Selected only confirmed I was particularly lovely tonight, and I was so bewildered, I had to turn my back on them to suppress my grin.

It was then that I felt something was off. There was a pang of tension that seemed to be floating through the room, and it was far more powerful than the pride over my dress or the sense of admiration coming from the boys. It was so weighty, it nearly gave me a chill.

I looked around, searching for a clue. Mom and Dad were in a corner, trying to be discreet. I could tell by Dad's tensed brow and Mom's gestures that something was wrong. What I wasn't sure of was if I could go talk to them. Was a few days of silence enough?

"Hey!" Baden had snuck up on me.

"Hi."

"Did I startle you?"

I focused politely. "No, I'm fine. A little lost in thought. Do you need something?"

"Well, I was wondering if I could invite you out for dinner or something this week? Maybe another jam session?" He strummed an invisible guitar, biting his smiling lip.

"That's sweet, but traditionally, I'm supposed to do the asking."

He shrugged. "So? Didn't that cooking thing happen because those guys invited you?"

I squinted, trying to remember. "Maybe technically."

"So, since I didn't grow up in the palace, I can't ask, but Kile can?"

"I assure you, Kile has less of an advantage than you'd imagine," I answered with a laugh, thinking of all the years of frustration.

Baden stood there, silent and unbelieving. "Sure."

I was completely shocked when he walked away, hands in his pocket and footsteps steady. Had I done something rude? I was being honest. And I hadn't actually turned him down.

I tried to shake off the snub, focusing on my duty for the evening: being charming and gracious, and trying to convince everyone that I was falling in love.

Dad passed me, and I gently grabbed his arm. "What's wrong?"

He shook his head and patted my hand. "Nothing, darling."

The lie shook me more than Baden's dismissal. People whirred around the room, giving commands and checking notes. I heard Josie laugh, and someone shush her immediately after. The boys talked to one another, all a little too loud to be considered appropriate. Baden was sulking next to Henri, ignoring everyone, and I pressed my hands to my stomach, calming myself.

Next to Henri, just offstage in the dark, I saw a waving hand. It was Erik, standing on the sideline, waiting to take his hidden seat. Once he had my attention, he gave me a thumbs-up, but the expression on his face let me know it was a question. I shrugged. He pressed his lips together, then mouthed the word *sorry*. I gave him a tight smile and a thumbs-up back, which wasn't quite right but was the only thing I could do. Erik shook his head at me, and I was strangely comforted. At least someone seemed to understand how I was feeling.

Taking a deep breath, I went over to sit between Mom and Ahren.

"Something's wrong," I whispered to him.

"I know."

"Do you know what it is?"

"Yes."

"Will you tell me?"

"Later."

I sighed. How was I supposed to perform with worry hanging over my head?

The updates were dispensed, and Daddy spoke briefly, though I couldn't concentrate on anything he was saying. All I could see were the lines of stress around his eyes, the way his shoulders wore the strain of whatever was troubling him.

Partway through, Gavril stepped toward the middle of the set and announced that he had a few questions for the Selected, and I watched them all straighten their ties or cuffs and move into more assertive stances in their chairs.

"So, let's see . . . Sir Ivan?" On the near side of the first row, Ivan raised his hand, and Gavril faced him.

"How are you enjoying the Selection so far?"

He chuckled. "I'd be enjoying it more if I could manage to get to see the princess one-on-one." Ivan winked at me, and I felt my face set on fire.

"I imagine the princess has a hard time getting to everyone," Gavril said graciously.

"For sure! I'm not complaining, just being hopeful," he added, still chortling like this was all a joke.

"Well, maybe you can press Her Royal Highness tonight and sway her into making time for you. Tell us: what do you think the most important job of a future prince would be?"

Ivan's laughing stopped. "I don't know. I think just being good company is important. Princess Eadlyn is forced into lots of relationships for work, and I think it would be nice to be one of the people she always wanted to be around. Just for, you know, fun."

I tried not to roll my eyes. You *are* a forced relationship, honey.

"Interesting," Gavril commented. "What about you, Sir Gunner?"

Gunner was a bit on the short side, and he looked almost petite sitting beside the gangly Ivan. He tried to straighten himself, but it was no use.

"I think any future prince should be prepared to be available. You've already mentioned the princess's busy schedule, so anyone in her life should try to put himself in a position to be helpful. Of course, I don't know what that looks like yet, but it's important to think of how your life and priorities might change."

Gavril made an approving face, and Dad clapped, which led others to follow. I joined in, but it felt strange. This was a legitimate question, and I wasn't sure I liked it being turned into entertainment.

"Sir Kile, you've lived in the palace your whole life," Gavril said, walking across the stage. "How do you think your life might change were you to become prince?"

"I'd definitely need to focus more on my hygiene."

"*Pfffft*!" I covered my mouth, so embarrassed, but I couldn't stop laughing.

"Oh! Sounds like someone over there agrees."

Behind Kile, Henri belatedly joined in the laughter. Of course, he'd heard the comment on a delay. Gavril noticed him and moved back.

"Sir Henri, yes?" Henri nodded, but I could see the pure terror in his eyes. "What's your opinion on all this? What do you think a future prince's most important role might be?"

He tried not to let his fear show as he leaned to the side to hear Erik. Once he understood he nodded.

"Oh, oh, yes. The preence should being for preensess . . . ummm . . ."

I stood. I couldn't bear it. "Henri?" I called. All eyes turned to me, and I waved him over to come join me in the middle of the set. He carefully came down from his seat. "And Erik? You, too."

Henri waited for his friend to come around from behind the set. Erik looked nervous, not prepared to be in the spotlight; but Henri mumbled something to him with a smile, and he eased as they found their way with Gavril to the front.

I linked my arm around Henri's, and Erik stood just behind him, going into shadow mode.

"Gavril, Sir Henri was raised in Swendway. His first language is Finnish, so he requires a translator." I motioned to Erik, who gave a quick bow, ready to go back into obscurity. "I'm sure Henri would be happy to answer your question, but I think it would be much easier without Erik hiding behind the risers."

Henri smiled as Erik conveyed all this to him, and I felt strangely proud when he reached across and gently squeezed my arm.

Pausing to collect himself, Henri gave his answer. I could see he was thinking about his words, and even though he'd been thrown off, he was deliberate as he spoke. Finally, he came to a finish and all eyes fell on Erik.

"He says that any future prince should remember that it isn't simply one role to fill but several. Husband, consultant, friend, and dozens more. He would need to be prepared to study and work as hard as Her Highness and be ready to set his ego aside to serve." Erik put his hands behind his back, and I could see he was trying to remember the last of Henri's words. "And he would also need to understand that there is a weight she carries that he never could and be ready to sometimes just be a clown."

I giggled, happy to see Henri's huge smile when Erik was done. The entire room erupted in applause, and I got up on tiptoes to whisper in his ear.

"Good, good."

He beamed. "Good, good?"

I nodded.

"Your Highness, this is an extraordinary complication in the Selection process," Gavril gasped. "How do you manage?"

"Right now, with two things: patience and Erik."

There was a smattering of laughter across the room.

"But how could this work? At some point it would have to change."

This was the first time in my life that I'd ever wanted to run over, grab my chair, and fling it across the room at Gavril Fadaye.

"Yes, probably, but there are certainly worse things than a language barrier."

"Could you give us some examples?"

I motioned for Henri and Erik to go sit down, and worked very hard not to laugh at how quickly Erik moved. Henri gave me an affectionate smile as he left, and that inspired me.

"Well, since this began with Henri, let me use him as an example. We have to work hard to communicate, but he's an incredibly kind person. Whereas Jack and Burke spoke perfect English but behaved rather poorly."

"Yes, we all saw the story of Burke's fight, and let me say, I'm happy to see you were unharmed by that outburst."

Uninjured? Sure. Unharmed? That was questionable. But no one would want to hear about that.

"Yes, but they seem to be the exception, not the rule. There are so many candidates I could brag about."

"Oh? Well, don't let me stop you!"

I smiled and peeked back to the boys. "Sir Hale has incredible taste and works as a tailor. I would not be surprised to see all of Illéa covered in his designs one day."

"I love that dress!" he called.

"I made it!" I yelled back, unable to contain my pride.

"Perfection."

"See," I said, turning back to Gavril. "Told you he had good taste." I looked around again. "Of course, I've already mentioned Sir Baden's musical skills, but they're worth bringing up again. He's so talented."

Baden gave a quick nod, and, if he was still irritated, he was covering it well.

"Sir Henri, I've discovered, is an amazing cook. And it takes a lot to impress me in that department because, as you know, the palace chefs could rival anyone in the world. So trust me when I say you're jealous of me because I've gotten to taste his food."

More laughter filled the studio, and I caught a glimpse of Dad in a monitor looking so, so delighted.

"Sir Fox . . . now, some might not be aware of what a valuable skill this is, but he has the ability to make the best out of any situation. The Selection can be stressful, and yet he is always looking at the bright side. He's a pleasure to be around."

I shared a gaze with Fox, and, even with the gash on his head and his bruised eye showing slightly through the makeup, he looked as far from menacing as possible. I was glad I'd let him stay.

"Anyone else?" Gavril questioned, and I scanned the boys. Yes, there was one more.

"Most people have a hard time believing that I don't know Sir Kile backward and forward because we've lived in the same place our whole lives, but it's true. The Selection has allowed me to get to know him much better, and I've now learned that he's a very promising architect. If we ever needed a second palace built, he's the first person I'd call."

There were some sweet sighs around the room at the idea of childhood friends finally becoming possible lovers.

"Although, I can confirm, he needs help in the hygiene department," I added, sending the room into laughs again.

"It sounds like these are some truly amazing young men!" Gavril called, beginning another round of applause for them.

"Absolutely."

"So, if you're so impressed, I have to ask: has anyone got a special place in your heart just yet?"

I found myself fiddling with my hair. "I don't know."

"Oh, ho!"

I giggled, looking down. This wasn't real . . . was it?

"Does it happen to be anyone you mentioned?"

I slapped his arm playfully. "Oh, my gosh, Gavril!"

He snickered, as did most of the room. I fanned myself with a hand and turned back to him.

"The truth is, it's still difficult to talk about this so publicly, but I'm hoping to have more to say in the future."

"That's wonderful news, Your Highness. Let me join all of Illéa in wishing you luck as you look for your partner."

"Thank you." I nodded my head modestly and casually peeked over at Dad.

The expression on his face was one of disbelief, almost as if he was optimistic. It was bittersweet for me, to feel so unsure about the whole thing but to see that even the slightest glimmer of possibility took so much worry out of his eyes.

For now, that would be enough.

CHAPTER 27

"It's bad."

I lay on Ahren's bed, curled in a ball while he sat upright, telling me everything Mom and Dad didn't want to.

"Just say it."

He swallowed. "It always seems to start in the poorer provinces. They're not rebelling, not like when Mom and Dad were kids. . . . It's more like they're uprising."

"What does that mean exactly?"

"They're rallying to end the monarchy. No one is getting what they want out of the caste dissolution, and they think we don't care."

"Don't care?" I asked, astonished. "Dad's running himself ragged trying to fix it. I'm dating strangers for them!"

"I know. And I have no idea where that performance tonight came from, but that was spectacular." I made a smart face, acknowledging the praise, but I was starting to question just how much of tonight was planned and how much was genuine. "But even then, what are we supposed to do? Perform forever?"

"Ha!" I scoffed. "As if you'd ever be asked to perform. It would always be me, and I can't. I feel like I'm suffocating as it is."

"We could all step down," he suggested. "But then what would happen? Who would take over? And if we don't step down, will they run us out?"

"Do you think they'd do that?" I breathed.

He stared into the distance. "I don't know, Eady. People have done far worse things when they're hungry or tired or unwaveringly poor."

"But we can't feed everyone. We can't make everyone earn the same amount of money. What do they want from us?"

"Nothing," he said honestly. "They just want more for themselves. I can't say I blame them, but the people are confused. They think their lives are in our hands, but they're not."

"They're in their own."

"Exactly."

We sat in silence for a long time, considering what this meant for us. Truthfully, though, I knew it would hit me harder than anyone else if the people followed through on this. I didn't know how things like this happened, but governments changed. Kingdoms rose and fell; entire ideologies took over, shoving others to the side. Could I be brushed into the gutter?

I shivered, trying to imagine a life like that.

"They already threw food at me," I murmured.

"What?"

"I've been so stupid," I answered, shaking my head. "I've grown up believing that I was adored . . . but the people don't love me. Once Mom and Dad step down, I can't imagine there would be anything preventing the country from getting rid of me."

It was a tangible thing, like I was being held aloft by this idea, and now that I knew it was a lie, my body felt heavier.

Ahren's face grew worried. I waited for him to contradict me, but he couldn't. "You can make them love you, Eadlyn."

"I'm not as charming as you or as clever as Kaden or as adorably rambunctious as Osten. There's nothing that special about me."

He whacked his head on his headboard as he groaned. "Eadlyn, you're joking, right? You're the first female heir. You're unlike anything this country has ever known. You just have to learn how to use that, to remind them who you are."

I'm Eadlyn Schreave, and no one in the world is as powerful as me.

"I don't think they'd like me if they knew who I really was."

"If you're going to whine, I'll kick you out."

"I'll have you flogged."

"You've been threatening me with that since we were six."

"One day it'll happen. Heed my warning."

He chuckled. "Don't worry, Eady. The chances of people organizing enough to do anything are slim. They're venting.

Once they get this out of their system, things will go back to normal, you'll see."

I nodded and sighed. Maybe I was fretting for nothing, but I could still hear the hateful yelling during the parade, and I could still see the hateful remarks from my kiss with Kile. This certainly wouldn't be the last we heard about abolishing the monarchy.

"Don't tell Mom and Dad I know, okay?"

"If you insist."

I hopped up and kissed Ahren's cheek. I felt bad for girls who didn't have brothers. "See you tomorrow."

He grinned. "Get some sleep."

I left his room with every intention of going back to mine. But as I walked, I realized I was hungry. Now that I'd been to the kitchens, I kind of liked it down there. I remembered seeing some fruit, and there was cheese in the refrigerator. Certainly it was late enough that it couldn't bother anyone, so I trotted down the back stairs.

I was wrong in assuming that it would be completely empty. There were a handful of young men and women rolling out dough and chopping vegetables. I took it all in for a moment, entranced by how efficient and driven they were. I loved that, in spite of the hour, they all seemed alert and happy, chatting with one another as they went about their work.

They were so interesting that it took several moments for me to notice the head of floppy blond curls in the back corner of the room. Henri had hung his shirt on a hook, and his blue undershirt was covered in flour. I moved quietly, but as the staff recognized me, they curtsied and bowed as I passed, alerting Henri to my presence.

When he saw me he tried to brush the mess off himself, failing completely. He pushed back his hair and turned to me, smiling as always.

"No Erik?"

"He sleep."

"Why aren't you asleep?"

He squinted, trying to piece together the words. "Umm. Sorry. I cook?"

I nodded. "Can I cook, too?"

He pointed to the pile of apples and dough on the table. "You want? You cook?"

"Yes."

He beamed and nodded. Then, giving me a once-over, he paused before grabbing his dress shirt and wrapping it around me, tying the sleeves together in the back. An apron. He wanted me to have an apron.

I smiled to myself. It was only a nightgown after all, but there weren't enough words between the two of us to argue over it.

He picked up an apple and took the peel off in one long strip. When he was done, he set it on the counter and picked up a different knife. "*Pidäveitsi näin,*" he said, pointing to the way his fingers held the handle. "*Pidäomena huolellisesti.*" He turned his other hand into a claw, tucking his fingers away as he held the apple. Then he started cutting.

Even with my inexperienced eyes, I could see how he was using the minimum amount of force to do his work and how his simple stance protected his hands.

"You," he said, passing me the knife.

"Okay. Like this?" I curled my hand up like he had.

"Good, good."

I wasn't nearly as fast as he was, and my slices weren't half as uniform, but by the way he grinned, you'd have thought I made an entire feast by myself.

He worked with the dough and mixed cinnamon and sugar and prepped one of the fryers along the wall.

I wondered if he was in charge of desserts at home or if they were simply his favorite.

I helped toss the apples and stuff the dough, and though I was terrified of the hot oil, I did sink one of the baskets. I squealed when the oil came alive, popping and dancing all over the place. Henri only laughed at me a little, which was kind.

When he finally placed the tray in front of me, I was dying of hunger and nearly too excited to wait. But I did, and he gestured that I should try, so I plucked up one of the fritter-doughnut-pastry things and bit in.

It was heaven, even better than the rolls he'd made the other day. "Oh, yum!" I exclaimed as I chewed. He broke into a laugh and picked one up himself. He seemed pretty satisfied, but I could see in his eyes he was evaluating what he'd made.

I thought they were perfect.

"What are these called?"

"Hmm?"

"Umm, name?" I pointed to the food.

"Oh, *omenalörtsy*."

"*Ohmenalortsee*?"

"Good!"

"Yeah?"

"Good."

I smiled to myself. I'd have to tell Kaden I was seriously mastering the names of several Swendish desserts.

I ate two, feeling a little sick once I was done, and then I watched as Henri passed the plate around to the cooks, who all praised his skills. In the deepest core of myself, I hated that he didn't understand the words they were using.

Delectable. Flawless. Perfection.

I got the sense that if he had understood, he'd have said they were being too generous. It was hard to be sure though. That was just my assumption about who he was. I really didn't know.

And, I reminded myself, *you don't want to.*

There were times when it was getting harder and harder to remember that.

When Henri finished his rounds and the plate came back with hardly a crumb left, I gave him a shy smile.

"I should sleep."

"You sleep?"

"Yes."

"Good, good."

"Um. Tonight? The *Report*?" I asked, trying to keep things simple.

He nodded. "*Report*, yes."

I placed my hand on his chest. "You were so sweet."

"Sweet? Umm, the sugar?"

I laughed. "Yes. Like sugar."

He brought his hand up to cover mine as it was still pressed against his heart. His smile dwindled as he looked at me and swallowed. He shrugged as he held me there, seeming only to want to make the moment last. He held my hand for the longest time, and I could see he was sorting through words in his head, trying so, so hard to find one that he knew I might understand. . . .

But there was nothing.

I wanted Henri to know that I saw what he felt. I could tell in every smile and every gesture that he really cared about me. And, despite my best efforts, I cared about him, too. I worried about how much I would regret it, but there was only one way to express that feeling.

I closed the distance between us and placed a hand on his cheek. He stared into my eyes as if he'd discovered something truly valuable, something rare that he might never see again. I nodded slowly, and he lowered his lips to mine.

Henri was scared. I could feel it. He was afraid to touch me, afraid to hold me, afraid to move. I didn't know if it was because I was a princess or because he'd never done this before, but that kiss was so vulnerable.

That made me love it even more.

I pressed my lips into his, trying to tell him without words that this was okay, that I wanted him to hold me. And finally, after a moment of hesitation, he responded. Henri held me like I was delicate, like if his grip was too tight, I'd crumble. And his kisses were the same way, only now, instead of being driven by fear, they were motivated by what felt like reverence. It was an affection almost too beautiful to endure.

I pulled away, slightly dizzy from the kiss, noting that his eyes looked pained, but he wore the tiniest smile.

"I should go," I said again.

He nodded.

"Goodnight."

"Goodnight."

I moved slowly until I was out of his sight, then I ran. My head was swimming with thoughts that I didn't understand. Why did it bother me so much when Gavril picked at Henri? Why did I have to keep Fox when he should have left? Why did Kile—for goodness' sake, Kile!—keep popping into my mind?

And why was it so terrifying even to ask those questions?

When I got to my room, I flung myself into bed, feeling disoriented. As angry as I was at Gavril for bringing it up, it did bother me that I couldn't speak to Henri, that I couldn't communicate anything intimate to him because of how uncomfortable it would be to go through Erik. As unnerved as the thought made me, if I was going to tell anyone something personal, it would probably be Henri. I felt safe around him, and I knew he was smart, and I admired his passion. Henri was good.

But I didn't speak Finnish. And that was bad.

I rolled over onto my back in frustration, yelping when something dug into my spine. Reaching around, I felt that it was a knot. I was still wearing Henri's shirt.

I untied it and, despite how absurd it was, pulled it up to my nose. Of course. Of course he smelled like cinnamon and honey and vanilla. Of course he smelled like dessert.

Stupid Swendish baker with his stupid spices.

This was making me asinine!

This was why love was a terrible idea: it made you weak.

And there was no one in the world as powerful as me.

CHAPTER 28

At breakfast I was struck by a number of things. First was Henri trying to catch Erik up on everything that had happened the night before. Erik's eyes kept darting over to mine and then back to Henri, and he looked like he was trying to calm him down. I thought for sure Henri would be elated today as the second person in the Selection to get a kiss. Instead, he seemed frantic.

Across from Henri, Kile's confused gaze flipped back and forth between him and Erik, as he clearly didn't know enough words to follow even a fraction of the conversation. He slowly spooned food into his mouth without trying to interject.

I also noticed that Baden was trying to get my attention. He gave me a small wave and nodded toward the door. I mouthed "Later" and did my best not to be irritated by him neglecting protocol again.

But the worst by far were Mom and Dad surreptitiously peeking over at me, obviously wondering how much I knew about the uprising.

I cleared my throat. "So, did I do okay last night?"

Dad's face finally broke into a smile. "I was impressed, Eadlyn. After such a trying week, you were incredibly poised. When Henri got up there and you were so generous with him, it was a wonderful thing to watch. And I'm happy to see that maybe some of them are . . . appealing to you. Gives me hope."

"We'll see where that goes," I hedged, "but I did promise you three months, and I think it will take me at least that long to figure any of this out."

"I know exactly what you mean," he said, looking as if a thousand memories were flooding his head. "Thank you."

"You're welcome." I watched his sweet, wistful smile, and I could see how much this whole thing meant to him. "Will you be disappointed? If I get to the end and there's no engagement?"

"No, dear. *I* won't be disappointed." He only barely accented the word, but it sent me into a sudden tailspin of worry.

What would it mean for me when I got to the end and was still single? If we weren't just dealing with post-caste confusion anymore and trying to quell an outright rebellion, three months wasn't enough to fix this. In fact, two weeks had already disappeared in a rush.

This wasn't going to be enough.

And then I understood why they might want to keep any hint of unrest from me: If I thought this was completely pointless, would I quit? If I quit, then there really was nothing.

"Don't worry, Daddy," I said. "It's all going to be fine."

He put his hand over mine and gave it a squeeze. "I'm sure you're right, dear." Then, taking a deep breath, he went back to his coffee. "I meant to tell you; the background checks are done. If we had made a few calls before the Selection, we would have known that Burke had anger issues and that a girl at Jack's school reported him for inappropriate behavior once. It also turns out Ean spends almost all his time alone. I don't think that's anything worth sending him home for, but we should watch him."

"Ean's actually been pretty generous."

"Oh?"

"Yeah. But I have noticed he's a bit of a loner. Not sure why though; he's a good conversationalist."

Dad sipped his coffee and stared at Ean. "That's strange."

"Anyone else I need to worry about?" I asked, not wanting him to linger on Ean. Isolated didn't mean troublemaker.

"There was one who had some bad grades, but nothing to kick up a fuss about."

"All right then. The worst has passed." I tried to look encouraging.

"I certainly hope so. I'm going to have a special team continue to look into this. I wasn't as diligent as I should have been, and I'm sorry for that," he confessed.

"But on the plus side, I could have actual dates to talk about next Friday."

He chuckled to himself. "True. So maybe give someone you haven't talked to yet a chance. I promise, it is actually possible to meet with all of them."

I surveyed the mass of boys. "I might not be in the office this week."

He shook his head. "Not a problem. Get to know them. I'm still pulling for you to find someone, even if part of you thinks it's pointless."

"I might remind you, that wasn't your goal when you proposed this."

"All the same."

"There are just so many. Anyone you don't like?"

He squinted. "As a matter of fact . . ." Dad gazed over each of their faces, trying to find one in particular. "That one. Green shirt."

"Black hair?"

"Yes."

"That's Julian. What's wrong with him?"

"This might sound trivial, but when you were complimenting the others last night, he didn't smile or clap for any of them. Not a good attitude to have. If he can't stand being in their shadows temporarily, how would he handle being in yours for the rest of his life?"

For all the mental time I spent debating how much he honestly believed in me as a leader, that statement made it all a waste. Of course he saw me as a leader.

"And this might also sound trivial, but I don't think you'd make attractive children."

"Daddy!" I yelled, causing a bit of a stir. I buried my head in my hand as Dad doubled over in laughter.

"I'm just saying!"

"All right. I'm leaving. Thanks for the insight."

I practically bolted from the hall, though I made sure my pace was only slightly faster than what might be considered ladylike. Once I was alone it turned into an all-out sprint. In my room, I filed through the remaining applications, looking for anything that might make one person more exciting than another. I paused on Julian's picture. Dad was right. No matter how I combined his nose and my eyes or my mouth and his cheeks, every variation looked awful in my head.

Not that it mattered.

I'd send him home soon enough, but probably only once a few dates went bad and he had company. The solo eliminations had all been rather awful. For now I had to make a plan. Ten dates. That was the goal before I had to face another *Report.* And I'd need to get at least three of them in the papers. How could I make them look magnificent?

Mom was in the Women's Room with Miss Lucy, meeting with a mayor. There weren't very many ladies holding down those positions, so I knew them by heart. This was Milla Warren from Calgary gracing our home today. I hadn't planned on making this an official visit, but now I had no choice.

I curtsied, greeting Mom and her guest.

"Your Highness!" Ms. Warren sang, standing to give me a deep curtsy. "It's a pleasure to see you, and during such an exciting time!"

"We're very happy to have you as well, ma'am. Please sit."

"How are you, Eadlyn?" Mom asked.

"Good. I have some questions for you later," I added quietly.

"No doubt a little boy talk, eh?" Ms. Warren asked with a wink. Mom and Miss Lucy indulged her with a laugh, but while I smiled, I thought she should know the truth.

"I don't think the Selection is quite what you imagine."

She raised her eyebrows. "Please, give me thirty-five men fighting over me any day!"

"Honestly, it's more work than anything," I promised. "We make it look exciting, but it's challenging."

"I can back that up," Mom said. "No matter what side of the situation you're on, it's hard. There are long hours of nothing happening followed by bursts of events." She shook her head. "Even now, just thinking back on it, I feel tired."

Mom rested her head on her hand and flicked her eyes toward me. There was something in her expression, that motherly, accepting look, that made me feel understood and comforted.

But there was the same worry there, the hint of stress that Dad was wearing this morning. She brushed off the moment and focused on Ms. Warren. "So, Milla, the last I heard, things were going well in Calgary."

"Oh, yes, well, we're a quiet bunch."

She'd stopped by on little more than a social call, and I sat there holding my perfect posture until she decided to leave. Which only happened because I slipped a note to the maid asking that she come in and tell Mom she was needed urgently.

The second Ms. Warren was out the door, Mom straightened her dress. "Let me go see what this is all about."

"Relax, it's just me." I studied my nails. They needed some work.

Mom and Miss Lucy stared.

"I wanted to talk to you and she wouldn't stop, so I made an appointment. Sort of." I flashed a cheeky smile.

Mom shook her head. "Eadlyn, sometimes you can be a little manipulative." She sighed. "And sometimes it's a gift. Ugh, I didn't think I could take much more."

I giggled conspiratorially with her and Miss Lucy, glad I wasn't alone.

"I feel bad for her," Mom said guiltily. "She doesn't get out much, and it's hard to do her job alone. But I didn't appreciate how she spoke to you."

I made a face. "I've had worse."

"True." She swallowed. "What did you need?"

I glanced at Miss Lucy. "Of course," she answered to my unspoken request. "I'm around all day if you need me." She curtsied to Mom, kissed me on my head, and left. It was such a tender gesture.

"She's so good to me," I said. "The boys, too. Sometimes I feel like I ended up with several mothers."

I smiled at Mom, and she nodded. "I kept the people I

love close, and they have fawned over you since the moment they knew you were coming."

"I really wish she had children," I said sadly.

"Me, too." Mom swallowed. "I guess by now it's common knowledge that she's faced a long struggle with no success. I'd do nearly anything to be able to help her."

"Have you tried?" I felt like there was little the Schreaves couldn't accomplish.

Mom blinked a few times, trying not to cry. "I shouldn't tell you this; it's private. But, yes, I've done everything I could. I even went so far as to offer to be a surrogate and carry a baby for her." She pressed her lips together. "It was the one time I regretted being queen. It appears my body isn't always mine, and there are certain things I'm not allowed to do."

"Says who?" I demanded.

"Everyone, Eadlyn. It's not exactly a traditional thing to do, and our advisers thought the people would be upset by it. Some even argued that any baby I carried would have to be in line for the throne. It was ridiculous, so I had to let it go."

I was quiet for a minute, watching my mother recover from a heartbreak years old, and one that wasn't even her own in a way.

"How do you do that?"

"What?"

"It's like you're always giving pieces of yourself away. How do you have anything left for you? I feel exhausted watching you sometimes."

She smiled. "When you know who matters most to you, giving things up, even yourself, doesn't really feel like a sacrifice. There are a handful of people who I'd lay down my life for without a second thought. And then there are the people of Illéa, our subjects, who I lay my life down for in a different way."

She lowered her eyes and touched up her already immaculate dress. "You probably have people you'd sacrifice for and you don't know it. But you will, one day."

For a second I wondered if we were actually related. All the people she was thinking about—Dad, Ahren, Miss Lucy, Aunt May—were important to me, too. But mostly I needed them to help me, not the other way around.

"Anyway," she said, "what was it that you needed?"

"Oh, so Dad has deemed that the remaining boys aren't complete lunatics, so I'm focusing on dates this week," I answered, leaning forward. "I'm looking for ideas that would be easy but look great on camera."

"Ah." She lifted her eyes to the ceiling in thought. "I'm not sure how useful I can be in that department. Nearly all the dates I had with your father during my Selection were walks around the garden."

"Seriously? How did you two even get together? That's so boring!"

She laughed. "Well, it gave us a lot of opportunities to talk. Or to argue, and the majority of our time spent with each other was filled with one or the other."

I squinted. "You guys fought?"

"All. The. Time." For some reason that brought a smile to her face.

"Honestly, the more and more I hear about your Selection,

the less sense it makes. I can't even imagine you and Dad fighting."

"I know. There were a lot of things we needed to work through, and truthfully, we liked having someone who'd be honest with us, even when it was hard to take."

It wasn't that I didn't want someone honest in my life as well—if I ever chose to get married, anyway—but he'd need to find a better way of delivering his words if he wanted a chance of sticking around.

"Okay, dates," she said, sitting back in her chair and thinking. "I was never good at archery, but if there's someone who is skilled at that, it might look nice."

"I think I can do that. Oh, and I've already done horseback riding, so that's out."

"Right. Cooking, too." She smiled to herself as if she couldn't believe I'd allowed that date to happen.

"And it turned out disastrous."

"Well, Kile and Henri did great! And Fox wasn't terrible."

"True," I amended. I found myself thinking about Henri and me cooking alone in the kitchen, the date no one knew about.

"Sweetheart, I think instead of going for something flashy, you might try simpler dates. Have tea, take a walk in the gardens. Meals are always a good standard; you can't eat too many times. It might look better than you riding a horse anyway."

I'd been trying to avoid anything that might be too personal. But those types of dates gave the impression of closeness, which was something I thought the public wanted.

Maybe she was right. If I went in with a list of safe topics and questions, perhaps it wouldn't feel so bad anyway.

"Thanks, Mom. I'll probably give that a go."

"Any time, sweetie. I'm always here for you."

"I know." I fidgeted with my dress. "Sorry if I've been a pain lately."

She reached across to me. "Eadlyn, you're under a lot of stress. We understand. And short of becoming an ax murderer, there's nothing you could do to make me love you less."

I laughed. "An ax murderer? That's your limit?"

"Well . . . maybe even then." She winked at me. "Go on. If you're doing several dates this week, you should make a plan."

I nodded and, for reasons I wasn't entirely sure of, scuttled into her lap for a second.

"*Oof!*" she complained as my weight settled.

"Love you, Mom."

She wrapped her arms around me tightly. "I love you, too. More than you could ever know."

I kissed her cheek and hopped up, thinking of the week ahead and hoping it would somehow appease everyone. But those thoughts were driven from my mind when I stepped into the hallway and found Baden there, waiting for me.

CHAPTER 29

Baden stood and then crossed the hall. The midday sun was filtering in through the windows, making the space warm and covering everything with a slight hint of yellow. Even his dark skin looked brighter somehow.

"Stalking me?" I asked, trying to be playful.

The hard set of his eyes told me he wasn't in the mood. "I wasn't sure how else to get ahold of you. You're so hard to find."

I crossed my arms. "Clearly you're upset. Why don't you tell me what it's all about so we can move on?"

He made a face, displeased with my offer. "I want to leave."

I felt like I'd run full speed into a brick wall. "Excuse me?"

"Last night was embarrassing. I asked you out and you shot me down."

I held up a hand. "I never actually said no. You didn't let me get that far."

"Were you going to say yes?" He sounded skeptical.

I raised my arms and let them drop. "I'll never know, because you got an attitude and walked away."

"Are you seriously going to lecture me on having a bad attitude?"

I gasped. How dare he?

I got closer to him, though even at my full height I was dwarfed by his frame. "You know I could have you punished for speaking to me that way, right?"

"So now you're going to bully me? First you reject me, then you use me for a little snippet of entertainment on the *Report*, and now I've had to spend my entire morning tracking you down after you told me you would meet with me during breakfast."

"You're one person out of twenty! I have work to do! How self-centered can you possibly be?"

His eyes widened, and he pointed at his chest. "Me? Self-centered?"

I tried to tuck my heart away, refusing to let him hurt me. "You know, you were one of my favorites. I was going to keep you around for a long time. My family liked you, and I admired your talent."

"I don't need your family's stamp of approval. You were nice to me for all of an hour, then you disappear and it's like nothing happened at all. I have the freedom to leave, and I'm ready to go."

"Then go!"

I started walking away. I didn't have to endure that.

He yelled down the hall, taking one last stab at me. "My friends all told me I was crazy to put my name in! They were so right!"

I kept going.

"You're pushy! You're selfish! What was I thinking?"

I turned a corner, even though it didn't lead to where I was going. I could find my way eventually. I held it in, keeping the brave face I'd always been taught to have. No one could know how much that hurt.

After a trip that took twice as long as it should have, I finally made it to the third floor. I started crying the second I hit the landing, unable to stay composed any longer. Baden's words repeated themselves in my head, and I clutched my stomach, feeling them like literal blows.

Before any of the boys had shown up, I'd had a list of ideas for how to get rid of them. I'd planned on making them so angry they'd say plenty of the things Baden just had . . . but I'd done nothing to provoke him. And he said them anyway. What was so wrong with me that I got rejected simply for being myself?

And his last words did exactly what he wanted them to. It looked like I'd had millions of choices when I drew the names nearly a month ago. How many men hadn't entered because they already objected to me on some level?

Did people think I was pushy? Selfish? Which were the public enjoying more: the sweet moments between me and the boys or the moments when I looked like a failure?

I straightened up to head to my room, only to see that Erik was waiting outside my door for me and had undoubtedly just watched my crying fit.

I swiped at my face, trying to clean it up, but there was no hiding the puffy eyes or red cheeks. Erik seeing me like this was almost as bad as the original issue, but the only way to make it *seem* as if it was nothing was to *act* as if it was nothing.

I walked over to Erik, achingly aware of the sadness in his eyes, and he bowed as I approached.

"I feel like maybe I've come at a bad time," he said, the tiniest hint of sarcasm in his voice.

I smiled. "Ever so slightly," I answered, acknowledging my hurt against my better judgment. "Still, I'm happy to help you if I can."

Erik pressed his lips together, unsure if he should go on. "I wanted to talk to you about Henri. He didn't send me!" he insisted, holding up a hand. "I think he'd come to you himself if he could speak on his own. But he's embarrassed." Erik swallowed. "He, uh . . . he told me about the kiss."

I nodded. "I figured."

"He's afraid he's crossed a line. He said something about holding on to you and that he probably should have let go, but then he didn't and—"

I shook my head. "That makes it sound much worse than it was. He . . . we . . ." I stood there, lost. "We were trying to communicate, and when the words didn't work, well, that did."

For some reason I was upset admitting this to Erik, even though he already knew everything.

"So you're not cross with him?"

I heaved out a breath, almost laughing because the idea was so bizarre. "No. He's one of the kindest people I know. I'm not upset with him in the slightest."

Erik nodded. "Would it be all right if I told him as much?"

"Absolutely." I wiped at my eyes again, pulling off smudged eyeliner in the process. "Ick."

"Are you okay, Your Highness?" His voice was so tender but, mercifully, lacking pity. I almost explained what had happened to him, but it was borderline inappropriate. It was one thing to talk about Henri; it was another to discuss the other suitors at length.

"I am. Or will be. Don't worry about me; just make sure Henri is all right."

His expression changed slightly, and I could see the weight of that role in his eyes. "I do my best."

I studied him. "Henri really wants it, doesn't he?"

Erik shook his head. "There is no 'it.' He wants you."

After Baden's heart-shattering speech, it was hard to imagine this was possible, but Erik confirmed it as he went on.

"He talks of you endlessly. Each day in the Men's Parlor, I'm translating political science books to him or trying to explain the difference between the absolute monarchy you have here and the constitutional monarchy he grew up with in Swendway. He even—" Erik paused to chuckle. "He even studies the way your brothers walk and stand. He wants to be worthy of you in every way."

I swallowed, overcome by this admission. Smirking, trying to dull the feeling, I replied, "But he can't even speak to me."

"I know," he answered solemnly. "Which is why I wonder . . ."

"Wonder what?"

He rubbed his hand over his mouth, trying to decide if he should continue. "It's easiest to learn new languages when you're a child. And it can be taught later in life, but the accent will probably always be bad. Henri simply has a difficult time retaining it. At the rate he's going, it would be *years* before you'd be able to carry on the most basic conversations. And the nuances of languages—slang and colloquialisms—would take years beyond that. Do you understand what that would mean?"

That I wouldn't be able to communicate with him for who knew how long. By the time the Selection should end, we still would hardly know each other.

"I do." Two small words, but they felt massive, like they were filling up the entire hallway, crushing me.

"I just thought you should know that. I wanted you to be aware of what things might look like if you had developed feelings for him, too."

"Thank you," I breathed.

"Do you?" he asked suddenly. "Have feelings for him?"

I'd been so emotional already that the question sent me into a tailspin. "I honestly have no idea how I feel about anything."

"Hey." He reached out a hand before thinking better of it. "I'm sorry. I was being nosy. That's really none of my business, and you're obviously having a rough day. I'm an ass."

I wiped at my nose. "No. You're trying to be a good friend. To him, to me. It's no big deal."

He tucked his hands behind his back. "Well, I am, you know?"

"Huh?"

He sighed, seeming embarrassed. "Your friend. If you need one."

It was such a simple offer, yet generous in a million ways. "I couldn't imagine having a better one."

He beamed but was quiet. It seemed like the times when we were silent were some of the easiest.

Eventually he cleared his throat. "I'm sure you have work to do, but I hate leaving you alone when you feel so bad."

"No. I kind of prefer it."

Erik gave me a halfhearted smile. "If you say so." He bowed. "Hope your day gets better."

"It already has," I promised, walking around him to get into my room, a kind smile on my face.

"Miss?" Neena asked as I came through the doorway. I couldn't imagine how awful I looked.

"Hi, Neena."

"Are you all right?"

"Not exactly, but I'll get there. Can you bring me the Selection forms, please? I have work to do."

Though the confusion on her face was plain, she did as I asked. She also brought a box of tissues.

"Thank you." I thought I was past the worst of it, but I did tear up again as I looked at the pictures, wondering who was maybe here despite having reservations and hating each of them on the off chance it applied to them all.

"Neena, could you get me some paper?"

Once again she obeyed, bringing a cup of tea along with a notebook. She really was too good.

I tried to plot out my week. Apsel's application said he played the piano, so I'd arrange for us to work on duets tomorrow morning; and in the early evening I'd walk outside with Tavish. Monday would be tea with Gunner and a photography walk with Harrison. Dad would probably love that.

I finished my plans and set down my pile of papers beside me. Without a word, Neena started a bath. I sipped the last of my tea and put the cup back on the table next to the pot so she wouldn't have to go hunting for it later.

In the bathroom, steam was filling the air, and I planted myself in front of the mirror, pulling pins out of my hair. Between the soothing water and Neena's calming presence, I was free from most of Baden's harsh words by the time I was ready to dry off.

"Do you want to talk about it?" Neena asked quietly, pulling a brush through my hair.

"There's not much to say. People will throw food at me, people will throw words at me, and I have to be stronger than that if I'm going to survive."

She let out a disapproving sound, and I watched her troubled eyes in the mirror.

"What?"

Neena stopped brushing for a minute, looking at my reflection. "For all my problems, I'd never trade them for yours. I'm so sorry."

I pulled myself up. "Nothing to be sorry for. This was what I was born to do."

"That's not fair though, is it? I thought eliminating the castes meant that no one was born into anything. Does that apply to everyone except you?"

"Apparently."

It didn't matter that Apsel's skills were so good I praised him endlessly. And it didn't matter that the photos of Tavish and me in the garden were positively beautiful. With all the work I put in, neither of those things were headline material Monday morning.

Above the pictures of me and my dates was an entirely different story.

IT'S WORK! screamed the headline above a candid shot of me yawning. An "exclusive source" had shared that I felt the Selection process was "more work than anything" and that "we make it look exciting." All I could think about was how badly I wanted to hurt Milla Warren.

I couldn't blame her completely though. Baden's exposé on how staged the Selection was helped nothing. He described me at length as frigid, two-faced, and distant. He spoke of our one charming moment alone and then my intentional disconnection from him, and said there was no way he could have stayed in the palace, living under such a lie. I knew it was likely that he was paid an exorbitant amount of money for his story and that he was probably worrying about a mountain of debt for his education. But I felt certain he would have said it all for free.

Juxtaposing those stories with the one of my weekend dates cheapened everything about them. It was a waste of effort and worse, it was visibly taking a toll on Dad. Weeks had passed, he still had no idea how to address the caste issues, and pockets of rioters were calling for the end of the monarchy.

I was failing in every possible way.

After breakfast I went to my room, looking at my plans for the day. Were they worthless now? Was there a way to make these dates better?

I heard a knock and turned to see Kile standing at the door. I ran into his arms without a second thought.

"Hey," he said, holding me tight.

"I don't know what to do. Everything's just getting worse and worse."

He pulled back and lowered his eyes to meet mine. "Some of the guys are confused. They don't know if they're being used. Eadlyn," he continued in a whisper, presumably so

Neena wouldn't hear his words, "I know our first kiss was for show. Is it all for show? If it is, you need to come clean."

I stared into his eyes. How had I ever thought he was anything less than smart and funny and handsome and kind? I didn't want to respond in a whisper, so I signaled for Neena to leave, and once she had closed the door behind her, I faced him again.

"It's complicated, Kile."

"I'm a very intelligent person. Explain."

His words were calm, an invitation more than a demand.

"If you had asked me the night before everyone came, I would have said it was all a joke. But it's not anymore, not to me." The words shocked me. I'd fought caring about these boys, and I was still terrified of them getting closer. Even now, Kile was walking the edge of my comfort zone, and I was unsure how I'd manage if he pushed himself over the line.

"You matter to me," I confessed. "A lot of you do. But do I think I'll get married?" I shrugged. "I can't say."

"That doesn't make sense. Either you want this or you don't."

"That's not fair. When your name was called, did you want to participate? Would you say the same thing now?"

I didn't realize how tense he'd become until he let out a breath and closed his eyes. "Okay. I can understand that."

"It's been harder than I thought, with so many disasters along the way. And I'm not as good at showing my emotions as other girls, so it comes across like I don't care, even when

I do. I like to keep things to myself. It looks bad, I know, but it's real."

He'd been around me long enough to know it was true. "You need to address this. You need to say something publicly about that story," he insisted, his eyes focused on mine.

I rubbed my temple. "I'm not sure that's a good idea. What if I somehow make it worse?"

He poked my stomach, something we hadn't done since we were children. "How can the truth make anything worse?"

Well, that confirmed all my anxieties. Admitting how much this meant to me now might also mean owning up to the origins of this particular Selection. With the way things were going, that wouldn't win me any sympathy.

He turned me around and pointed me toward my table and chairs. "Here. Let's sit for a minute."

I sat beside him, piling up some of the dress ideas I had been working on.

"Those are impressive, Eadlyn," he remarked.

I gave him a weak smile. "Thank you, but it's really just a bunch of scribbles."

"Don't do that," he said. "Don't make it seem like it's not important."

I remembered those words, and they soothed me.

Kile pulled over a handful of the pencils and started some sketches of his own.

"What are you drawing?" I asked, looking at the little boxes.

"An idea I've been experimenting with. I've been reading

about some of the poorer provinces. One of their bigger issues is housing right now."

"Because of the manufacturing boom?"

"Yeah." He continued to sketch, making practically perfect straight lines.

Dad did what he could to encourage more industrial growth in some of the primarily agricultural provinces. It was good for everyone if things could be processed where they were grown. But as that took off, more and more people moved to be closer to those areas, meaning not everyone had adequate housing.

"I know a little bit about how much it costs to get supplies, and I figured out that it'd be possible to build these smaller huts, basically like family cubicles, fairly inexpensively. I've been playing with the idea over the last few weeks. If there was someone I could get the design to, they might be able to implement it."

I looked at the little structure, barely as big as my bathroom, abutted against an identical box. They each had a door and a side-facing window. A little tube at the top caught rainwater, and a small bucket collected it by the door. Vents lined the top, and a small tarp jutted out in front, shading the front of the space.

"They look so tiny though."

"But they'd feel like a mansion if you were homeless."

I exhaled, thinking that was probably true. "There can't be space for a bathroom in there."

"No, but most people use facilities inside the plants. That's what I read anyway. This would be strictly for shelter, which means workers would be more rested, have better health . . . and there's just something special about having a place to call your own."

I watched Kile, his eyes focused on the extra little details he was adding to his work. I knew that hit home for him, that he was aching for anything that truly belonged to him. He pushed the paper away gently, adding it to the others.

"Not nearly as exciting as a ball gown, but that's all I know how to draw," he concluded with a laugh.

"And you do it so well."

"Eh. I just wanted to distract you for a minute, but I don't know what else to do."

I reached over and held his hand. "That you came at all is enough. I shouldn't let myself sulk too much anyway. I need to come up with a plan of action."

"Like talking about it?"

I shrugged. "Maybe. I have to speak with my dad first."

I could tell he thought I was being silly, but he didn't know what was going on. Not really. And even as someone in the know, it was hard to understand.

"Thanks for coming, Kile. I owe you one."

"You owe me two. I'm still waiting for that chat with my mom." He winked, not too upset I hadn't delivered yet.

My promise was still in the back of my head, and I'd had more than one opportunity to bring it up with Miss Marlee. But now I was the problem, not her. It was getting harder to imagine the palace without Kile around.

"Of course. I haven't forgotten."

He poked my stomach again, and I giggled. "I know."

"Let me go talk to my parents. I need to figure out what to do."

"Okay." He put an arm around me and walked me out the door, parting with me at the stairs. From there I went straight to the office, nervous about how tired Dad looked when I came in and cleared my throat.

He popped his head up from the papers, shoving the stack of them into a drawer as if I wouldn't see. "Hey, sweetie. I thought you were going to be working on the Selection side of things this week."

"Well, that was the plan, but I'm wondering if that will even be of any help right now."

He was crestfallen. "I don't know how this happened, Eadlyn. I'm sorry."

"I'm the one who should be sorry. Baden exaggerated things, but the barest points of his story were real. And with the mayor, I said those things out loud, it's true. But I was simply venting about the work of it all. Ask Mom; she was there. Everything got twisted around."

"I already spoke to her, honey, and I'm not upset with you. I just can't understand why Milla would do that. It's like everyone is taking aim at us right now. . . ." He kept opening his mouth like he wanted to say more, but he was so confused by the overwhelming unhappiness of the public, he didn't know where to start.

"I'm trying, Dad, but I don't think it's good enough.

Which made me wonder if maybe we wanted to try something different."

He shrugged. "I'm up for most anything at the moment."

"Let's switch the focus. No one trusts me right now. Let's bring Camille in for a visit and let people see how in love Ahren is with her. He always does much better in the spotlight. I can come in and talk about their influence on me, and then we can pick up with the Selection shortly after, try to blend one love story into another."

He stared at his desk, contemplating. "I don't know where you get some of your ideas, but that's inspired, Eadlyn. And I think Ahren will be beside himself. Let me make a call and see if she can even come before we say anything, all right?"

"Absolutely."

"I want you to plan a party for her. You two should know each other better than you do."

As if I didn't have anything else to worry about. "I'll start at once."

He picked up the telephone, and I went back to my room, hoping this would be enough to get things back on the right track.

CHAPTER 30

Two days later I was standing on the tarmac next to my giddy brother, who was holding an obnoxiously large bouquet in his hands.

"Why don't you get me flowers like that?"

"Because I'm not trying to impress you."

"You're worse than those boys back at the palace," I said, shaking my head. "She's going to be the queen of France. Girls like us are hard to amaze."

"I know." He looked idiotically happy. "Guess I'm just y."

 stairs lowered from the plane, and two guards came efore Camille. She was a willowy thing, blond and ith a face that looked eternally well rested and person and in print, I'd never seen her wearing remotely resembled a frown.

rotocol to follow, but Ahren and Camille

bypassed it, running into each other's arms. He held her tightly and kissed every corner of her face, ruining half of his flowers in the process. Camille laughed as he peppered her with affection, and I felt a little awkward standing there, waiting for it to end so I could say hello.

"I have missed you so!" she cried, her accent making each word sound like a surprise.

"I have so much to show you. I asked Mom and Dad to make you a permanent suite so you will always have the best room when you come."

"Oh, Ahren! So generous for me!"

He turned, grinning from ear to ear, suddenly recalling my presence. "You remember my sister, of course."

We curtsied to each other, and she rose elegantly. "Your Highness, so nice to see you again. I bring gifts for you."

"For me?"

"Yes. Here is a secret," she said, leaning in. "You can wear all of them."

I perked up. "Wonderful! Maybe I'll have to use some of it at the party I'm throwing for you tonight."

She gasped and placed both hands on her chest. "For me?" She turned her blue eyes on Ahren. "Really?"

"Really."

It was strange to see him with this look in his eyes, like maybe he was in the middle of an act of worship, prepare to sacrifice anything to please Camille.

"Your family is so good to me. Let's go. I'm dying to s your mother."

I tried to keep up with them on the ride back to the pa

but Ahren spoke mostly in French for her benefit, and since I had chosen to master Spanish, I was completely in the dark. Once we got home, Mom, Dad, Kaden, and Osten were all waiting on the front stairs for us. Positioned on the edges of the steps, trying to be inconspicuous, were several photographers.

Ahren exited first, holding out his hand to help Camille. When I scooted over and reached for him, it turned out he'd already run off with Camille, who was rushing into my mother's arms.

Mom, Dad, and Kaden all knew French and were greeting her warmly. I walked over to Osten, who looked like he was itching to climb on something.

"What are you up to today?" I asked.

"I don't know."

"Go find the Selected guys and ask them awkward questions. Report back."

He laughed and went running.

"Where's he off to?" Dad asked quietly.

"Nowhere."

…'s all go inside," Mom announced. "You should nap …night. Eadlyn's been working so hard on this party, …o be wonderful."

… everything. The music was live—suitable for …and there was a mix of foods, both from Illéa …ll as some of those delicious apple fritters … me. I couldn't wait for him to see.

Mom looked radiant as always, and Dad didn't seem quite so worn-out. Josie was right at home, and I was pleased because for once she hadn't stolen a tiara. Kaden was like a little ambassador, walking around the room and shaking hands.

I was, of course, staying close to the happy couple, which was both captivating and draining. Ahren looked at Camille like she hung the sun in the sky every morning. It was beautiful, the way he watched her, enchanted by every breath that came out of her mouth. But I felt strangely detached from it all because no one had ever done that for me, and I'd never done that for anyone else.

I found myself jealous of Camille. Not for having the unwavering love of my brother—which I knew to be one of the steadiest forces in the world—but because everything about her came so effortlessly.

What had the French queen done to raise her like this? Camille was delicate and sweet, and yet no one would think to try and walk all over her. I kept up with international affairs, and I knew her people cherished her. Last year on her birthday an impromptu party started in the streets in her honor and lasted for three days. Three days!

I thought my education was fair and well-rounded, which meant one thing: my shortcomings had nothing to do with how or what I was taught but with me alone.

The realization forced me to step away from her and Ahren. Standing near her only made me feel worse. Before I could get too far, Ean was in front of me, holding out his arm.

"Long time, no see."

I rolled my eyes. "I see you every day." I laced my arm through his all the same.

"But we don't get to speak. I've been wondering how you're doing."

"Excellent. Can't you tell? I'm running around like a crazy person trying to date while being accused of faking it all, and my brother is in love with a perfect girl, and I know eventually she's going to steal him away."

"Steal him?"

I nodded. "When they finally do get married, which will require her mother's express approval and a lengthy engagement to plan what will surely be the most ostentatious wedding anyone has ever seen, he'll have to live in France with her."

"Hmm," he said, leading me to the dance floor and placing a hand on my waist. "I can't do much about your brother, but, if he does end up leaving, you still have someone you can always depend on."

"Would you happen to be speaking about yourself?" I teased, swaying to the music.

"Of course," he replied. "My offer still stands."

"I haven't forgotten it."

As I took in the room with all its trappings and important guests, it was hard to deny just how well he fit in with the crowd. Ever since Ean had arrived, he'd carried himself with a kind of poise that few people possessed. If I hadn't known better, I would have guessed that he grew up in a palace as well.

"If there's any truth to that article, you don't have to torture yourself with these little boys. I will be everything you could ask for in a husband. I will be faithful, kind, and a true helper. I will never demand love from you. And I will be more than happy simply to live by your side."

I still couldn't understand his motivation. In some ways he could do so much better.

"I thank you again for your offer. But I haven't given up on the Selection yet."

Ean cocked his head to the side, smiling slyly. "Oh, but I think you have."

"And why is that?" I tried to match his know-it-all attitude as best as I could.

"Because I'm still here. And if you were really hoping to find love, I can't see why you would keep me around."

We were both grinning at the audacity of his statement as I stopped dancing, pulling my hands away slowly. "I could send you home right now, you know."

"But you won't," he assumed, that impish grin still plastered to his face. "You know I can give you the one thing you really want, and you're the only one who can give me what I want."

"Which is?"

"Comfort. Comfort in exchange for freedom." He shrugged. "I think that's a pretty good deal." He bowed. "See you tomorrow, Your Highness."

I couldn't stand that he was probably the only person here more calculating than I was. He knew exactly what

I wanted and how far I was willing to go to get it, which was irritating.

I was close to the side door of the Great Room and slipped into the hallway for a moment to be by myself. I rubbed my cheeks, so tired of smiling. It was cooler out here and much easier to think.

"Your Highness?"

Erik came down the hall in the smartest suit I'd seen him in to date. His hair was neater than usual, slightly slicked back. He looked taller, prouder. My jaw fell open at the change. He looked positively gorgeous.

"You clean up nice," I said, trying to get my expression somewhere close to normal again.

"Oh." He looked down. "I was aiming for appropriate."

"You did much better than that." I pushed myself off the wall to face him.

"You think? Hale told me I should consider thinner ties."

I giggled. "Well, Hale is pretty gifted when it comes to style, but you look very good."

He stood there, clearly ill at ease with the praise. "So, are you enjoying the party?"

I peeked back into the room. "It's a success, don't you think? Good food, excellent music, a wide range of company . . . it might be the best party I've ever thrown."

"So diplomatic," he said.

I turned back to Erik and smiled. "I feel like I'm the one competing tonight."

"With who?" he asked, shocked.

"Camille, of course." I looked back into the room, trying to hide behind the door as I watched. Erik came beside me, and we both followed her as she danced with Ahren across the floor.

"That's ridiculous."

"That's kind of you, but I know better. She's everything I try to be." I'd thought this to myself before, but I'd never admitted it to anyone. I wasn't sure how Erik managed to make me want to confide this in him.

"But why would you try to be her when Eadlyn is more than enough?"

I whipped my head back to him, as if the concept was unimaginable. I was in a constant state of striving; I was never enough.

Erik's words nearly brought tears to my eyes, and I reached down to take his hand as I'd done in my bedroom not that long ago.

"I'm so glad I got to meet you. However this whole thing ends, I think I've been enlightened just by crossing paths with some of you."

He smiled. "And I'll never be able to express what a privilege it's been to know you."

I think I meant to shake his hand, but we ended up standing there, connected in silence for a while.

"Did you put your name in?" I asked suddenly. "For the Selection, I mean?"

He smiled and shook his head. "No."

"Why not?"

He shrugged, searching for an answer. "Because . . . who am I?"

"You're Eikko."

He stood there, slightly dazed at the sound of his given name. Finally, he smiled again.

"Yes, I'm Eikko. But you barely know me."

"I know Eikko as well as he knows Eadlyn. And I can tell you, you are enough as well."

He rubbed his thumb against the back of my hand, the tiniest movement. And I could sense we were both wondering what would have happened if his name had been in one of those baskets. Maybe he'd be one of the contenders, maybe he wouldn't have been picked at all . . . it was hard to say if the risk would have been worth it in the end.

"I should get back in there." I pointed over my shoulder to the party.

"Of course. See you."

I focused on my posture and stood as tall as I could, which was much more impressive in these heels Camille brought me. I walked into the room, graciously greeting everyone with a bow of my head. I could have stopped a dozen times, but I pushed on until I found Henri.

"Hello," he greeted.

I meant to go see him a dozen times this week. But between dating at top speed, doing damage control, and planning for Camille, I hadn't gotten to speak to Henri at all. I could see that he was anxious, and though I was sure Erik conveyed everything I'd said, I think we both knew we needed to actually speak, just the two of us.

"Okay?" I asked.

He nodded. "And you okay?"

I nodded.

With that he let out a massive sigh, and the bright face I'd come to expect was back again. I tried to think of all the disagreements and misunderstandings I'd had in my life. There was no way any of them was ended with less than five words. But that was genuinely all I needed from Henri to know his regret at possibly offending me without wishing at all that he could take back that kiss.

Maybe Erik had nothing to worry about. Maybe Henri and I could communicate just fine.

"Dance?" I asked, pointing to the floor.

"Please!"

I was nearly as tall as him in these shoes, and he wasn't much of a dancer, but what he lacked in grace he made up for with enthusiasm. He spun me several times and even dipped me twice. When I came up the second time, laughing, I spotted Erik over his shoulder.

I could have been wrong, but his shy smile looked a little sad.

CHAPTER 31

CAMILLE LOOKED FLAWLESS ON THE front of every paper and a few of the gossip magazines that tended to equate our family with movie stars and singers. She brightened the mood in the Women's Room simply by sitting there, and Aunt May came to visit for a few days solely to see her.

I knew why I had problems with Josie. She was bratty and juvenile and tried so hard to be me that I felt like I had to be overly guarded when she was near. But it was more complicated with Camille. Even her perfection was a quiet thing, as if she hardly noticed it at all. So though I really, really wanted to hate her, I knew that would look much worse for me than for the sweet, unassuming French girl.

"How is your mother?" Mom asked Camille, and something about her tone made it seem like she felt obligated to inquire about Queen Daphne. It was the one subject that seemed to take any effort between them.

Mom handed her a cup of tea, and Camille happily took it, pausing as she thought through her answer.

"Very well. She wanted me to send you her love."

"I've been seeing pictures of her lately, and she looks the most content I've ever seen her." Mom placed her hands in her lap, smiling kindly. This comment felt more genuine.

"She is," Camille agreed. "I don't know what's come over her, but she has never been more joyful. And her happiness only makes me happier." Her eyes grew soft at the thought of her mother, and again I was forced to wonder exactly what was going on in the French palace.

"So," Josie said, crossing her legs quite dramatically and taking over the conversation. "Any chance we'll be hearing wedding bells in your future?"

Camille bashfully looked away, and everyone laughed.

"Perhaps," she hedged. "I know Ahren is the one, but we both want to find the proper time."

Miss Marlee sighed. "So I suppose in the middle of the Selection is not at the top of the list."

"Never!" Camille laid a hand on my lap. "I wouldn't take this moment from such a dear friend!"

Miss Marlee and Miss Lucy clutched their hands together at the thought.

"Which reminds me." Camille straightened up. "Eadlyn, you have told me nothing. What are these boys like?"

I chuckled. "More trouble than they're worth."

"Oh, stop," Mom teased.

"Please don't tell me anything about Kile! Ick!" Josie protested. Her mother swatted her leg.

"I need an update, too!" Aunt May insisted. "I missed a lot. I saw there was a fight!"

"There was." I rolled my eyes, remembering. "The truth is, I'm still getting to know most of them," I admitted. "There are a few standouts, but things change from day to day, so it's hard to measure who might be better than anyone else."

"Measure?" Camille sounded sad. "There is no measure. Isn't there one person who fills your heart and takes up all your thoughts?"

As she said it, a name popped into my head. And I was so surprised that anyone came to mind at all that I didn't have time to absorb exactly who it was.

I forced myself to concentrate on the conversation. "I guess I'm just not as romantically inclined as some people."

"Obviously," Josie muttered under her breath.

Either Camille didn't hear her or she dismissed it. "I believe you will find a wonderful husband. I cannot wait to see!"

The conversation drifted away, and I listened quietly. I wasn't sure if I needed to stay in the room all day or if I was supposed to go work with Dad. It seemed like I'd been doing everything wrong lately, and I didn't want to add to my running list of mistakes.

And I liked girl talk, but I needed a little break. I excused myself and made my way into the hall, not sure of where I would go. Fifteen minutes. I promised myself after that I'd go back and be vibrant and engaging.

By pure luck I caught Hale on his way out to the gardens, holding a tray with carafes of water on it. He saw me and broke into a giant smile.

"Where are you off to?" he asked.

"Nowhere really. Taking a break from the Women's Room."

"Some of the guys are playing baseball outside, if you want to come."

I went over to the window and, sure enough, maybe eight of the boys were out there tossing a ball.

"Where did they even get that stuff?"

"Osten."

Of course. Osten had everything. I watched the boys roll up their pant legs and slide off their dress shoes, pushing one another jovially.

"I've never played baseball," I admitted.

"All the more reason to join us."

"Can you play?"

"I'm more of a pitcher than a hitter, but I do all right. And I'll teach you." Hale's face was so genuine, I really believed he'd take care of me out there.

"Okay. But I'll probably be rotten."

"Since when are you rotten at anything?" he said, leading us out the doorway.

Kile was there, as were Apsel, Tavish, and Harrison. Alex was there, too, and I hated to admit that I'd been very tempted to send him back to Calgary ever since Milla blabbed to the papers. I was still considering it.

Henri was stretching next to Linde, so I instinctively looked for Erik. He was there, sitting on one of the stone benches.

"Your Highness!" Edwin called, getting my attention. "Are you here to watch?"

"No, sir. I'm here to play."

Several of the boys clapped or cheered, though I seriously doubted any of them considered me a positive addition.

"Okay, okay," I said loudly, raising my arms. "Just keep in mind that I need to be back inside in a few minutes, and I've never played before. At all. But I thought I'd give it a quick go before I get to work again."

"You've got this!" Tavish assured me. "Here, give me your shoes. I'll put them by mine."

I slipped off my heels and placed them in his hands.

"Ugh, these are heavy. How do you lift your feet?"

"Strong calves?"

He laughed and carried my shoes to the side.

"All right, Eadlyn's up first then," Kile insisted.

I had a general understanding of how the game worked. Three outs, four bases. What I was lost on were the mechanics.

Hale was standing out in the middle of the diamond, practicing his pitches with Apsel. Raoul, who was going to be catching, came up behind me.

"Here's what you need to do," he said. He had a thick

Hispanic accent, but his instructions were nice and clear. "You grab the bat here and here." He demonstrated, clutching the bat firmly toward the bottom. "Legs apart, and keep your back foot dug into the grass, okay?"

"Okay."

"Just watch the ball."

"Watch the ball . . . all right."

Raoul passed me the bat, which weighed much more than I expected. "Good luck."

"Thanks."

I stood at the makeshift base, trying to do everything Raoul had told me to. I supposed if Hale was pitching, then he and I were on different teams. All the same, he was grinning when he saw me in my stance.

"It'll come in slow, okay?"

I nodded.

He threw the ball, and I swung well above it. The same thing happened the second time. I wasn't sure what happened with the third, but I ended up spinning around.

Hale laughed and so did Raoul, and while I typically would have felt embarrassed, this didn't seem too bad.

"Eadlyn! Eadlyn!"

I recognized my mother's voice instantly, and I faced the open windows of the Women's Room. Everyone was there, and I waited for her to order me back inside.

"Get them!" she yelled. "Hit it!"

Aunt May raised her arms in the air. "Go, Eady!"

The rest of the girls joined in, shouting and clapping.

I laughed and turned back to Hale. He gave me a nod. I returned it, gripping the bat.

I finally connected with the ball, sending it low and to the left. I shrieked, dropped the bat so I could pick up my dress, and bolted to the first base.

"Go, Eady, go!" Kile screamed.

I saw Henri chasing the ball, so I headed to the second base, watching him the whole time. I wasn't going to make it. Impulsively I lunged, falling into the base.

I beat him!

Everyone erupted. It wasn't even still my turn, and it wasn't like I'd won, but it felt huge. Suddenly, Edwin lifted me up off the ground and hugged me, swinging me around.

Moments later, Mom and Josie and all the other ladies were outside, slipping off their shoes and demanding a turn.

Someone alerted Dad and my brothers to the game, and Kaden showed everyone what a superior athlete he was. Mom and Dad stood off to the side, arms around each other. The Selected boys patted one another on the back, and Ahren snuck away with Camille, kissing her every step of the way.

"Go, Henri!" I yelled when he came up to bat. Erik sneaked up beside me and joined in.

We were both a little too dignified to jump around, but we pumped our fists in the air.

"Isn't this great?" I said. "I love that he can just play without worrying about words."

"Me, too," Erik agreed. "And I can't believe you hit that ball!"

I laughed. "I know! It was completely worth getting my dress dirty for."

"Agreed. Is there anything you can't do?" he teased.

"Plenty," I said, soberly thinking over my many faults.

"Like what?"

"Umm . . . speak Finnish?"

He laughed. "Okay. So one thing. That's forgivable."

"What about you?"

Erik looked around. "I couldn't run a country."

I waved my hand. "Trust me, if I can learn to do it, anybody could."

Mom rushed up, embracing me. "This was a great idea."

"The boys did it," I explained. "I happened to be in the right place to get an invitation."

I looked past her, watching Dad walk up to the plate.

"Go, Daddy, go!"

He lifted his arm, pointing into the distance, and Mom shook her head. "Not gonna happen," she mumbled.

As she guessed, he completely struck out. We clapped for him anyway, celebrating as the game continued on, with no one keeping score.

For just one moment we were happy. My family and friends swarmed around me, laughing and clapping and enjoying the sun. Mom wrapped me up in another hug, kissing my head and telling me how proud she was of my hit—though I didn't even try again the whole time. Osten ran in circles, disrupting things and making everyone laugh. Josie had stolen one of the boys' dress shirts and was wearing it open over her dress, looking silly and completely delighted.

It was a bubble of pure joy.

There were no cameras around to capture it, no reporters to tell the world about it. And for some reason, that made it so much better.

CHAPTER 32

I WANTED TO LIVE IN that place, to forget about all the worries hanging over my family, threatening to drop at any moment. But the peace was gone by dinner. Some of the Selected boys who missed out on the game were complaining that they should have been told about it. The ones who were present, they claimed, had gotten an unfair amount of additional face time with me, and they were asking for some sort of group date for them.

They elected Winslow to tell me this, and he stood in front of me with puppy dog eyes relaying the collective dejection of the group. We were outside the dining hall, where he caught me as I was heading back to my room.

"We're simply asking for another group date to keep things fair."

I rubbed my temple. "It wasn't exactly a date. There was

no planning involved, and my family was with me for most of it, including my younger brothers."

"We understand that, and we're willing to do any planning if you'll agree to come."

I sighed, frustrated. "How many people would it be exactly?"

"Only eight. Ean asked not to be included."

I smirked to myself. Of course Ean wanted nothing to do with a bunch of boys grumbling about more time. It made me wonder if I should go grab him right now for a date simply to make a point. I suspected he'd hoped for just that.

"You organize the date, and I'll do my best to make time for it."

Winslow beamed. "Thank you, Your Highness."

"But," I added quickly, "please pass along to the others that griping like this does not elevate my opinion of you. If anything, this is a bit childish. So you'd better make this the date of your lives."

Winslow's face fell as I walked past him and up the stairs.

Two more months. I could do this. Admittedly, there were as many lows as there were highs, but I sensed the worst had passed. I was feeling less intimidated by the boys after the game, and I felt sure I could give Dad the time he needed.

I still wasn't quite certain what to do with my heart.

I rounded the stairs to the third floor, catching Ahren leaving his room. He'd changed out of his suit coat and into a vest, and I felt sure he was heading to Camille's new suite.

"Do you ever stop smiling?" I asked, unable to believe his

face could hold that pose for so many days straight.

"Not when she's here." He straightened his vest. "Do I look okay?"

"As always. I'm sure she doesn't care one way or another. She's as head over heels for you as you are for her."

He sighed. "I think so, too. I hope so."

It was like he was already gone. In his mind, he was in Paris, showering Camille with kisses and debating what to name their children. I felt him leaving me. . . . I wasn't ready.

I swallowed, daring to say what I'd been deliberating over for a very long time. "Look, Ahren, she's a great girl. There's no denying it. But maybe she's not the one."

His smile finally faltered. "What do you mean?"

"Just that you might want to consider other options. There are so many eligible girls in Illéa that you've completely bypassed. Don't rush into something that you can't undo. If you and Camille broke up, it would be nothing. If you got divorced, we could lose our alliance with France."

Ahren stared at me. "Eadlyn, I know you're hesitant to fall in love, but I know how I feel about her. Just because you're scared—"

"I'm not scared!" I insisted. "I'm trying to help you. I love you maybe more than anyone. I'd do nearly anything for you, and I thought you'd do the same for me."

Every ounce of happiness left his face. "I would. You know I would."

"Then, please, think about it. That's all I'm asking."

He nodded, running his fingers over his mouth and

cheeks, looking concerned . . . almost lost.

Ahren brought his eyes to mine, gave me a tiny smile, and opened his arms for a hug. He held me tightly, like he'd never needed a hug so badly in his life.

"I love you, Eady."

"And I love you."

He kissed my hair and let me go, continuing on to Camille's room.

Neena was waiting for me with my nightgown ready. "Any plans for the evening? Or do you want to dress for bed?"

"Bed," I assured her. "But wait until you hear what these boys are doing now." I told her about the demanded group date, adding that Ean had excused himself from it.

"Smart move on his part," she agreed.

"I know. I keep wondering if that warrants a special date, just for him."

"A real date or a spite date?"

I laughed. "I hardly know. Ugh, what am I supposed to do with all these boys?"

"Weed 'em out. Ha! I found a piece of grass we missed earlier." She pulled the blade around for me to see before tossing it in the trash.

"That was so much fun," I said. "I'll never forget Mom's face, hanging out of the window telling me to go for it. I was sure I was in trouble!"

"I wish I could have seen that."

"You really don't need to hide in my room all day. It's

always clean, and it doesn't take too long for me to get dressed in the morning. You should come with me places, see more of the palace than this room and yours."

She shrugged. "Perhaps."

But I could hear in her voice that she was excited about the possibility. I wondered if I should train Neena for travel. It would be nice to have her with me next time I went abroad. But if she really was planning on leaving within the next year or so, it might not be worth it. I knew I couldn't keep one maid forever, but I dreaded the thought of someone replacing her.

I went down for breakfast the next day and noticed that Ahren didn't come. I worried he was upset with me. We never stayed cross with each other for long, but I hated when that happened at all. Ahren felt like a piece of me sometimes.

I didn't notice until a bit later that Camille didn't make it either. I assumed one of two things had happened: Ahren had come to his senses and told her that he needed to consider other options, and they were both in the process of avoiding each other . . . or they'd spent the night together and were maybe still in bed.

I wondered what Dad would think about that.

Then I realized that a few of the boys were missing as well. Maybe Camille and Ahren weren't wrapped in each other's arms after all. It was possible there was a bug going around. That was far more likely . . . and much less exciting.

I left the dining hall to find Leeland and Ivan waiting for

me. They both bowed deeply.

"Your Highness," Ivan greeted. "Your presence is requested in the Great Room for the greatest date of your life."

I smirked. "Oh, really?"

Leeland chuckled. "We were up all night working. Please say you're free right now."

I checked the clock on the wall. "I have maybe an hour."

Ivan perked up. "That's plenty of time. Come with us." They both offered their elbows, and I grabbed on to them, allowing myself to be escorted into the Great Room.

Along the back wall, a small stage had been set up and covered with what appeared to be tablecloths from our Christmas supplies. Spotlights that we sometimes brought out for parties were aimed at the center of the stage, and as we approached, the boys all shushed one another as they stood in a line.

I was brought to the lone chair right in front of the stage, and I took my seat, simultaneously curious and confused.

Winslow spread his arms wide. "Welcome to the first ever Selection Variety Show, starring a bunch of losers competing for your attention."

I laughed. At least they owned it.

Calvin jumped off to the side and sat at the piano, playing music that had a ragtime feel, and everyone left the stage except for Winslow.

He bowed very solemnly. But when he stood back up, he smiled hugely, bringing three beanbags in front of him. Then he started juggling. It was so silly, I had to laugh. Winslow turned to the side, and from offstage someone threw a fourth beanbag. Then a fifth and sixth. He managed to keep them going for a couple of tosses before they all fell to the ground, with one slapping him on the head.

Everyone lamented but applauded his efforts, even me.

Lodge got out a bow and arrow and a target covered with balloons, then managed to shoot and pierce each one. As they burst, glitter flew out of them, slowly settling on the floor. All the while, Calvin played on, switching up tunes for each act.

Fox, who I was surprised would rope himself into another group date, got onstage and drew. Horribly. I was sure Osten had made better stick figures as a child, but since this show seemed to either be highlighting their strengths in a ludicrous way or shrugging off their weaknesses as comedy, it ended up being quite charming. I was trying to think of a way to inconspicuously pilfer the picture he drew of me, which was little more than a balloon-shaped head and some brown waves of hair coming off it. I'd been drawn and painted countless times . . . but they never came out that sweet.

Leeland sang, Julian hula hooped, Ivan bounced a soccer ball for an incredibly long time, and Gunner read a poem.

"Our lovely Princess Eadlyn,

It's hard to rhyme your name.

And though we really ticked you off,

We love you all the same."

I giggled the whole way through it, as did most of the boys.

The grand finale was the eight of them cluttered onstage dancing. Well, trying to dance. There was a lot of grinding and hip shaking, to the point that I blushed a few times. In the end I really was impressed. They'd organized the whole thing overnight, both trying to entertain me and apologize at the same time.

There was something really sweet about it.

I applauded them as they had their final bow, giving them a standing ovation.

"All right, I should go to work . . . but what if I get some drinks in here for us instead and we talk for a bit?"

They all answered affirmatively over one another, so I sent for tea and water and some cold drinks as well. We didn't bother with rolling out tables and instead sat on the floor. Sometimes these pain-in-the-neck boys could be so nice.

Ahren didn't come to dinner either. I watched as the Selected boys filed in, and all our guests, then Mom who was running a little late . . . but no Ahren.

Dad leaned over to me. "Where is your brother?"

I shrugged, cutting my chicken. "I don't know. I haven't seen him today."

"That's not like him."

I glanced around the room, looking at the remaining nineteen candidates. Kile gave me a wink, and Henri waved. Every time I looked at Gunner, all I could think about was his silly poem. Fox nodded his head at me as our eyes met, and when Raoul stretched, I remembered the care he took teaching me to grip a bat.

Oh, no.

It had happened. Even with the boys I hadn't spent much time with, I knew that each of them had a hold on me in some way. I already knew that some of them claimed a spot in my ever-terrified heart, but how had it come to pass that they *all* mattered?

I felt a heaviness settle in my chest. I was going to miss these loud, strange boys. Because even if I miraculously found one to stay with me in the end, there was no way to keep them all.

I was thinking about how worried I used to be about losing my quiet house when Gavril walked in, one of the news staff we kept around for the *Report* trailing him.

He bowed in front of the head table, looking at Dad. "I'm so sorry to bother you, Your Majesty."

"Not at all. What's wrong?"

Gavril glanced at all the watching eyes. "May I approach you?"

Daddy nodded, and Gavril whispered something in his ear.

Dad squinted in disbelief. "Married?" he asked only loud enough that probably Mom and I could hear. He pulled back to look into Gavril's eyes.

"Her mother approved. It's been done, all legal. He's gone."

My body turned cold, and I ran from the room.

"No, no, no," I mumbled, rushing up the stairs. I went to Ahren's room first. Nothing. Everything looked pristine, no sign of packing or an urgent exit. But, more important, no sign of my brother.

I tore from the room, heading to Camille's suite. I'd peeked in the day before and had seen her trunks spilling open with so many outfit choices, they probably could have filled my closet. The trunks were still there, all but the smallest. And no Camille.

I fell into the wall, in far too much shock to process this. Ahren was gone. He'd eloped and left me here alone.

I stood there in a daze, not sure what to do. Could I get him back? Gavril said something about legal. What did that mean? Was there any way to undo this?

My world felt dimmer, slightly misaligned and wrong. How was I supposed to do anything without Ahren?

I ended up in my room without realizing I'd even walked there. Neena held out an envelope to me.

"Ahren's butler delivered this for you about half an hour ago."

I snatched the paper from her hands.

Eadlyn,

On the off chance that the news has not reached you by the time this letter does, let me tell you what I've done. I've gone to France with Camille, and, pending her parents' approval, I intend to marry her immediately. I'm sorry to have run off without you and to have excluded you and Mom and Dad from what I always knew would be the happiest day of my life, but I felt I had no choice.

After speaking with you last night, the last few years made perfect sense to me. I always assumed your dislike for Camille stemmed from you both being in the same situation. You're young, beautiful women who will inherit a throne. And you and she handle this position in vastly different ways. She is open to everything, while you keep people at a distance. She deals out her power with humility, while you wield yours like a sword. I hate to be so blunt, though I'm sure you already know this about yourself. Still, it brings me no joy to say it.

But your positions are not the reason you dislike her so. You don't like Camille because she's the only person who could ever separate you and me.

Your words hit me so hard, Eadlyn. Because I wanted to believe you. I wanted to hear you out and consider your suggestions. I knew that if I did, one day you'd convince me to give up everything for you. Maybe even put your crown on my head. And, heaven knows, I would have done it. I would do anything for you.

So before you could ask for my life, I gave it to Camille.

I wish you could find love, Eadlyn. The reckless, relentless kind that consumes you. If you could, then maybe you'd understand. I hope someday you will.

My happiness with Camille is tarnished by one thing: that I may be estranged from you if you choose not to forgive me. That sadness will be great, but far more bearable than my separation from my soul mate.

Even as I write this I miss you. I cannot imagine us being so far apart. Please find a way to forgive me and know that I love you. Maybe not as deeply as you'd like, but still.

As a testimony to my desire to always be there for you, I want to give you one last piece of information, something that may help you in the coming months.

More provinces are protesting the monarchy than you could guess. Not all of them, but plenty. And while it pains me to tell you this, the problem people have with the monarchy stems from one person: you.

I don't know why—perhaps because of your youth, perhaps because of your gender, perhaps for reasons none of us could believe—but they worry. Dad's aging beyond his years. The stress of the amount of things he's accomplished in his reign is bigger than his predecessors', and the general population thinks you will ascend soon, and they are not prepared.

I hate saying those words to you, but you've already kind of guessed at this. I didn't want to let you dwell on those thoughts, hoping you could move past it. And I only tell you this because I think you can change their minds. Stop holding everyone at bay, Eadlyn. You can be brave and still be feminine. You can lead and still love flowers. Most important, you can be queen and still be a bride.

I think those who cannot know you the way I do would finally have a glimpse of this side of you if you consider finding a mate. I could be wrong, but just in case this is the last time you ever want to speak to me, I must give you the only piece of advice I can.

I hope you can forgive me.

Your brother, your twin, your other piece,

Ahren

CHAPTER 33

I STARED AT THE LETTER for the longest time. He left me. He left me for her. When the finality of it hit me, I was consumed by a wild rush of rage. I picked up the closest breakable thing and flung it across the room with every ounce of strength I had.

I heard Neena gasp as the glass shattered against the wall, and that brought me back. I'd completely forgotten she was there.

Through heavy breaths I shook my head. "I'm sorry."

"I'll fix it."

"I didn't mean to frighten you. It's . . . he's gone. Ahren's gone."

"What?"

"He eloped with Camille." I ran my fingers through my hair, feeling slightly unhinged. "I can't imagine why the queen would have authorized something like this, but she unquestionably did. Gavril said it was legal downstairs."

"So what does that mean?"

I swallowed. "With Camille in line for her throne and Ahren as her prince consort, his primary duty is to France now. Illéa is nothing more than the country he was born in."

"Do your parents know?"

I nodded. "But I'm not sure if he sent them letters as well. I should go to them."

Neena came over and smoothed out my dress and my hair. She took a tissue to my face, blotting away any imperfections.

"There now. That's how my future queen should look."

I threw my arms around her. "You're too good to me, Neena."

"Hush. Go to your parents. They need you."

I stepped back and swiped at the tears that were so, so close to falling. I went down the hall, knocking on the door to Dad's room, which they generally shared.

No one answered, so I risked a quick peek inside.

"Dad?" I stepped into the huge space. I hadn't been here in so long—maybe since I was a child—and I couldn't remember if it had always been this way. The room looked more like something Mom would have decorated than him. Warm colors on the walls, books everywhere. If this was his retreat, why didn't it feel like him at all?

Without Mom and Dad joining me, I felt like I was intruding and turned to go.

But I was stopped in my tracks by the sight behind me. Several large, framed pictures covered the wall. There was one of Mom and Dad when they were my age, with him in his full suit and sash next to Mom in a cream-colored dress. I saw them on their wedding day, their faces covered in cake. Then there was Mom, her hair slicked back with sweat, holding two babies in her arms as Dad kissed her forehead, a tear falling down his cheek. Several candid shots, like a kiss or a smile, had been blown up and changed to black-and-white, making them seem more classic than casual.

Two things became instantly clear. First, the reason Dad's room didn't feel like it was completely his was because it wasn't. He had all but turned it into a shrine to Mom. Or rather, a shrine to the two of them and how deeply they loved each other.

I saw it every day, but it was different seeing the images they both looked at before falling asleep each night. They were meant to be, even after dozens of obstacles, and they liked to be reminded of it constantly.

Second, I could see why Ahren would give me up—give all of us up—for a chance at this. If he even got a scrap of the love Mom and Dad had, it would be justified.

In that moment I knew I needed to tell them what Ahren's letter said. They would understand—perhaps better than anyone on the planet—why he had to go. They'd certainly understand better than I could.

They weren't in the dining hall, or Dad's office, or Mom's room. In fact, the hallways were abnormally empty. There wasn't a single guard in sight.

"Hello?" I called into the dimly lit air. "HELLO?"

Finally, a pair of guards came running around the corner.

"Thank God," one said. "Go to the king and tell him we've found her."

The second guard raced away while the first faced me and took a deep breath. "You need to come with me to the hospital wing, Your Highness. Your mother has had a heart attack."

As quiet as it was, it sounded like he was screaming. I couldn't think of what to say or do, but I knew I had to get to her. Even in heels, I outpaced the guard, running as fast as I could.

The only thoughts passing through my head were how wrong I'd been about so many things, how snippy I'd been with her when I'd wanted my way. And I was sure that she knew I loved her, but I needed to tell her one more time.

In front of the hospital wing, Aunt May sat next to Miss Marlee, who appeared to be deep in prayer. Osten, mercifully, wasn't present, but Kaden was there trying so hard to look brave. Lady Brice was there as well, pacing on the outskirts of the scene, but the true fear of the moment was summed up in Dad.

He clung to General Leger, holding on to him for dear life, his fingers digging into the back of his uniform. He was unabashedly crying, and I'd never heard such a painful sound. I hoped I never would again.

"I can't lose her. I don't know. . . . I don't . . ."

General Leger grabbed him by the shoulders. "Don't think about that now. We need to believe she'll be fine. And you need to think about your children."

Dad nodded, but I could tell he didn't quite believe he was capable.

"Daddy?" I called, my voice breaking.

He turned to me and opened his arms. I bolted right to him, squeezing him. I let myself cry, not concerned with pride at the moment.

"What happened?"

"I don't know, honey. I think the shock of Ahren leaving was too much. Heart problems run in her family, and she's been so anxious lately." His voice changed, and I knew he wasn't really talking to me anymore. "I should have made her rest more. I should have asked her for less. She did everything for me."

General Leger grabbed his arm. "You know how stubborn she is," he said kindly. "Do you think for one second she'd have let you make her slow down?"

They both shared a sad smile.

Dad nodded. "Okay, so now we wait."

General Leger let him go. "I need to go home and tell Lucy and get fresh clothes. I'll call her mother if you haven't already."

Dad sighed to himself. "I didn't even think about it."

"I got it. And I'll be back within an hour. Whatever you need, I'm here."

Dad let me go and embraced General Leger once more. "Thank you."

I walked away, going to stand by the door. I wondered if she could sense I was near. I felt so angry. At everyone, at me. If the people hadn't asked for so much or if I had done more . . . I wasn't ready to lose my mother.

I kept thinking that I couldn't live my life for other people, that love was nothing but chains. And maybe it was, but so help me, I needed these chains. I let myself feel the weight of Ahren leaving, the weight of my father's worry, and, most important, the weight of my mother's life hanging in the balance. These things didn't make me weaker; they held my soul to the earth. I wasn't going to run from them anymore.

I turned at the sound of the footsteps, aware that a mass of people was approaching. I was humbled, moved beyond words, to see each of the Selected come around the corner.

Kile looked at me. "We've come to pray."

Tears filled my eyes, and I nodded. The gentlemen scattered, some leaning in a corner and others perching on benches. They bowed their heads or lifted them, all for my mother. They'd caused such an upheaval in my life . . . and I was so glad they did.

Hale kept his fist to his mouth, rocking on his feet nervously. Ean, as I expected, was very steady, arms crossed in concentration. Henri leaned forward on his bench, his curls flopping over his eyes; and I was happy to see that, even though he didn't need to come, Erik stood beside him.

Kile found his mother, and they held each other. Kile was actually moved to tears for Mom, and, strangely, that tenderness made me feel stronger.

My eyes moved from him to the other remaining boys,

and I thought again of how each of them had grown on me in his own way . . . and I looked over at Dad. His face was red from crying, his suit was all rumpled, and I could see the distress in every molecule of his body, horrified at the thought of his wife dying.

It wasn't all that long ago that he'd stood where I did, that my mom's face was one of many in his world. And yet, despite all the impediments and all the time that had passed, they were still deeply in love.

It was obvious in everything, from their shared room to the way they fretted over each other to the way they seemed to be incapable of not flirting with each other even after being married so long.

If anyone had told me I might consider that a possibility for myself a month ago, I'd have rolled my eyes and walked away. Now? Well, it didn't seem so far-fetched. I didn't expect to find what my parents had or even what Ahren had found with Camille. But . . . maybe I could find *something*. Maybe there would be one person who'd still want to kiss me when I had a runny nose or would rub my shoulders after a long day of meetings. Maybe I could find someone who didn't seem so scary, who made letting him past the wall seem natural. But all that still could be asking for too much.

Either way, I couldn't slow now. I knew that for my sake—for my family's sake—I had to finish my Selection.

And, when I did, I'd have a ring on my finger.

ACKNOWLEDGMENTS

SPECIAL THANKS TO:

You, for being a generally cool person, but mostly for picking up a fourth book when you thought there'd only be three.

Callaway, for everything, but mostly for doing dishes and math, so I don't have to.

Guyden and Zuzu, for being the cutest kids ever, but mostly for giving me snuggles when I'm having a rough day.

Mom, Dad, Jody, for all your encouragement, but mostly for being as weird as I am.

Mimi, Papa, Chris, for being so supportive, but mostly for watching the kids over Christmas break so I could sleep.

Elana, for being a really incredible agent, but mostly for making me feel certain that if anyone tried to pie me in the face, you'd tackle them for me.

Erica, for being a very talented editor, but mostly for letting me call you about eighteen times a week without complaining.

Olivia, Christina, Kara, Stephanie, Erin, Alison, Jon, and

a gazillion other people at HarperTeen, for being generally awesome people, but mostly for making my life much easier even though we, like, never see one another.

God, for being God, but mostly for making a world where things like kittens wearing bowties are a reality.

And to anyone else I forgot—which is undoubtedly a lot of people—because I'm generally forgetful, but mostly because I'm so tired now, I'm typing this with my eyes closed.

Love you all!